THE LIGHT OF MEN

BY

ANDREW SALMON

THANK YOU FOR YOUR INTEREST

BEST REGARDS,

CORNERSTONE BOOK PUBLISHERS

DEDICATION

For Mirjam
Without whose unwavering support
and encouragement this novel would
not have been possible.
All my love, Andrew.

Airship 27 Presents
"The Light of Men"
by Andrew Salmon
Copyright © 2008 Andrew Salmon

Cover by Rob Davis
Illustrations copyright © 2008 by Rob Davis
Production and design by Rob Davis
Edited by Ron Fortier

Published by Cornerstone Book Publishers
New Orleans, Louisiana
www.cornerstonepublishers.com

ISBN: 1-934935-29-8
      978-1-934935-29-3

Printed in the United States of America

10 9 8 7 6 5 4 3 2 1

In him was life;
and the life was the light of men

~John 1:4

CHAPTER ONE

The train whistle shrieked across the deepening twilight. A lancing, yellow beam beneath a thick column of agitated smoke washed over the exhausted prisoners strewn about the platform, heralding the arrival of the transport. The emaciated prisoners rose slowly as though jerked by invisible strings. Another blast from the whistle urged them upright but they did not hurry, their work had long since become routine.

Forming strict ranks of three, they stood disinterested and downcast. Only the animal gleam of hunger in their eyes betrayed any emotion. The thundering locomotive loomed out of the black autumn night. Hissing and spitting like an enormous snake, it slowed, trailing its long body behind. Its single bright orb threw light on the armed SS men on either side of the track and turned the skeletal faces of the staring prisoners ghostly pale.

Staff cars rolled up to disgorge SS officers who took up vantage points above their men and the prisoners. Silver eagles clutching swastikas gleamed and winked from their caps as they looked down on the scene about to unfold.

At the arrival of the officers, the prisoners shrugged off their disinterest. The hiss of steam subsided only to be replaced by a new sound from the cars. Rumbling, chaotic murmurs and muffled cries seeped from between the slatted walls of the cattle cars.

"Water! Water!"

All along the sixty cars of the train the litany roared. Desperate faces pressed themselves between the slats, gulped air, then vanished and were replaced by others. The cars creaked and swayed with the shifting of the teeming, invisible mass they contained.

Barked orders. The SS men leapt to the doors. The shouts aroused the people in the cars and the volume of their pleas grew. The men drew the bolts which cracked like rifle shots.

Men, women and children were packed 150 to a car. When the doors rumbled open, the dead poured out like water from a pitcher. They toppled into the pools of sickly yellow haze cast by the light poles overhead.

"Everyone get out! Bring your hand baggage with you! Leave heavy baggage inside!"

Men jumped down, then turned with hands outstretched for the women, children and the elderly. The light baggage followed.

"Men to the left! Women to the right!" shouted a dozen SS noncoms who had come forward. With no trace of emotion in their voices and with an air of calm efficiency, they moved amongst the filthy, hungry arrivals, asking, "How old? Healthy?"

The prisoners marched forward. Their striped garb and hairless knobby heads gave them an eerie similarity. In rows of threes, they moved towards the train with an odd, embarrassed step with arms rigid at their sides, heads dangling in front.

In minutes, the cars were empty. Individual clouds of breath rose above the crowd, turning to a pinkish color as they rose to mingle with the smoke from the crematorium. The sickly sweet smell of burning flesh descended on the new arrivals, winding its way through the fetid odor from the cars and their contents.

A third of the way down the length of the train, a young man leapt gracefully down from a boxcar. He moved easily through the crowd. No wife clung to his threadbare, torn coat. No children hid themselves behind his soiled black trousers. He carried no backpack, no luggage of any kind.

He was tall, slim, well proportioned with an athletic build barely concealed by his loose work shirt and tattered trousers. The cold

October wind ran through his short, brown hair but did not furrow his high forehead. It did not pinch his long, thin nose or raise a blush on his high cheeks. The stench of human waste, in the car, on his clothes, all around him, sent no waves of nausea through him. He stood passive amidst the crowd, his dark eyes, set wide apart, gazed in the direction of distant thunder promising rain.

An SS man quickly made his way toward the young man. In his wake, columns of men and women formed. At the same time, a flushed, handsome peasant woman was struggling with an SS noncom behind the young man. The scuffle sent her thin, bony husband crashing into him. He turned.

"Women to the left!" the SS soldier spat. He held the woman by her scarf as she tried to tear away. The husband dug a claw-like hand into the guard's shoulder as the woman fought to break free. Enraged, the guard released the woman, raised the butt of his rifle and struck the husband on the side of the head. The spindly man dropped senseless at the young man's feet. The guard dragged the woman off. She could only stare open-mouthed, rigid with shock.

The young man went down on one knee to examine the fallen man. Blood poured from the side of the man's head. His eyes held a vague, opaque stare.

"What are you doing here?" the husband asked the young man in his delirium.

The young man did not reply. The husband was a stranger who, in his semi-conscious state, mistook him for someone else.

"I lose nothing when I lose my life," the dying man said. He clasped the young man's hand.

A rifle butt hit the young man between the shoulder blades. "Up, you! Or do you want to join your friend in the great beyond?" There was ire in the guard's laughter.

The young man rose, letting the frozen claw drop away. He moved quickly to the right and did not look back.

Sorting was easier now. Terror and hunger had overcome curiosity. In less than ten minutes the new arrivals were separated into two ragged columns. The column of women, children, the sick and aged were ordered forward first. Families called to each other across the

"I lose nothing when I lose my life."

widening gulf but their words were swallowed by the sickly sweet cloud overhead. Soon wives, children, grandparents dwindled to an obscure mass at the end of the platform -- a twisting stream winding its way to the large iron gates and the crematorium.

The striped prisoners marched into the cars to remove the dead and the heavy baggage left behind. Dead infants, old men, bodies trampled beyond recognition dropped from the cars like heavy, black sacks.

The order was given and the column of men moved forward as if linked by a giant rope tugged by invisible hands. Some of the prisoners marched alongside the column, shining their lights in each face, begging for bread or valuables. The men, eyes rigid on the gates, mouths dumb with something beyond their understanding, ignored their faceless tormentors.

Between the wrought iron letters atop the gate, the young man watched the last of the light kiss the snow-topped mountain peaks behind the spire of the crematorium. He read the words: Arbeit Macht Frei -- Work Will Free You -- then the light was gone. Only the glow of the crematorium remained.

The road the new arrivals were marched along was made up of the broken tombstones from the Jewish cemetery in the neighboring village of Jenseits. Births and deaths, old and young passed beneath the weary feet of the straggling column. The road stretched for three hundred meters. On either side ran high barbwire fences bearing signs that read: Danger High Tension. Beyond the wire, rows of barracks squatted in the deepening gloom. From high on the smooth walls pierced tiny windows through which pale, skeletal faces watched them with too-large eyes.

The new arrivals were ordered into long barracks. No heat emanated from the gurgling radiators. Terrified eyes glared at the dripping sink against the far wall. Thirst leapt into their throats despite the sign, which said, "Wassen Trinken Verboten."

An SS man entered.

"Form rows of five! Two yards between each man!"

His harsh voice echoed along the length of the barrack. The men instantly obeyed. Only the shuffling of feet accompanied this motion.

The men were still too numb to speak or question.

"Strip!" the man barked again when the rows had been formed to his liking. "You have ten minutes!"

Hand luggage boomed to the ground as the last syllable of the guard's orders died away. Like pack animals the men shrugged out of their burdens.

"Woolen garments on one side, the rest on the other!"

Small mountains of garments rose up next to each of the shivering men. No one looked around. No one questioned. Each man stared at the bare back of the man in front. The front ranks stared at the sink into which dripped rhythmically the tainted water.

"Tie your shoes together," cautioned the SS man. "You don't want them stolen."

In minutes the new arrivals were reduced to bare, clenched skin and blue lips below fixed stares. The SS man, satisfied at the speed of the new group, opened the door to leave. A blast of cold air rushed in, sending small convulsions over the men. The SS man deliberately closed the door then opened it again, smiling at the effect. The door closed behind him.

Four men with razors came in after him. With quick swipes and prodding, the new arrivals were shaved. The young man watched as great tufts of hair from the naked peasant in front of him collected like the hump of a camel poking out of the floor. All body hair was removed, carpeting the cold damp floor. The buzz of the razors fell silent. The new arrivals stood naked and alone.

Voices. The new arrivals began to speak for the first time since having left the train. A din of questions quickly silenced by the guards who had rattled in undetected.

"Outside! Outside! On the double!"

The exhausted men called up reserves forgotten in primordial memory and ran out the doors into the cold night. Kapos -- prisoners with white armbands embossed with a large black "K" -- beat them with axe handles. A youth, no more than fifteen was struck down. An older man, his father, seeing this, roared like a lion and charged the Kapo. In seconds the man was clubbed senseless while the naked youth sobbed in the mud.

The young man had to step around the fallen youth and received a solid blow to the kidneys for breaking ranks. He staggered but kept up with the rest. He heard the dull thumps of the axe handles as the fallen youth was bludgeoned behind him. This sound was quickly lost in the desperate breathing of the rest of the column, which had doubled its efforts to distance themselves from the slaughter at their backs.

A sign proclaimed 'Bathhouse' in a dozen languages. Outside the double doors of this barrack stood a barrel of petrol. Each prisoner was doused before entering the bathhouse. This was done to kill any vermin the men may have acquired during their time on the train.

Once inside, steaming hot water rained down on them. It pierced their frozen skin, providing the first comfort they had felt in a long time. They splashed about in the hot shower, some even spat jets of water out of their mouths. Smiles were born and died, a laugh echoed, strange and alien.

The comfort was short lived. After five minutes the water stopped. Naked and shivering the men stood about uncertain as to what would happen next. Some found their voices. Questions were asked, "Where are we?" "What will become of us?" But these newly shorn prisoners who had once been men had no answers.

Every mouth closed as the door banged open. Before them stood another of those comical fellows with the striped pajamas. However, by this time, he was not so comical because the new arrivals saw themselves reflected in his round head and pinched features. His sunken eyes held the promise of the same affliction being visited upon them. They were large, round, the whites yellowed and they seemed to look past the new arrivals at some nightmare they could only guess at.

"This is Kozentrationlager Gutundbose," his voice boomed over the heads of the naked men like a judgment. "We are five kilometers from the town of Jenseits, which rests 500 kilometers west of Frankfurt. You will be given shoes and clothes."

"Where are our wives?" a voice rang out.

"What have they done with the children?" asked another.

"You will work," the prisoner continued, ignoring their questions.

"On Sundays, there are concerts, football matches. Work well and you will receive coupons for water and tobacco. The water is no good, don't drink it. Don't worry, the soup is water enough."

The young man was close to the speaker and took in every word while examining the inverted red triangle on the prisoner's jacket. His speech completed, the prisoner turned and left, banging the door shut behind him.

Four Kapos entered and were on the new arrivals in a flash, herding them outside into the cold night.

The Clothing Room was some distance from the Bathhouse so the Kapos double-timed the new arrivals. A clinging, icy mist began to fall, chilling the prisoners. Panting and wheezing, they were queued up once more and led into a barracks. Inside were very long tables upon which were piled heaps of striped clothing. This line moved quickly as the prisoners behind the tables began throwing garments at the first in line. Each new arrival was issued, arbitrarily, a shirt, jacket, pants, underpants, a cap and, if fortunate, socks and shoes. The frozen men, ignoring the wretched odors of death, disease and human waste quickly donned these soiled, ragged garments.

The young man found himself in the possession of the top half of a priest's cassock, the back of which contained three small holes rimmed with dark red circles. He slipped it on without comment, pulling the striped jacket over it. He had been issued shoes -- a wrecked pair of black work boots -- but no socks. The brim of his cap was hard with dried sweat and perched uncomfortably on his shaved skull.

The Kapos screamed at the new arrivals and led them back outside where their new garments were little protection from the elements. Shoed feet rumbled across the frozen mud, bare feet slapped in time as the great, faceless mass were driven the one hundred yards to the next hut.

Inside, they were ordered to line up alphabetically then were filed past a skilled official clutching a pointed tool with a short needle. They were all given numbers tattooed on the inside of their left forearms.

When it was the young man's turn he watched the skilled man as he worked the needle. Colored smoke rose up before his rapt eyes. The needle bit and stung the soft flesh of his arm. In blue characters an inch high his number -- 96432 -- was pressed into his skin.

With their freedom, clothes, hair and names taken from them, the new arrivals were marched outside. They ran with their thoughts dimly glowing behind their terrified eyes. SS men had taken over the herd. The Kapos joined the new arrivals but the SS did not cudgel them.

Some of the men tried rubbing their sides to produce heat as they ran but the sergeant ordered them to run with their hands above their heads. The young man ran easily, his breathing unlabored.

They were led up a road, which ran perpendicular to the one they'd come in on. To their surprise, they did not stop at the rows of barracks squatting in the light rain, but continued along the packed dirt road into the glare of the lights surrounding the roll call area. This was a dead open area extending from the front gate to the barracks.

The new arrivals ran across this area to the end at the right of the gate. Here they stood at attention for forty minutes in the freezing rain awaiting the return of the work parties to the camp.

Normally the SS men would have passed the time by tormenting the new arrivals but the rain had dampened their enthusiasm and they huddled in a small hut to watch the rain run down the scraped, smooth heads of the new prisoners.

As time crept by, the new arrivals moved only their eyes as they looked about like newborns at this strange world. The exertion required to keep their bodies absolutely rigid was too much for some and they fainted. This brought a curse from a guard who came out of the hut and mercilessly beat the prisoner until he got back in ranks or was dead.

The young man listened to the rain, watched it drip from the barbwire gate. Towers squatted like monsters every thirty feet along the wire, the SS men huddled in their great coats like turtles, blowing on their hands. All was quiet save the drumming of the rain and the odd cough from the guard's hut.

A group of prisoners emerged from one of the barracks just as the rain began to taper off. Hastily, and silently, they set up their instruments, casting a quick glance at the arrivals.

From around the bend in the road beyond the gate, in columns of five, the prisoners came up the road, marching with that unnatural gait like crude, jointless puppets. The band took up the Emperor's Waltz and the men marched, downcast and ragged, in time to the music.

Another prisoner had appeared before the new arrivals. His uniform bore no dirt, contained no holes. The SS men acknowledged him as they emerged from the hut.

The prisoner's faces were exhausted, drawn, jaundiced. The weary stamp of their filthy shoes filled the roll call area, drowning out the gay music. The last column entered, staggering under their burden. On their backs they carried the dead or those too exhausted to march. This column took their place at the head of the ranks so that the dead too could be noted and recorded.

Rules dominated in death as they did in life. Corpses were laid with their heads square to the feet of the first rank, legs stretched out, hands folded on their belly cavity, Their heads precisely lined up with the muddy shoes of the first rank.

The prisoner with the clean uniform called the roll, taking a moment to record the numbers of the dead. Satisfied, he turned to the bored SS sergeant with the results.

"Abspene!" the prisoner barked after the SS men had marched off.

Stiff ranks broke up like wind tossed leaves. Amidst the confused, turbulent movement, a small detail was assembled to tote the dead and exhausted to the crematorium.

The new arrivals followed the prisoners now dragging themselves along to the barracks. A Blockaltester -- barrack commander -- waited outside each barrack for them. Without steel bowls attached to their belts, he picked out the new arrivals amongst the prisoners trudging aimlessly in stark contrast to the imposed rigidity of their earlier marching.

"Attention!" he shouted. "I'm only going to say this once. The Altesters are in charge. Disobey and you'll go up the chimney. Their ranks are their armbands! 'LA' means Lageraltestor. As far as you lot are concerned, he is the boss in Gutundbose. 'Kapo' stands for Kameradpolizei. Do what they say when they say it and you'll live longer. You will work under a 'Vorabeiter'. He's the foreman. If he knocks you down, well, get up and wait for more. Last, but not least, me. I am the Blockaltester for this barrack, Block 12. When I tell you to do something, do it. Or else. I'll show you what I mean."

His fleshy face flashed red. Eyes ablaze, he leapt into the crowd of new arrivals and seized a reed-thin man. With grunts of effort and pleasure, he swung his axe handle at the man who cried out once or twice before crumpling lifeless at the Blockaltester's feet.

No one moved a muscle. Silence reigned. The young man regarded their new lord and master with interest. Hands planted firmly on hips, the Blockaltester glared at the new arrivals, daring them to act. Seeing the defenseless man beaten to death in front of them would have outraged them outside but, here, they accepted in numb silence. Inside the camp was a different world.

"Now get inside you piles of shit before I finish off every last one of you!"

Once inside, the cold air was replaced by the fetid, close stench of too many prisoners in too confining an area. There was no talking in the Block. Prisoners regarded the new arrivals over the rims of their bowls. The last meal of the day had been doled out. There would be no food for the new men.

The new arrivals hesitantly eased their way down the tight walkway between the tiered, wooden bunks. Prisoners slurping soup on the floor did not make way for them. The look the veterans had for the new arrivals was a strange mixture of distrust, curiosity and envy. Into their midst had come strong, well-fed men. Their skin had not the yellowish gray of the veterans. Their bellies were not yet distended from starvation. Muscles still hid their bones from view. The old veterans knew that the arrival of new, strong prisoners only made them look even weaker, more jaundiced and brought them closer to the crematorium. When the next selection came, they would be taken. These new arrivals were their replacements. This pattern of logic made its way through the mind of each prisoner as they gulped their soup and ate their bread over the bowl so as not to lose any crumbs. Their resentment urged them to lash out at the new arrivals.

One of the new prisoners found the courage to ask for a portion of a veteran's bread. The starved veteran bore the green triangle of the convict and slapped the hand of the new arrival away. He added a kick to the man's groin.

And so it began. The new arrivals huddled together as kicks and punches rained down on them. Veterans too weak to do physical harm spat on their victims. There was nowhere the new arrivals could turn. They could not ask to be fed. They had no bowls or spoons and the only way to get them was to steal or trade but they did not know this. Nor did they understand the hate the veterans had for them.

What passed for sanity here slowly took possession of the veterans. They returned to their places on the floor and bunks. The new arrivals remained huddled in a corner of the room.

The young man, a bruise on one cheek, a cut on his chin, took in his surroundings. The prisoners were packed into one-story wooden barracks. Tiers of wooden planks ran along the walls with a narrow walkway between them. There were three rows one on top of the other, the highest coming to just below the ceiling. Each tier held straw pallets. On the pallets, the prisoners were packed like sardines. There was no room to move. One had to lie perfectly straight on one's back or side. It was clear even to the untrained, frightened eyes of the new arrivals that the tiers were full. There was no bed for them this night.

The young man found it curious that after the harsh reception they had received, the veterans ignored them completely. A few large eyes glared at them from the dark recesses of the beds but most slept or conversed in low whispers.

Daring to stand, the young man challenged the veterans. He met every gaze that turned his way as he cautiously, then more quickly, examined the berths in search of a bed for the night. He noticed that the veterans supported their heads beneath a bundle made of the same striped material as their clothes. Few of the prisoners lying abed were wearing trousers so he assumed these served as makeshift pillows.

He walked the length of the block. At the far wall he stopped. A prisoner was lying on a third level pallet but not like the others. His mouth hung slack and dry, his eyes were half-closed and upon further observation, the young man noticed that this prisoner's chest did not rise and fall. Two other prisoners had noticed their dead comrade and were easing claw-like hands beneath the lifeless head, making it move side-to-side as if trying to deny it was dead. The veterans weren't sure if he was dead, which explained their hesitation to rob the corpse.

The young man didn't hesitate. He crawled up onto the top tier. He shoved the skeletal, probing arms away while trying to place his body between the corpse and the robbers. Weak fingers sought his throat, frail kicks struck his knees and shins. The young man lashed out, quick chopping swings, hitting one veteran on the bridge of the nose, the other in the ribs. They left him alone.

He rolled the corpse over with one hand; the yellow exposed teeth clicked against the rough wall. With his other hand, he uncovered the bundle the corpse's head had been resting on. He found a bowl and spoon wrapped in the corpse's pants and a pair of shoes. A rock hard piece of bread was in one pocket, a shoelace in the other. He tossed the bread at the complaining veterans he had struck and kept the rest. The prisoners fought for the bread.

The young man guessed that the pants would not fit him since the corpse was no more than a skeleton. But they could be traded, as would the prisoner's ragged, worn out shoes under the bowl. The corpse clattered like a wooden puppet as the young man shoved it over the side of the bunk. The corpse fell amongst the new arrivals clustered on the floor, causing a great commotion.

The corpse seemed to dance as the new arrivals kicked and screamed in fright. This brought a holy babble of protests from the veterans. A dozen languages hurled curses and threats as the new prisoners tried to rid themselves of the thing. A few veterans, wearing the green triangle of convicts fell on them with punches and kicks. But they quieted down only after a veteran grabbed one of the corpse's reed-thin arms and hauled it away.

The young man watched from above with great interest then settled back on the hard, fetid straw. Blood, urine and mud smells assailed him as he placed his head on the dead man's bundle.

So passed the first night

CHAPTER TWO

S hrill whistles shattered the solemnity of the icy morning. In the barracks the sleeping dead awakened, exploding into activity. The block shook to its foundations. The new arrivals were trampled and kicked as the veterans dressed themselves feverishly. They dressed quickly not only to cut the numbing chill which had seeped into their bones but also to procure a good place in the bread line queuing up in five minutes.

Clouds of rank dust filled the foul air as prisoners shook their torn blankets and carefully made their beds. Although they consisted of rotting straw, it was a camp rule that the beds be trimmed with sharp corners and be completely flat on top. The Blockaltester had his cronies examine the beds while the prisoners used the latrines and washroom.

For the new arrivals, all was chaos. No one answered their questions, no one offered advice. Some mimicked the veteran's actions, following them outside. Others crouched on the hard floor and wept. The Kapos would see to them. For many this day would be their last on earth.

The young man pulled on his trousers and jumped down amongst the throng. He used the wire from the corpse's pants to attach his bowl to his belt. He had no alternative but to carry the extra pants, shirt and shoes with him to the bathhouse. If not, they would be stolen in an instant.

The young man moved outside. The air was crisp, the sun just beginning to light the day. A throng of prisoners was scurrying towards a large block, which the young man assumed was the latrine. Some of the prisoners urinated while running so they could bypass the latrine and head directly to the Washroom. He followed them.

The Washroom was a large, long barrack, badly lit and drafty. Beneath a layer of frozen mud ran a brick floor. There was a sign against one wall. The young man studied it while others pushed roughly by him.

There was a cartoon of a prisoner stripped to the waist about to soap his head. Beneath the image, in German, was a caption which read: 'Like this you are clean.' Beside this was a Semitic image of a prisoner dressed from head to toe in dirty clothes. A tattered beret on his shaved head. This prisoner was cautiously dipping one finger into the water. The caption read: 'Like this you come to a bad end.' On the opposite wall was hung a sign depicting an enormous louse with the writing: 'A louse is your death' and a brief rhyme: *After the latrine, before eating, wash your hands, do not forget.*

The young man removed the priest cassock and jacket he had been given and wadded them up with his shoes, bowl and spoon from the corpse, placing the bundle between his knees as he saw the veterans do.

Outside once more he found his way back to the block. A long line had formed for bread and he was at the back of it. He traded the corpse's pants to move up two spaces. The line moved quickly. He accepted the hard, course chunk of bread thrust at him by the food distributor. He tucked the bread inside his shirt.

Only thirty minutes had passed since the inmates had been deep in exhausted sleep. A buzzer assailed them and they quickly began forming up in the roll call area. The young man was amazed, as he took his place outside his block, that these strict, unmoving ranks comprised the prisoners who, just minutes before, had been dashing from one place to another and cursing anyone that stood in their way.

Beneath the watchful eye of the SS, the Roll Call Officer went through the ranks like a thresher, separating the new arrivals from the veterans. His task was made relatively easy since the new prisoners bore no colored triangles or numbers on their jackets. This was the first order of business before roll call could be conducted.

The young man rejoined the group he had come in with and they were marched to the Labor Records Office for processing before being assigned to a work Kommando.

Here their names were entered onto index cards as well as the reason for their incarceration. When all of the new arrivals had been catalogued, Kapos marched them to the Tailor Block so they could have their numbers sewn onto their uniform. The entire procedure from roll call area to Labor Records Office to the Tailor Block was conducted at a dead run. Many of the new arrivals collapsed in the process. No food and water coupled with even less sleep highlighted by terror decimated the ranks. Those too exhausted to continue had to lie, sobbing and groaning until after roll call when a small Kommando would be organized to carry them to the crematorium.

The young man knew he must use the things he had taken from the corpse because they would be taken from him in the Tailor's Block. The new prisoners were lined up outside the wood barrack with shouted orders and generous use of the Kapo's clubs.

"Hurry up with this, scum!" an SS sergeant said to one of the Kapos. "Then get them into a work detail. This isn't a country club."

The young man saw his chance. He was at the back of the line so only had a short time to make his move. He called to the Kapo behind him. His first call brought the Kapo's club down on his kidneys followed by an order to shut up.

"Please, sir," the young man persisted. "I have something for you."

Greed blazed from the Kapo's wary eyes.

"All I ask is to be assigned to Pietor Chekunov's detail."

He was taking a chance. If he so desired, the Kapo could just take what was offered and there was nothing the young man could do about it. But the Kapo was surprised by the request and moved closer.

"What do you have?"

"Bread and a pair of shoes."

The Kapo snorted at the ignorance of the new prisoners. Bread was gold in the camp. It was the only thing that kept one alive and this fool wanted to trade his life so he could slave away with someone he knew outside.

"Very well," the Kapo said. "Give them to me. I'll see what I can do."

The young man pulled the hard chunk of bread out of his shirt and the shoes from the pockets of his trousers. Bread and shoes vanished into the Kapos loose-fitting clothes. He shoved the young man back in line.

Inside the Tailor Block, the chatter of sewing machines filled the air. The SS non-coms working the machines moved quickly and efficiently. Another train was due later that morning and all the new arrivals had to be processed by then.

The files bearing the prisoner's name, number and crime had only been brought over fifteen minutes prior to the arrival of the prisoners. Each prisoner, upon entering, would give his name and number to the stout SS man at the desk, answer yes or no when his name was checked against the list. Once identity had been established, the guard would plunge his flabby hand into a row of trays containing different colored triangles. There were Red for Politicals (a white stripe added for repeat offenders), Green for habitual criminals, Purple for Jehovah's Witnesses, Black for vagrants, Pink for homosexuals, Brown for gypsies and Yellow for Jews. Next to the tray there were small piles or armbands and variations of the triangles -- some contained "K's" to denote war criminals or, if foreigners, the letter of their nationality was printed on the badges.

"96432," the young man said, showing the arm bearing the number.

"Aaron Dieter," the guard read.

"Yes."

The guard took a moment to re-check his list. There must be some mistake, he thought. The file said vagrant but what we had here was a filthy Jew. "Drop your trousers!" he ordered.

Aaron did so.

The guard used his club to prod Aaron's genitals to see if he had been circumcised. He had not. The guard resumed his seat, squinting at Aaron as if he had somehow fooled the guard. Aaron looked straight ahead. Finally, the guard, satisfied with the result of his bodily inspection and the cassock Aaron was wearing, picked up a black triangle and flung it Aaron.

At the machines, he had to hand over his jacket and trousers. The black triangle was sewn on to the left breast of the jacket. An inch below that, a dirty strip of cloth bearing a crudely stitched number was affixed. A similar strip was place on his right trouser leg. The garments were tossed back at Aaron and a guard pushed him roughly forward.

Back outside, the Kapos herded the prisoners back together. They were hurried back to the roll call area where endless numbers were called off then checked and rechecked by the RCO. Aaron replied when his number was called. He had managed to stay near the Kapo he had made the arrangement with.

A group of prisoners stood off to one side as the roll was completed; no one had seen their arrival. They were better dressed than the others. Each wore a navy jacket against the chill. Long hardwood clubs hung from their waists. Their calloused hands clenched and loosened.

"Labor details -- fall in!"

The Labor Kapos surged forward, the fronts of their coats fanning outwards. They herded the new prisoners towards the main body of the camp, which was breaking up into work details. They shoved the new prisoners in twos and threes arbitrarily into any work detail short of men. Aaron looked back and thought he saw the Kapo he had bribed whisper to his comrade but he could not be sure.

Aaron fond himself amongst a group of two dozen men. From the white, chalky dust on their uniforms, he assumed he would be put to work in the quarry.

A beefy hand clamped down on his shoulder. It was the Kapo he'd seen talking with the one he'd bribed. "You!" The Kapo's breath was in Aaron's face. "Over there!"

He was given a powerful kick that propelled him forward into a group of about a dozen men. They also had chalky residue on their uniforms.

The band had set up in a patch of morning sunshine; the sound of their tuning undercut the chatter of the prisoners.

"Form fives!"

The prisoners lined up in orderly ranks, kicking up clouds of dust. The band struck up the Blue Danube, which almost drowned out the Kapos.

"Move out! Double time!"

The prisoners shuffled forward. At the gate, they removed their caps and thrust their hands rigidly against their trouser seams. The clatter of the band was deafening as the prisoners filed through the gate.

The road turned sharply to the right and began sloping downward. Many of the weaker prisoners showed relief as they let gravity aid their progress. The veterans knew well that after ten hours of backbreaking labor, they would have to march uphill back to the camp.

Straight ahead in the distance lay an open, gray area. This was the quarry. From here, the camp had been constructed as well as the SS quarters a mile and a half from the camp. Beyond the quarry lay the small town of Jenseits in which a munitions factory had been secreted. In trying to halt the Allied advance, it had become necessary to expand the factory. Thus the quarry detail had been increased and worked longer hours.

The prisoners were run right into the quarry. They were not ordered to halt until they reached the tool shed. It was preferable to be at the front of the ranks in order to be issued a shovel or pick. Those at the rear would dig with their bare hands when the tools ran out or be given the backbreaking job of carting the rubble away.

The sun was well up by this time. Puffs of wind made the skeletal branches of the trees surrounding the quarry clatter. Gray stone burned white in the glare that cast the prisoners' faces deeper in shadow. The air carried only the barest trace of remembered spring to temper the autumn daggers it flung at the prisoners. It shrieked through the dry, dead shrubs, kicked up the loose dirt and flung it at their tattered pant cuffs while it stung their faces.

Aaron had seen Pietor Chekunov slip to the back of the line and followed him. By the time his row moved up, all of the tools had been distributed. Instead he was given a wooden pole. At each end of the pole a bucket hung from a rope. Aaron saw that Pietor had received the same apparatus. He judged the slim-shouldered sparse man could not last long at the demanding task but Pietor made no complaint.

Aaron, Pietor and the others scattered into the quarry like flung seeds upon stones. There were no assigned workstations for the carriers so he stayed close to Pietor.

The pale, thin arms of the pick-men hefted their tools in the air then brought them down on the hard stone. Only pebbles were produced by the weak effort. Soon they fell into a steady rhythm under the threatening presence of the Kapos. A couple of SS men had accompanied the Kommando and now lazed and smoked in the shade of the quarry wall.

Aaron used his hands to scoop up the fragments and dumped them in the bucket. When both buckets were full, he easily placed the pole behind his head and moved off in the direction the other dumpers had taken.

The dumpsite was an open area at the edge of the quarry separated by a thin stand of trees. Past the trees loomed a large mountain of rocks. Cold wind stirred the dust into blinding clouds, giving the trees a ghostly appearance. Aaron dumped his load, returned to the pick men.

This work continued all morning. Aaron spoke to no one but he observed the prisoners very closely. What was immediately noticeable was the presence of the Politicals in every supervising position. Three-quarters of the Kapos were Politicals and those prisoners, bearing the red triangle, who worked the quarry had the best picks. Those forced to do the most physically draining tasks such as carting the rubble or digging through the rocky earth with bare hands were homosexuals, Jehovah's Witnesses or transients like himself. The green badge of the criminal comprised the rest of the Kapos.

During the half-hour lunch break, Aaron approached Pietor. They did not speak but Aaron took a moment to study the prisoner. Aaron had judged him to be no more than five foot five inches tall. His frame was thin and wiry but that seemed to be close to its normal appearance so he had not endured all the hardships of camp life. His number, 52228, was low which told Aaron that Pietor had been in camp a while. He had a wide face with high, prominent cheekbones and sunken cheeks. His deep-set black eyes, set close together, above a Roman nose accented his small, thin, colorless lips and proud, square jaw. But what struck Aaron the most was Pietor's large spherical head. No bump or scar marred its smooth circumference. His ears were wide and stuck out more than up. His head was free even of stubble. The eyebrows, too, had been removed. Only dark shadows indicated the new growth beginning to sprout.

Towards late afternoon, Aaron saw Pietor staggering off to the dumpsite. One of the Kapos -- a criminal -- followed him. Up until that time, no Kapo had escorted a prisoner to the dumpsite. The choking, blinding dust was not to their liking so they avoided the area even though trees screened it. The Kapos knew well that none of the prisoners would use the trees to cover an escape attempt. Where could the prisoners go? Dressed as they were, who would help them? Even if they were fortunate enough to reach Jenseits, every hand there would be turned against them. Like old plough horses, the prisoners could be left unattended only to return after they had dumped their loads.

Now a Kapo had decided to follow Pietor. No other dumper made his way to the dumpsite, which was curious in itself. The work continued but each carrier seemed unable to fill his baskets or had a problem rope that had to be adjusted. The SS men were napping in the shade and missed this sudden loss of efficiency created for their benefit.

Aaron shouldered his pole and followed the two men. He hurried forward, the heavy buckets swinging like pendulums. The Kapo followed Pietor behind the stand of trees with Aaron a few yards behind.

Picking up the pace, Aaron cleared the cluster of trees in time to see Pietor slide the pole from his shoulders and turn on the Kapo.

"What!" the Kapo demanded.

"I have a message from Krueger," Pietor said in his slightly high, rich voice. "The last payment was short."

"I play fair with him!" the Kapo said, angrily. " Schummer took a bigger bite. You know the damned SS -- always after more."

"That's not how Krueger sees it."

"You call me a liar? I teach you!"

The Kapo drew his club and smashed it into Pietor's face. He fell heavily, sending up a cloud of dust. Before Pietor could regain his feet, another blow knocked him back down.

"Enough! Enough!" Pietor squealed.

"I say when is enough, you dog!" The Kapo moved forward.

Pietor scrambled backwards, his back slamming into the trunk of a tree. His face was covered in dust, making the blood pouring from his nose scarlet. His open mouth was a black, wet hole of pain. The Kapo grabbed hold of his collar and pulled him up. Pinning him against the tree, the Kapo smashed the club into Pietor's face again. He sagged but the Kapo hauled him up.

Aaron took a quick look around to ensure that they were not being observed. Satisfied, he moved forward quickly. As the Kapo drew his arm back, Aaron came up behind him and grabbed the man's wrist, stopping the impending blow. The Kapo grunted, trying to wrench his arm loose. Aaron released him and he swung around to face his next victim.

"Filthy bastard!" he shouted.

The first punch caught Aaron high the left cheek, snapping his head back but his eyes never left the Kapo's. The Kapo, enraged, swung his club in a blur at Aaron's head. Aaron brought both hands up. With his left he delivered a stiff chop just below the Kapo's elbow, numbing the hand. With the other he caught the wrist. With a quick, strong jerk, the Kapo's wrist snapped with a wet, muffled crack.

Howling, the Kapo crumpled into the dust with Aaron still holding his injured arm.

Meanwhile Pietor slowly managed to stand. With his returning senses came the realization of what had just transpired.

"Kill him! Kill him!" hissed pale Pietor, jerking his square chin at Aaron.

"That will not be necessary," Aaron said.

"If he lives we're done for. Kill him! I have protection. We'll be safe after he's dead!" Pietor looked upward as if to damn the heavens for creating this situation. He let his gaze drop to the sprawled Kapo. He kicked some dust onto the prone body. "You sick fool."

A gust of wind shook the tree Pietor was leaning against like an invisible hand. Aaron regarded Pietor for a moment, puzzled over the peculiar look in the man's eye.

Aaron sank down on his haunches and regarded the injured Kapo. "What is your name?"

"Dravek!"

"Well, Dravek, it seems you have taken a nasty fall. Look, you've broken your wrist."

"You wish you never born," Dravek threatened.

Aaron twisted the man's hand, grinding the broken bones together. Dravek's mouth gaped as he fought back a scream. Aaron's other hand clamped over his mouth. The Kapo's face drained of color, his bulging eyes rolled up.

"Kill him!" urged Pietor.

"Here's what we'll do. My comrade and I will return to work. In five minutes, you may notify the guards about your clumsy accident. Do you understand?"

"You -- " The Kapo's struggles, fuelled by rage, increased.

"You are right." Aaron looked up at Pietor. "I will kill him now."

Aaron dropped the broken arm and wrapped both his hands around the Kapo's throat. Pietor leaned forward, a gleam in his bloodshot eyes. The pleading in the Kapo's eyes as his face distorted and turned blue told Aaron he wished to be more cooperative.

"Do you understand?" Aaron asked again.

Dravek nodded his head, coughing and spluttering.

"Very well." Aaron stood. "Remember, five minutes."

Aaron took up his pole while urging Pietor to do the same. As they rounded the stand of trees, their buckets empty, Pietor spoke up.

"You should have finished him."

"Don't you see," Aaron replied. "It is much more believable to fall and break one's wrist than to break one's neck."

"I'm protected -- "

"If he is found dead, then suspicion and security will be increased above and beyond the present intense level. We cannot allow that to happen?"

"We?'

"Yes, there is much to be done." Aaron stopped and stared into the other's eyes. "I need your help, Pietor Chekunov."

CHAPTER THREE

Aside from Dravek stumbling into camp and reluctantly informing the guards that he had fallen and broken his wrist, the rest of the workday passed without incident.

Aaron did not speak again with Pietor but he could sense the Russian's eyes on him while he worked. The sky grew dark with an impending storm and the dying of the light. At the SS men's signal, the Kapos blew their whistles, ending the day's work. The tools were cleaned, inspected -- several of the new prisoners were beaten mercilessly for not cleaning their tools satisfactorily -- and returned to the shed.

The prisoners formed ranks, the last row supporting the dead and those two weak to walk. They would have to be carried back to camp so their deaths could be recorded, their bodies burned.

It began to rain heavily as the men marched back to camp. Music welled up from inside the camp as they approached the gate. They marched beneath the clutching talons of the Nazi eagle above the gate.

Eager for the day's meager ration to say nothing of their need to get out of the icy rain now falling, the prisoners formed ranks quickly in anticipation of roll call. But it did not come. The last of the work parties returned and still it did not begin. The veterans knew what was to come. The new arrivals felt only hunger gnawing at their bellies.

12,000 men stood silently in the pouring rain. Across double strands of electrified barbwire, 8000 Jews stood waiting. The quiet swelled as the rain filled the mouths of the silently screaming dead.

Without warning, the roll began. Hour after hour passed as prison clerks checked the numbers. The line of dead at the front of each squad of men grew.

"Caps off!" shouted the Roll Call Officer in respect to the Senior Camp Inmate who rarely appeared for the roll, but whose presence was felt everywhere in camp. "Caps on!"

"Left face!" the RCO's voice thundered over the loud speakers.

This was that the veterans had expected. There would be a punishment.

A woman was led out of the Jail Barrack. Her zebra-striped dress hung in rags on her ravaged body. She fell and was dragged to her feet. The prisoners saw her back as a mass of torn red flesh. Blood soaked through her clothing turning any area it touched darker than the rain did. Blood also ran down the insides of her legs. The gallows was in the prisoners' line of sight. She was dragged there.

Aaron recognized her as they drew closer. It was the woman who had jostled with the guard on the platform. Her face was badly bruised, lips swollen, one eye puffed shut, but he felt the flame from her remaining eye, squinting through her matted hair.

She fell again at the foot of the gallows. The SS men left her there as they checked with the man above on the raised platform fixing the rope. He indicated that all was ready so they grabbed her by the hair and raised her up. She had fallen so heavily into the thick mud that they struggled to draw her out. The moist earth sucked her down and they fought against the pull.

Aaron became aware of a slight murmuring around him as he watched the scene unfold. Someone behind him whispered a prayer while others wished the deed would be done so they could get their soup. Some of the criminals laughed while expressing their dismay over hanging her before they could have a turn on her. A prisoner two over from Aaron wept silently. All were shamefully relieved that it was she, not them, who was about to die.

One of the guards put a sign around her neck that bore her crime
-- she had struck an Aryan. He punched her for good measure,
snapping her head back. She swayed and almost fell, then fixed him
with her one blazing eye. He turned and read out her crime for the
prisoners. First in German, then in her native language. He stepped
back. The guard behind her bound her hands, jerked the crude noose
tight around her neck.

For an instant, she stood alone on the platform. The guards
dwindled away beneath her flaming eye radiating its gaze over the
assembled prisoners. She drew a shaking breath. The sign bearing
her crime rose and fell on her exposed chest as the guard reached up
for the lever which would mean her death.

"Revenge!" she screamed, the cords on her neck standing out.
The flaming eye closed tight and the rain wept large drops from her
soaked hair.

The trap door fell open and her frail body plunged through,
jerking to a sudden, final stop. Rain and blood ran down her face,
dripped from her lifeless feet still kicking feebly like the last embers
of a dying fire.

The punishment over, the order was given to disperse. A thunder
of running feet erupted from the compound. Teams of men carted
the dead to the furnaces while food distributors rolled their kettles
of thin soup to the barracks.

Aaron watched Pietor disappear into Block 6. He would go there
after the food had been distributed.

Aaron's Block became a symphony of slurping noises the minute
the soup was distributed. He received his portion and downed it
quickly after throwing a squatter out of the sleeping place he had
taken from the corpse.

At the end of the workday, unless otherwise specified, the prisoners
were free to do whatever they wished until lights out. Many opted
for the rarest and most precious commodity in camp: rest. Others
moved about the compound, talking or just taking air. The more
cunning of the prisoners used the time to organize the next day's
survival. Although death could come at any time from any direction

there were a few precautions the prisoners could take. This period of free time was the opportunity to trade for bread, better shoes, cigarettes, a piece of rope for a belt or wire to hold a rotted pair of shoes together. Medicine was very rare but it too could be had for the right price. A few rotted carrots or the meat of a stray dog or cat which had wandered into the camp were just a few of the precious items to be traded for by those able to see beyond the next minute. This type of foresight was rare and dangerous in the camp but as long as one didn't look too far into the future, say, to the time of liberation -- a time no inmate dared to believe would ever come -- then it was possible to survive minute to minute.

Aaron didn't waste any time tracking down Pietor. He found him outside, smoking and talking with two other men. One wore the red triangle, the other wore green.

"Pietor Chekunov," he said, approaching the prisoners. "It is time."

"Time for what?"

"I wish to see Senior Camp Inmate Hans Krueger. He will no doubt want to hear all about Dravek's accident this afternoon."

"Believe me, comrade." Pietor walked away from the other two and went off with Aaron. "He already knows."

"Will you take me to him?"

"Yes, of course. You saved my life did you not?"

The Administration Block lay outside the camp. Since the Senior Camp Officers were all political, they were permitted to live outside the barbed wire. Power was all they desired and ruling over the prisoners, there was no need for them to escape. Also, the barrack being outside the appalling conditions in camp, gave easier access to the main road so the SS could travel to and from the barrack without having to enter the camp. The Block lay in the shadow of a guard tower manned by an SS non-com with a machine gun. The surrounding terrain was open and flat. These two elements acted as excellent deterrents to any prisoner who considered attempting escape under the pretext of visiting the Senior Inmates.

Pietor led Aaron out through the gate under the watchful eye of the SS and onto the porch that ran along the side of the barrack. The

Block lay lengthwise to the camp and was divided right down the middle. The half facing the camp contained the offices for the Senior Inmates and clerks as well as their living quarters -- spacious and comfortable by camp standards. The half facing the road housed the working offices of the SS clerks and junior officers that acted as the eyes and ears of the Kommandant who lived in the small village the prisoners had been forced to build for the SS guard contingent a quarter mile from the camp. The SS avoided Jenseits since the Allied bombing had begun two years before. The town had yet to be hit but one never knew.

There was a bench to the left of the entrance. Pietor motioned Aaron to take a seat while he went inside to inquire if Krueger would see them. He returned a moment later, relaying Krueger's orders that they wait until called for.

"I want to thank you for saving my life," Pietor blurted, breaking the silence.

"Think nothing of it," Aaron replied. "Getting me this far has been thanks enough."

"I'll do you one better, comrade." Pietor got up and faced the camp. Night had fallen, prisoners moved like ghosts between the dark mass of the barracks. In the distance, the glow from the crematorium cast its eerie radiance. The faint crackling of the barbwire reached them as some poor soul sought oblivion by throwing himself on the electrified fence. "All this," he began, sweeping a raised hand across the camp. "All this works. There is a system here. You are new, comrade, so it is better to tell you now while you can still think. Later, you brain won't hold anything other than basic needs. And you'll end up like them."

He pointed at several shambling figures moving about near the wire. Their empty, watery, staring eyes flickered like candles far away. With clenched teeth and fixed stares they shuffled aimlessly, interfering in trades and discussions. The other prisoners kicked and cuffed them until they moved on.

"Muselmänner!" Pietor declared. "Living coffins. Broken men with all intellect and reason beaten and starved out of them. This is the fate of anyone trying to survive here without learning the system.

Your business with Krueger is your business but let me tell you that
your fate is the Muselmann's unless you belong to a group. Kapos.
Politicals. POWs, Jews. Each is a network supporting the individual.
Any of these mean survival. Alone, a man cannot live."

Aaron listened intently.

"You are quick and resourceful," he went on. "Comrade, you
belong with us. Tell Krueger you will be his and he will keep you
alive. He saved my life before we were placed here."

"What manner of man is he?"

"Strong and proud," Pietor replied, awe in his voice. "A leader of
men. A visionary. He answers to no man save the Kommandant."

"Remarkable under these conditions. Listen to me, Pietor. I have
come to offer myself to Krueger. That is my task this night."

"You will do great things here. I feel it. Let me explain how we
survive."

With quick efficiency, Pietor explained Kozentrationlager
Gutundbose. The men's camp contained twenty-seven barracks.
The large horseshoe shaped structure just inside the gate was the
camp kitchen. To the right of that was Block Six, Pietor's block.
Blocks sixteen and seventeen were the Prison Hospital. On the left
south corner, Crematorium One, next to it, almost operational, was
Crematorium Two. Three thousand SS watched the camp in three
shifts. There was a large structure on the east side of the camp Aaron
pointed out and was told that it was the Storeroom for property taken
from those who were gassed in the Bathhouse next to Crematorium
One. One small Block outside the wire between the Crematorium
and the SS quarters was the Brothel. Only Aryan Politicals and the
SS guards were permitted to use it. A fact to which Pietor expressed
a great deal of regret. North of the double row of barbed wire lay the
Jewish Camp.

"The SS have a multitude of rules," he went on, "which I will come
to. But we prisoners have some vital methods. First of all, don't get
sick. Never report to the Hospital Block. It is frequently liquidated
to avoid overcrowding. Medicine is traded freely in camp so find
your cure there. Eat every scrap of food put in front of you. Even
the crumbs. Lick your bowl 'til it shines. Trade for extra rations.

You will have to. It is impossible to live for long on the daily ration. Everything can be traded in camp. Food, clothes, rags, paper, string, wire, everything has value. Remember that."

"And the SS?" Aaron asked. He had already observed much of what Pietor was relating. Ignorance of a prison rule meant going hungry, disobeying the SS, for whatever reason, meant death.

"There are too many to list," Pietor replied. "Watch carefully and learn. Never come within two yards of the wire. Don't sleep in your jacket or with your cap on. Never leave your Block with your jacket unbuttoned. Or with the collar raised. You must have five buttons on your jacket at all times. Keep your clothes clean. Never put your hands in your pockets. Always say Jawohl. Never question a Kapo or the SS. Much, much more. It is up to you to learn."

"Camp schedules?"

"Schedules?" Pietor snorted. "You High Numbers, always so full of ridiculous questions. Work is the only schedule. Work until you are unable to, then you go up the chimney. Sometimes six, seven days a week. Ten hours a day or twenty. The Germans make schedules as they wish. Recently we have worked six days and longer hours. Things are worse in the Jewish Camp. Every Saturday, after work, you must report to the camp barber, that is Block Eleven, to have your beard and head shaved. Sunday is the medical exam but the SS have tired of this so it cannot be counted on."

He resumed his seat. "That is all I can tell you. The rest you must learn yourself. If Krueger will have you, then you will survive. This war can't last much longer. We get sporadic reports and know the tide has turned. With Krueger's network you will survive until we are liberated. Have faith. We communists take pride in our leader and his accomplishments."

"I would think there was no place for pride in a concentration camp," Aaron observed.

"You speak the truth. If you want to survive, you best leave pride outside the gate, but, if you are of tougher mettle, then it can be smuggled in. But be wary, for here more than any other place on earth, it is a double-edged sword. Pride can fill you up when there is no soup but it can also slice through your guts when you must witness, or be a part of, things that should not be. Gutundbose tends to play on the baser instincts. High ideals are burned in the crematorium everyday."

The door opened and a mean-faced Kapo grunted and gestured.

"Come," Pietor said, standing. "It is time."

CHAPTER FOUR

A stone-faced Kapo led them down a dark hallway. The air bore a heavy solemnity. The block was silent in the early evening. The dim light and hushed movements of the Kapo gave the building the air of a church.

Two Kapos with stout clubs flanked the double oak doors at the end of the hall. The window on their right faced the camp and one light from the top of the fence shone in, highlighting their rough, hard features. Aaron found it amazing that Krueger was treated like a valuable dignitary, not an inmate. If not for the smell of the crematorium, the plain walls and chipped paint on the heavy doors, the block seemed more like a palace.

They were searched by the Kapos, then told to wait. One of them, the older of the two, rapped on the door and entered. The door banged shut in their faces. The same Kapo opened it a few seconds after waved them inside.

The room contained a large desk, a filing cabinet and three chairs. There were two small windows and a door to the left of the desk leading to Krueger's sleeping quarters. An overhead light cast cold white light over the room. Pietor raised a hand to his eyes until they adjusted.

The other door opened and in the shadow of the darkened room, a hulking silhouette was visible. The uneven wood floor groaned as the figure crossed the threshold.

Senior Camp Inmate Hans Krueger emerged into the light. He did not look at Aaron or Pietor but went directly to his desk. Krueger was a large, imposing man, boasting a considerable girth topped by a great barrel chest. Both of these titanic physical attributes he was somehow able to squeeze behind his desk. Hands red like the backs of crabs thudded onto the top of the desk. Sausage-like fingers drummed slowly. Ice blue, alert eyes flicked to Aaron. There was no challenge in his gaze -- just confident inspection, like a zookeeper examining his animals. One of the crab hands rose slowly to the broad expanse of weathered face. A thick, fat finger traced the thin white scar running from his right eye down his cheek like a tear, curling tightly towards the base of the bulbous nose before disappearing into the forest of beard. Large rubbery lips pursed out of the tangled expanse. Parted slightly, they revealed gray, round teeth like tombstones. The forest of beard undulated with the working of the jaw muscles as the finger explored.

No one spoke. Aaron thought it best not to begin the interview and Pietor had withered into craven silence in the presence of his lord and master. Krueger did not seem eager to get started. The profound silence in the room took on the anxious feeling of the calm before the storm.

The door swung open, shattering the silence. Three men all wearing Kapo jackets with red triangles entered the room. They stepped softly, respectfully, but their tread sounded thunderous after the silence. Two were in their late thirties, the third looked more like a boy than a man though he might have been anywhere from twenty to fifty years old. They removed their caps and took up places around Krueger.

"You are late," Krueger said, his voice rich and full.

The three did not attempt to explain themselves for no excuse would be tolerated.

"96432," Krueger said, fixing his piercing gaze on Aaron, "you wished to see me."

"Yes, sir."

"And why should I waste my time with you?"

"And why should I waste my time with you?"

"I ask only four minutes."

"Many can shower down the road in four minutes."

Aaron said nothing.

Krueger studied him for a moment before speaking. "Had you not come to the rescue of Pietor this afternoon... Does it surprise you that I would know this? Nothing escapes my notice in this camp, 96432. That is why I sent for you. Or, did you think Pietor has the courage to walk over here without my leave and insist on an audience?"

"If you sent for me, sir, why complain about time. The minutes are yours to give or withhold as you wish."

"You are quite right. Here, all time is mine. Life and death are the opening and closing of my eyes. What were you in life, 96432?"

"A farmer."

"You were not," Krueger said, quickly. "Lie to me again and your life is finished."

"A Jew, then," Aaron said. "That is all that matters here."

Krueger leaned back, regarding Aaron with newfound interest. "You gained admittance to the Men's Camp... You take risks, Jew."

"I am not circumcised. And you, sir, have my file on your desk. You have read and considered it. What more is there?"

Krueger frowned at Aaron's observation. He had read the file, knew all there was to know about the man sitting before him. However, the file was amidst the stack on his desk and it had nothing to say concerning Aaron's intuitive ability. He would have Jew 96432 watched. If he proved a threat, he would be removed. For him, this was the end of the matter. "Your time grows short. Pietor's life is barely worth four minutes. What is it you wish? An extra coat? Bread?"

"I ask two things."

"Two?" Krueger's eyebrows shot up. The man was either impertinent or suicidal.

"The first is information."

"What good is information in camp?"

"It will give me peace of mind."

"That, Jew 96432, can be had at a much cheaper cost to me," Krueger laughed. "In the crematorium can be found peace of mind.

In camp you may flee inside yourself where none can reach you. As a Muselmann, your life will be short but peaceful I assure you."

Aaron waited patiently for Krueger to finish. "You asked me what I wish, sir. I am prepared to tell you."

"Speak."

"I wish to know today's date."

"It is the thirty-first of October, one thousand nine hundred and forty-four. Next?"

"Thank you, sir," Aaron said, graciously. "I wish information concerning Professor Solomon Liebman. I assume he is in this camp, but I do not know which barracks."

"What is this Liebman to you?"

"We share a mutual acquaintance."

Krueger rubbed his jaw thoughtfully. "And if he is here?"

"Then I respectfully request to be placed in the same barrack."

"I see. Anything else?"

Aaron shook his head.

Krueger considered Aaron's request while his associates darted glances from him to Aaron and back again. The new arrival's demands were outrageous. Krueger might grant simple requests but he did not do favors like some errand boy.

"What makes you think he is here?" Krueger asked.

"Call it a belief."

"Truth has no greater enemy than conviction. Following one in pursuit of the other is dangerous."

"Conviction of thought and will to act are not the same thing."

Krueger was intrigued by the sudden opening of this doorway to higher thought. So much of his governing here dealt with matters on a more primitive level. Food. Shelter. Graft. The petty grievances of his lieutenants. "Whatever lives, obeys, Jew. Personal conviction liberates one to act. The will of the State liberates many. All must follow one or the other. Which is the stronger?"

"The will of the individual, for the State imposes its will. One must surrender to the State in order to embrace it. This is contrary to human nature."

"Human nature aspires to divinity. Does not the divine impose its will on the rest?"

Aaron gestured to the window where the glow of the Crematorium lit the twilight. "Listen to the roar of the fires. Smell the decay. Gods, too, decompose."

Krueger stared out the window, eyes vague, staring at something past what they looked upon. "To become new we must first become ashes. It is our naked self against the purifying flame. If we can endure, how much stronger must we become? The best steel goes through the fire. The weak fuel that flame, the flame hardens those who survive. It is the will of the State that the weak be destroyed so the strong can grow stronger."

"How will you keep the fire burning when the fuel is used up?"

"It will never be used up. Conflict provides the fuel."

"In that, I'm afraid, we are in agreement."

Krueger seemed to shake himself back into the present moment. He turned his gaze from the window and his eyes bore into Aaron. He cleared his throat. "We discuss the abstract and, though I find it mildly stimulating, we will focus on the here and now. Your first request was accepted because you saved Pietor's life. The second, however, requires a considerable effort on behalf of my people. Tracking down a single inmate in a camp of this size is an undertaking which goes beyond mere gratitude."

Aaron saw where this was headed. "What is it you wish from me?"

"Half your bread ration."

Pietor gasped and looked sharply at Krueger. To deprive a man of bread was to end his life. Aaron, however, was not fazed by this demand.

"Agreed," he said.

"Excellent."

"To whom shall I turn over the half-ration?"

Krueger leaned back in his chair and stared at Pietor. "It is said that once you save a life you are responsible for it."

"But he's a Jew!" Pietor interrupted. "Please, don't -- "

"Give the ration to Pietor."

Pietor squirmed in his seat, he opened his mouth to protest again but knew it would be folly to do so. Aaron was confused by this outburst but continued on. "When may I have the information?"

Krueger had gown tired of this exchange. Philosophical discussion aside, he'd challenged Aaron and found him to be a fool. Or was it cunning? Any man who would so readily agree to his demand had more to gain than to lose. What lurked behind the Jew's request? He seemed innocent enough but innocence can be worn like a garment. What lay beneath the robe? In all men there is a secret self, Krueger knew, concealed beneath a veneer of civilization. Such artifices as one's walk, manner of speech or position in society were easily penetrated. Subterfuge, deceit and ingratiation had been many a man's shroud during Krueger's rise through life. In camp, things were so much simpler. There was only oneself and cold reality, no blinds to hide behind. Coming to power here had been the simplest of undertakings. There were no secrets beyond his understanding, no truth he could not possess. Jew 96432 bore watching. He would learn the Jew's truth before dealing with him. He waved a hand dismissively. "Within a couple of days. I will send for you. Until then, Pietor knows what I expect from him."

Then he turned his attention to the Kapos. Aaron and Pietor, clearly dismissed, stood, bowed their heads slightly to Krueger and left.

CHAPTER FIVE

C Block had the privilege of being located a considerable distance from the bathhouse and the fires of the crematorium, the roar of which was reduced to a barely audible throb. C Block was the Men's Camp. It was divided into three sections. Barracks thirty-four through sixty-eight housed the majority of prisoners. Homosexuals and Politicals, Jehovah's Witnesses and criminals called these one-story hovels home. Barracks sixty-nine through one hundred and two were reserved for the Jewish population. Only a stone's throw from the Crematorium and gas chambers, it was the worst spot in the camp. The population of these barracks was reduced approximately every six months thus necessitating the proximity to the ovens.

The Men's Camp, however, had in recent months undergone a period of overcrowding that it could not compensate for. When the camp had first been put into operation, Barracks one through seventeen had been designated as the Quarantine Camp. Typhus and Dysentery, both of which had escalated in the last six months, had led to an enlarging of the Quarantine Camp to include Barracks eighteen through thirty-three. The healthy prisoners from these barracks had been absorbed into the barracks that remained or they had been gassed. Some went to Ka-Be, others were used for target practice but in the end, the move was completed. Now the greatly reduced Men's Camp slept eight to a bunk instead of five. The line-ups for the latrine were staggering. Many simply relieved themselves wherever they could. But one had to be cautious. This was against camp rules and could bring a bullet from the watchtowers.

Each camp consisted of two or more rows of barracks with one latrine per row. Seventeen barracks comprised a row plus two buildings for Block Leader and his Kapo. The rows were set up in a rectangle. To the north lay the crematorium and gas chambers as well as the storerooms for the victim's property. To the south, guard towers and barbed wire. Westward lay the rail connection which brought the trains in.

These conditions could be considered ideal compared to those of the Jewish Camp. Aaron and Pietor were struck immediately by the overpowering odor from the crematorium. They were alone on the east road bordering the Men's and Jewish Camps. The guards kept close watch over the two men since it was almost curfew. Any prisoner caught outside after the bell would be shot. The guards were not alone in their vigil. Saucer-wide eyes stared from gaunt faces at the pair as they neared the fence of the Jewish Camp. These ghastly apparitions silently stood watch, only their too-large eyes, wet and bleary, betrayed the spark of life in their frail bodies.

Pietor did not look at the starving, skeletal prisoners. He seemed fascinated by the moon which was on the rise. Aaron, on the other hand, studied them with great interest. When they had come upon the Jewish Camp they had been in the shadow of a road lamp. As soon as they passed out of the shadow into the glow from the next, the prisoners stirred to life. Feeble cries for bread or water emanated from the mass. Aaron moved closer to the barbed wire.

"Don't!" hissed Pietor. "The guards!"

Aaron resumed his place at his companion's side but did not take his eyes off the wretched prisoners. Pietor increased his pace and they were soon past the camp. The smell from the crematorium grew stronger as they approached Ka-Be. This area consisted of twelve sick wards, two small barracks for the nurses and a larger barrack for the doctor and his assistants. Pietor seemed to have more spring in his step as the Jewish Camp receded behind them.

"Where are we going?" Aaron asked.

"Storerooms."

"Why?"

"We need uniforms. We can't get into... "

Unfazed by the fear in Pietor's eyes, Aaron pressed. "Go on."

"We have to spend the night... there."

"In the Jewish Camp?"

"Yes."

"I am Jewish," stated Aaron.

"Not after tomorrow," Pietor said. "You heard Krueger. You are responsible for me. He has bound us together, it is the way things are done here. It is my punishment for what happened at the quarry. We're stuck with each other now. So for tonight we both are."

They were at the storerooms now. Pietor nodded to the prison guards and opened the door of the fifth barrack they came to. Aaron took in the sheer size of the storage facility. There were twenty-four barn-like buildings in three neat rows of eight barracks each. Signs above the doors indicated what was stored in each. He glanced up at the sign over the door Pietor had opened. Men's Coats it said.

Inside were endless stacks of clothes reaching nearly to the roof. Tight bundles of jackets of all shapes and colors were piled one on top of the other. And not just prison uniforms. Three-quarters of the space was filled with civilian coats being prepared for shipment back to the Reich. Men and women moved like ants around the mountains of clothes, sorting, counting, and numbering each bundle. Not a thread of cloth was allowed to go unaccounted for.

Aaron spotted Pietor at one of the four desks in front of the bundles. A young girl with a pinched, starved face was listening as he explained their needs. The girl punctuated each point with a quick bird-like nodding of her shorn head. Aaron moved towards the desk. The girl, her mission received, whisked away on feet that barely touched the rough wood floor.

"It won't take long," Pietor said as Aaron came to stand next to him. "God, I wish it would. I asked Molly to find something for you, too."

"Couldn't the jackets we are wearing be altered?"

"No. If the guards see a thread or a light patch where the numbers match up, we'll both go up the chimney."

"I see."

The girl returned with a small bundle under her arm. She quickly inspected the serial number on the jacket with her pencil-thin fingers, then handed them to Pietor who was removing the jacket he wore.

He gave the girl his coat. "Not too much starch, now."

She did not smile or chuckle at this weak attempt at humor.

"This will do," Pietor said, examining his new coat. "No blood, hardly a rip in it."

She nodded her head but did not speak.

Pietor fingered the yellow star on the breast of the jacket gingerly, then shrugged into the coat. Aaron did likewise. "We better get moving."

Aaron kept pace with Pietor as they made their way to the Jewish Camp. At the gate, the two SS guards, bandanas tied around their mouths and noses against the stench, barely gave them a glance as they stepped inside. The compound was deserted, as it was almost curfew. Just off the main road, behind Barrack 18, they rounded a large, sloping hill of soil left over from the excavation for the Crematoria. The hill bristled with grass shoots that swayed in the breeze. They moved deeper into the camp. Aaron found it strange that as their time was short, they did not simply enter the first barrack they came to. Instead Pietor led him between the rows, eventually stopping in front of Barrack Fifteen.

"Follow my lead," he whispered and stepped inside.

Their arrival went unnoticed. Men chatted in the cots arranged in tiers along either wall. Snores resounded from the darkened area at the rear. One feeble bulb lit the entire room, its light barely reaching a ten-foot radius. Four wooden tables were clustered around a small pot-bellied stove which hardly put a dent in the aching chill. Men sat at the tables, talking or just resting with eyes closed. Aaron and Pietor moved amongst the tables. No one offered any greeting.

The light would be put out soon so Pietor hurried them down the rows of bunks. If they did not find a bunk before lights out, they would sleep on the floor. Slowly, weak, tired faces began turning in their direction. A place to sleep was almost as valuable as a hunk of bread. The men lying on the bunks were preparing themselves for a fight. They would flail with feeble limbs at whoever threatened their place of rest.

Aaron and Pietor were almost at the far wall of the barrack and had not found a bed. Weak moonlight filtered through the small window set high in the wall but it did not help them in their search. Without warning, the lights went out casting the dark rear of the barrack into ghostly night. Feet could be heard shuffling towards them from the darkness. Four figures stepped into the moonlight. All four men had the same face, the same emaciated form. Beards of differing lengths and shades of color lent them a sort of individuality. Their features were hard, deep lines of sadness around the bloodless lips and bulging eyes. Their hunched, bony shoulders seemed to have been crushed by a great weight. Their scrawny necks pressed downwards as if by the weight of their skull-like faces.

And yet, despite all of the horror and revulsion these quasi-human figures generated, it was their eyes which held one's attention. For amidst the envy of the healthy bodies of Aaron and Pietor and the remembered images of the atrocities they had suffered or witnessed, there was pity in their eyes, a sadness for the two healthy men who would soon be turned into monsters like themselves.

No one spoke. No one moved. A man coughed, a racking explosion in the gloom. Finally one of the living skeletons moved forward, clear of the others. The tunic it wore hung like a tent on the stick figure. It extended a long, bony hand to Aaron and, at a time for sobs and lament, performed the one small action of humanity which sets it apart from the beasts of the field and conquers the beast in all of us. It smiled.

"Hello. My name is Jacob."

For fear of breaking the bones clearly defined in the prisoner's dry skin, Aaron gently clasped the offered hand and returned the faint smile. "My name is Aaron."

"Peter Schiller," Pietor said, offering his hand.

Jacob took Pietor's hand in a surprisingly strong grip. His deep brown eyes gazed intently into first Pietor's face, then Aaron's as if the answer to these strangers lay in their souls.

"Is there anywhere to sleep?" Pietor asked.

"We will find you a place." Jacob's voice was full and rich. His words sent a wave of grumbling through the crowd listening in the shadows. Hearing it, Jacob spoke up, "We will find them a place, brothers. Let us help them."

Hands reached from the shadows and led them forward. A faint flickering candle ahead cast silhouettes that writhed and danced on the wall behind them. It showed them one row of bunks. Owl-like faces peered over the sides of the bed as they passed. There were several gaps in the rows of faces. Jacob nodded at them, making the new arrivals aware of their existence.

"Sit," he said, indicating one of the lower bunks near the table on which rested the candle.

Aaron and Pietor sat upon the straw. Jacob sat opposite them. His two companions stood on either side of the bunk like sentinels.

"You are new here." It was not a question.

"Not me," Pietor said, quickly. There was no point in trying to lie his way past the interrogation. He would be found out immediately and killed as a spy. All he needed was a convincing reason to be there.

"And you?" Jacob turned his attention to Aaron.

"I arrived yesterday."

"From where?" Jewish prisoners usually handled all new arrivals. The Kanada Kommando knew every transport from point of departure to cargo.

"Krakow."

"How many in your shipment? When did it leave Krakow?"

"I do not know," Aaron said. "I have been locked in a cattle car for more days than I can remember. I cannot answer your questions."

Jacob expected no other answer than the one he had just received. An inexperienced spy might have tried to supply answers he thought were necessary to his acceptance. This prisoner was either a very good spy of he was telling the truth. Jacob believed the latter. He had the knack for judging character. Aaron was acceptable. This Peter Schiller on the other hand did not sit well with him. He turned to Pietor. "Tell us your story."

"I've been here three months. Transferred from Flossenburg."

"Why have I not seen you before?"

"Because I've been Major Goetz's valet from the day I arrived,"

Pietor replied without a moment's hesitation. Major Goetz was in charge of the SS troops assigned to guard the town of Jenseits which relied on camp labor to keep its factories running. His presence was felt by the conduct of the men under his command but Goetz himself never set foot in the camp unless ordered to by Kommandant Werner.

"How did you come to be here?"

"One of Goetz's boys hid himself in the pantry. There was a party last night with Werner and some other SS. Goetz had been using his boy all afternoon. Nerves, I guess. Anyway, one slipped away. He uses so many it is hard to keep track of them all. I stumbled upon him while the party was in full swing. Before I could brain the ignorant brat, Major Kurtz's wife saw him naked and crying. She screamed. Goetz told them the boy was my son and this was what he got for allowing me to see him, but the party broke up and I was sent here."

"If that was last night. Where were you all day?"

"Interrogation. Nobody laid a hand on me though. I think Goetz just wanted to scare me. He needs me. I always find him the best boys. No offense, but I don't expect to be here long."

Jacob took a moment to consider this. There was a party last night, that was common knowledge in the camp. For now he would accept Peter Schiller. They would be watched, however.

"You may sleep up top tonight."

They scrambled up to the top rows of bunks and squeezed in between the four or five emaciated sleepers who grunted and cursed at the intrusion. The candle still burned beneath them as Jacob discussed food distribution as well as other administrative problems.

The barrack was pitch dark but sound described their surroundings. Amidst the snores and nightmare cries, whispering could be heard from several parts of the barrack. There was a shuffling of feet, and the scrape of wood on the hard mud floor. Aaron leaned forward on the bunk, ears pricked to pick up every sound. The dull clink of a belt buckle on the beams did not fit the other sounds. Soft rhythmic whispers drifted from the blackness.

"Now!" a soft voice pleaded.

There was a loud scrape of wood followed by a loud whump which dwindled to a gentle creaking. A wisp of dust floated down from the ceiling. Someone sneezed.

Again the rafters shook. Then all was still.

A figure appeared out of the gloom into the light from Jacob's candle. His face was gaunt and wrinkled. Deep sadness filled his eyes.

"Are you all right, Joel?" Jacob asked but received no answer.

The man moved like a zombie past Jacob and crept up into his bunk. Sobbing came from the bunk slowly at first and then in great racking heaves which shook the whole frame of the bunk. No one reached out to the distraught man. No word of condolence was uttered.

"Jacob," Aaron said. "What has happened?"

Jacob did not look up from the candlelight. "Two of us are free."

"I do not understand."

"There are two choices in camp. And only two. You can live... day by day, hoping to find something worth living for or... you can escape by the only route available to us: Suicide." He raised his head and looked up at Aaron. "Do not weep for our dead comrades. They are free at last."

"Why does Joel weep?"

"Perhaps he weeps for his father and young brother whom he has just aided on their journey to a better place. Or he weeps because he lacked the determination to join them. The two choices carry two griefs. Each man's grief is his own. It is the one possession he is allowed to keep. They never take that away. And we do not intrude. The privacy to grieve or to think and live are the two constants in this place. One's mind is one's only solitude."

"Do you not try to reason with those who are beyond hope?"

"In the beginning, yes. But when reason fails, we leave them to make their choice."

"Was your choice a difficult one?"

"Yes. Choosing to live, I believe I chose wisely. What will your choice be?"

Once more the rafters shook. Several seconds later they shook again. The dancing flame of the candle moved about in the darkness enshrouding the entrance to the barrack. Harsh whispers made their way to the rear and caught the attention of Jacob and Aaron. Pietor's curiosity was also piqued. Aaron had thought his comrade asleep but the Russian leapt down from the bunk and moved stealthily towards the speakers. Aaron excused himself and followed. From behind Pietor's silhouetted back, he could see a mixture of faces both healthy and pale skulls floating around the swaying figures of the suicides. Pietor stopped several yards away from the small group, got down on one knee and, from the safety of the darkness, watched.

Aaron moved deliberately forward, making his presence known so as not to interrupt any private discussions that may be going on. There were five men clustered around the hanging corpses. The leader, spotted Aaron, and motioned him over with an emphatic hand. "Friend, join us."

The leader wore a rough coat tied securely by a wide leather belt he had somehow procured. He stood proud in his rags. When he spoke, the words gained strength from the fire blazing behind the dark, hooded gaze. His nose was large, flat, nostrils flaring. His thin-lipped mouth seemed to quiver with words unspoken and there was a general nervousness in his manner, his wiry frame like a coiled spring.

"Come, friend. I want to show you something."

Aaron moved forward into the feeble candlelight.

"What is your name?" the young man asked.

"Aaron. And you?"

"John," he replied. "So friend Aaron, I was just telling my comrades about this coward." He thumped the body hanging before him, sending it swaying and bringing more dust down from above.

"What were you telling them?"

"That this will be their fate if they wait like lambs for the slaughter. It's time for action! Only the truly blind can't see that."

Aaron did not know what to say so he held his tongue.

"We must fight!" John raved.

"Why don't you shut up so we can get some sleep?" said a voice from the darkened bunks.

John ran quickly in the direction from which the voice emanated. He gripped the upper brace and lifted himself up. "With the axe over your head you want to sleep? When they burn you, you'll thank them with your dying breath. I'm sure of that."

"Leave me alone!" the man whined. "Let me sleep."

"Sleep like the dead, friend, on a bed of fire that will never go out." He turned to his companions, seeing that he would not receive any fresh support for his cause save from, perhaps, Aaron. His followers were lowering the dead men from the rafters. They moved quickly, not overly careful, apparently eager to have the whole business dispensed with.

John did not seem discouraged by the lack of zeal demonstrated by his followers, but turned his full attention to Aaron who, fascinated by the young man, turned and beckoned Pietor to join them, but the Russian was content to remain in the shadows and observe from a distance. John took Aaron by the arm and led him to a narrow opening on one of the lower bunks. From above, a soft, lilting, mournful voice put forth a gentle song:

Lord, hear my prayer
and let my cry for help reach thee.

"You see, friend," John said. "This is our fate if we stick out our necks like sheep. The axe is above our heads, ready to fall, but it is up to us if we sit calmly and wait for it."

When I call answer me soon
for my days vanish like smoke

Aaron, intrigued, asked, "What do you suppose we do?"

"Fight!"

"Hey, keep it down!" another shout from the darkness.

"Shut up false prophet!" This brought a smattering of laughter from the prisoners.

"We have God on our side," John went on. "We are strong and good. We cannot fail."

my body is burnt up as in an oven.
I am stricken, withered like grass,
I cannot find the strength to eat.
Wasted away I groan aloud
and my skin hangs on my bones

"Our strength lies here," John said, tapping his forehead. He placed his hand over his heart. "And here."

"How could we fight them?"

"We can't!" another jeered. "Now go to sleep!"

"We fight them every day we stay alive. We are torture to them thus they torture us. They curse and abuse us because we defy their order. But I tell you, it will not always be so. Evil cannot survive in the presence of good. And we are good!"

My enemies insult me all the day long,
mad with rage they conspire
against me.

I have eaten ashes for bread
and mingled tears with my drink

"But you shall drink sweet wine," John addressed the singer. "When we have been delivered. However we cannot wait. Oh, dear Lord, snatch me not away before half my days are done! My strength is broken in midcourse, the time allotted me is short. Yes, brothers, our time grows short! Let us use it wisely. This shall be written down for future generations and a people yet unborn shall praise us. It shall be remembered how we did not go like sheep to our end but met it with swords in our hands. We must choose our time and storm the wires of the camp! So, brothers, be resolute and pray, stay strong and persevere. Be ready!"

He slowly slumped over onto his side as if weighed down by

a heavy burden. His breathing slowed and deepened and he slept. Aaron rose gently so as not to awaken the sleeper. He was eager to discuss the events of the night with Pietor but his friend was not in his place amongst the shadows. Aaron found him sound asleep on a bunk. The space beside Pietor was cramped but he eased into it and lay on his back. There was much to consider. Much to think about.

The soft voice was just barely audible, drifting in the deep black night. Sleep was washing over the lonely singer, slowing his words and giving them a dream-like quality:

*The Lord looks down from his
sanctuary on high,
from heaven he surveys the earth
to listen to the groaning of the
prisoners
and set free men under sentence of
death*

CHAPTER SIX

Krueger kept them three days in the Jewish Camp. Although their living conditions were unendurable, Pietor assured Aaron that he had no need for concern for this was Krueger's way of demonstrating who was in charge. Aaron did not think Krueger capable of such pettiness but held his tongue.

Their barracks, as well as the men from two others, were put to work preparing the camp for the fast approaching winter. In a chilling, ceaseless rain, the men repaired the barbed wire, dug trenches and most ridiculous of all, painted the guards' houses, kitchen, showers and the exterior of the Crematoria. The rain, driven by an angry wind washed the paint from the bricks and wood before it had a chance to leave the makeshift brushes the guards had provided for the job. One man, a doctor before the camp, insisted the brushes were made from human hair but nobody listened or wanted to believe what he said.

And through the entire ordeal, John preached. He worked hardest of all, twisting barbed wire until the drenched, shivering guards had to drag him from the fence. He dug the trench surrounding the camp until he could no longer stand straight. But for all his physical exertions, his spirit worked all the harder. For John preached as they marched double-time to their work station. He spoke to any that would hear as they huddled over their measly soup made more watery by the rain. On the afternoon of the second day, Aaron worked beside him on the wire. While blood and water ran from his torn hands, John whispered psalms to himself.

The man's faith, so evident by day, reached its peak in the barracks. All that his hands built by day, his words tore down by night. In the evening, as they shivered beneath their thin blankets, he told them to be thankful for the rain. It washed them clean, it was something to drink, it was baptism itself. For did they not see that the harder they worked the tougher they became. They were being baked in a kiln and would emerge new men. Every slap, punch and rifle butt which fell upon their shoulders and back would be returned to their persecutors a hundred fold.

Aaron found the young man fascinating. He listened every night. The fall of the suicides could not distract him from the words delivered in a voice much older than John's years. John was ridiculed for his behavior but each night Aaron spotted one or two new faces in the crowd at John's feet. No matter how much he urged, Aaron could not convince Pietor to speak with John. The quiet Russian preferred the shadows and this was vexing to Aaron.

On the evening of the third day, Jacob put a bony hand on Aaron's arm as he passed the wise man's bunk after listening to John speak. "Stay a moment."

"Certainly," Aaron replied.

He sat on the edge close to Jacob, the older man's face at Aaron's knee. He looked up at Aaron with large eyes. The block leader had not shown interest in John. Neither his words nor actions seemed to make any impression on the wise man. Some attributed this to the toll the work and rain had taken on Jacob's already weakened frame. He seemed to exude and urgency as if aware that his flame was going out.

"I see you every night at John's feet," he said through trembling lips. "Tell me, do his words interest you so?"

"Yes, very much."

"Good. For it is of words that I wish to speak." He raised himself up on bony elbows and stared into Aaron's calm features. "Do you know that, in camp, words can kill as efficiently as the gas chambers?"

Aaron made no reply.

"Outside, you may insult a neighbor or argue with a shopkeeper but, in the end, nothing comes of it but hard feelings which fade in time. Not so in camp. Words have power here. Do you know the proverb: 'Judge not lest ye yourself by judged?'"

"I have heard it."

"Good. Then I ask you not to judge John too harshly."

"I do not understand."

Jacob pulled himself up into a sitting position, his eyes level with Aaron's. "I am not a fool! I know why you have come among us. I would not speak to you in this manner if I did not."

Jacob had Aaron's full attention now. Aaron stared into the man's eyes, plumbing their depth. Satisfied, he got up to leave.

Jacob restrained him. "Wait, I will tell you a story. You listen to John every night, now you will listen to the truth."

Aaron took his seat.

"One bleak day," Jacob began, "a young man came into the camp with his father. The man's father was a very well respected rabbi. Not only in his own community but for hundreds of miles around. He was a man known for his great wisdom and charity. He was a great man. Men read his writing, mothers wished their sons to attain his stature amongst his fellow men. Scholarly men applauded him for his great works.

"This fame was a double-edged sword, bringing respect and honor but also the watchful eye of the SS. He, with his son, went into hiding before his people were herded into ghettos. With the help of a gentile comrade, the rabbi got what food and medical supplies he could lay his hands on into the ghetto. These errands of mercy proved to be his downfall. He was taken and arrested. Being a prime name on the lists of the SS, he was quickly dispatched here.

"His son, who had been arrested with him arrived in camp at the rabbi's side. The son, who worshipped his father, vowed to protect him at all costs and see him back in his synagogue one day. As they were led into the camp, word got around that a Jew of great importance had arrived. A Kapo told the guards and they prepared to receive him. First they beat him and knocked him down in the mud. The son, trying to protect his father, was knocked senseless by a rifle. Then, they ordered the rabbi to stand, and, in front of the men and woman who revered him, was ordered to dance. The rabbi, his face a fortress of dignity, danced for his tormentors. They told him to dance faster and faster until he collapsed, winded. The guards kicked him to his feet and pulled his beard. One guard ground a lit cigarette into the rabbi's cheek. Another, inspired by this action, lit the rabbi's beard on fire. They held him until the fire made him scream, then pushed him down to use the filthy mud to douse the flames.

"When he had regained his feet, his beard a smoldering wreck, his face bloody and bruised, he faced his persecutors in silence. Angered by this, they ripped his clothes from his back and displayed him for his followers who watched it all with cries of despair and anguish.

"Tired of their sport, the guards led those who were to be gassed to the showers. The rabbi, naked and humiliated, gathered his son up and headed in the direction of the others. As they made their way, many heard the rabbi begging God for deliverance and added their cry to his. Roused by the sound, the son joined in as well. The prayers reached a panicked intensity as they were stripped and herded to the showers. The rabbi and his son were in the back of the line and could just see the bathhouse over the heads of the great throng of men, women and children. As they neared the showers, they heard the muffled screams of the people being gassed ahead of them. A group of children in front of the rabbi grew frightened. He went to them and calmed them with soothing words. The guards saw this and after a moments discussion amongst themselves, led the children to a thin stand of trees to the right of the bathhouse. The rabbi and his son were pulled from the group along with some others and were told to follow the guards.

"The rabbi spoke to his comrades, telling them that they were to be spared along with the children and, though many had suffered, mercy for the little ones was something to be thankful for.

"When they were concealed in the trees, the guards took the

smallest of the children and tossed them into the air, using them for target practice before they hit the ground. Those too big to throw were seized by the ankles and smashed against the trees. The rabbi stared open-mouthed at this horror and then a great, low cry of despair rose up within him. When the slaughter was finished, they were told to pick up the bodies and carry them to the crematorium. The father, weeping with all the strength in his body could not move. He watched his son gather the corpses like kindling until the guard beat him down for disobeying and dragged him to the showers. The son never saw his father again, but the story has come down how the rabbi, his hands braced on either side of the shower doors, turned his face to the bland sky, shouting, "There is no God!" Then they pushed him inside.

"The deaths of the innocent saved the son. He was put to work. His name is John and he is a fool. Harmless, but a fool nonetheless. Must you condemn a fool who does not know the power of words?"

"I condemn no one," Aaron said, rising.

Weakened by the telling as much by the tale, Jacob lay back, his eyes boring into Aaron as he stood over him. "Yes, of course. I am mistaken."

Pietor moved past the two men and leapt easily up to the top bunk. Aaron joined him there but did not sleep, Jacob's words echoing in his mind.

The next morning, Pietor volunteered Aaron and himself for special duty in the Ka-Be. As they were led away, a Kapo under Krueger's control passed on the message that the camp leader would see them after supper, which was the sole reason for their volunteering. Aaron had wanted an opportunity to discuss with Pietor what Jacob had told him but that would have to wait until after they'd seen Krueger.

Under the watchful eye of the SS doctor, they removed the bodies of the men and women taken in the last selection for experimentation. The work was back breaking but passed the time.

Their work done, Pietor, with the aid of the same Kapo, led Aaron out of the Jewish Camp and back into the Men's Camp where dinner was being doled out. Before Pietor could lick his plate clean, a Kapo appeared to lead them to Krueger.

The Senior Camp Inmate welcomed them but it was plain that this was mere custom and had more to do with Krueger's mood than any constraints of civility. He listened with feigned interest to Pietor's report on the general state of the Jewish Camp, but it was clear that there was something he waited to hear. Aaron, baffled as to what it could be, was also intrigued by Pietor's detailed report. He had thought the Russian aloof and apathetic and was surprised how little had escaped the man's notice. And he had not forgotten that Krueger was to have information for them concerning Dr. Liebman. This was of paramount importance.

"Yes, yes, Pietor," Krueger said, waving away the rest of the report. "What have you to report?"

Pietor stood rigid as though at attention. "The subject, prisoner 76016, called John, full name John Siderman, is not in full possession of his mental faculties. He preaches salvation and spreads hope but it is all fantasy."

"I see," Krueger replied, turning his attention to Aaron. "And you, Jew 96432, what have you to say?"

"Sir?"

"You spoke with this Jew, Siderman, heard his words. Report!"

"He is a good man," Aaron began, not knowing what to say and not wishing to upset his only link with Liebman. "He preaches freedom and retribution and the coming of a new age. Ideas which have a profound effect on his listeners though they are few. No surprise considering the present circumstances."

"What affect did they have on you, Jew 96432?"

"He was... extremely interesting."

"Interesting. That's all?"

"Yes, sir."

Krueger leaned back in his chair and regarded them. "I distrust people who are... interesting. Men often turn to interesting individuals for guidance. Do you see him as a threat?"

"A threat to what?" Aaron asked.

Krueger laced his fingers on his desk and put his head down, eyes closed. He kept them closed as he spoke. "There is an order to all things. The camp is no exception. Why nature itself, on the surface random, chaotic, is a complex system of balance and counter-balance. There is order of the highest magnitude. Absolute chaos does not exist."

Aaron was thinking that this system could not apply to camp life where the random executions and punishments were unpredictable and were the product of the slightest whim of their jailors. Even disease was random, striking one prisoner but not the other though all were in the same state of malnutrition.

"We have order here," Krueger resumed. "More than ever possessed outside. For the camp is the natural order in microcosm. Men and women, even children, are stripped of all weapons save their spirit. They retain no defenses other than personal courage. We are truly ourselves in camp. Whatever does not kill us makes us stronger. 'Arbeit Macht Frei.' If we, as men, can endure, alone and defenseless, here, then how much stronger must we become? The weak in mind, body and spirit perish and so are examples to the strong. Is it not better that the weak be destroyed in order for the strong to grow stronger? We eat the bread of the weakling, we take his jacket when the snow comes. It is our right! We must survive and we shall. Nothing can be allowed to interfere until the unfit are ashes."

The ensuing silence was a profound one. Aaron could think of no reply he could vocalize. He understood now that Krueger was insane, but this madness was the most dangerous kind. It was not babbling lunacy but rather of the most cunning nature. It was the kind of madness which produced perverse genius. The same form which had swept like a plague through Germany in 1933: uncontrollable, unstoppable and deadly. He would have to deal carefully with Krueger else his mission would fail before it had begun.

"My patience grows thin," Krueger said.

"Sir," Pietor said, "I do not see Siderman as a threat just yet. Perhaps continued surveillance -- "

"And you, Jew 96432?"

"John Siderman is no threat," Aaron replied with conviction. "Not directly at any rate."

"The prisoner's worst enemy is the prisoner," Krueger said. "That is your first lesson, remember it. Hunger, desperation steal not only reason but innocence."

"John is an unknown variable," Aaron said. "Caution hurts no man. What harm a watchful eye?"

Krueger brought his great hands together in a resounding clap. "Then we are in agreement. You have done well and you shall be rewarded."

He snapped his fingers. One of the bodyguards at the door behind Aaron moved forward and handed them slips of paper. He held the paper gingerly in two fingers while Pietor, more accustomed to the habit of the camp, quickly folded his and shoved it down his trouser front.

"Thank you, sir! Thank you!" Pietor gushed.

Aaron examined the paper. It was a pass for the brothel. Not the standard pass for exactly five minutes duration but an extended one for a full hour. From what he knew of the black-market trade in camp, this was as priceless as medicine or cigarettes. They could eat well for a month with this. Or an easy work detail might be obtained and possibly kept for an extended period. On the other hand, a torn throat in the night might also be the reward for telling the wrong person of this prize for the pass could safely be used for a night of pleasure, an emotion as rare as beef in camp.

"Thank you, sir," Aaron said, placing the pass in his pocket. "May I respectfully ask after Dr. Liebman?"

"He is not in this camp," Krueger replied. "He is not amongst the lists of dead. He is not in Ka-Be. He has not escaped. Nor was he sent for scientific experimentation. Does that answer your question?"

"Yes, sir. Thank you, sir." This was distressing news for Aaron. Not that he was concerned for Dr. Liebman's welfare, but that it necessitated the taking of a calculated risk. A potentially lethal one. However, there was no alternative. "Sir, I respectfully request to work in the Sonderkommando."

A gasp came from the men at their backs. Pietor swung around in his chair to look at his comrade with complete and utter disbelief etched into his features. "No one volunteers for the Kommando! Are you mad?"

Krueger stretched out a huge paw to quiet Pietor. He examined the two men, then cleared his throat. It appeared even he was taken aback by Aaron's request. "Perhaps you have been misinformed, Jew 96432. If you expect better food or access to medicine..."

"No, sir. That is not what I am after."

"Well, then, perhaps my young associate is correct in his assessment of your mental stability. The Kommando is certain death. I sense a keen intellect in you, Jew 96432. Tell me why I should squander such a resource. What possible gain can come from my sending you there?"

This was the part Aaron had the most difficulty reasoning out. He'd considered entering the Kommando a possible course of action, necessary for locating Dr. Liebman, but only as a last resort. How to go about it, safely, was another matter. It was only Krueger's speech a few moments ago that gave him the key he needed to make the senior officer grant his request. He had to appeal to the man's greed and this newly revealed social order. It was going to be tricky.

"I will not lie to you, sir," he said. "I have a personal stake in the well being of Dr. Liebman. If I could assist him upon his arrival, I think I could provide for you a valuable ally. Dr. Liebman is an extraordinarily intelligent individual."

"Intelligence is nothing in camp. Resourcefulness, ingenuity and loyalty are the qualities I seek in underlings."

"If you will allow me to speak frankly, sir."

"Yes."

"This war will not last forever. The last reports I heard back in the world were not good for the Reich. The allied forces are on their way. It is inevitable." Aaron paused to let this sink in. He had everyone's attention now. "The camp will be liberated. The world will know what now it only suspects. The investigation following the end of hostilities will be thorough. Anyone who has bettered himself by the situation will be called to account for their behavior. It will take influence and ingenuity to ensure that no unfortunate mistakes are made."

Krueger's feature clouded with anger. "You threaten me!"

"Never, sir. I merely point out the coming need for resources."

"What makes you think I have not already seen to this?"

"I'm sure you have, a man of your vision. But why waste an opportunity to improve your situation? There are no certainties other than death and no plan is flawless, however brilliantly conceived. Dr. Liebman has a great deal of wealth on his person. It is most ingeniously concealed. He can pass any inspection the SS can come up with."

Krueger's eyes flashed greedily. "What does he carry?"

"Diamonds."

Krueger made a dismissive gesture and leaned back in his chair. "Bah! The SS has beaten them out of him by now."

"The SS do no know he has them. They do not even suspect."

"I am intrigued, Jew 96432."

"He is living under a forged identity. His papers are in perfect order. He is a Jew and is still a Jew. Circumcision did not permit any other course of action. His disguise is that of a poor man. The SS are not suspicious. I am sure he was beaten and searched as a matter of habit, but the SS know beforehand which of the prisoners they target. There is very little which cannot be purchased for favors these days. Information amongst the rest. Dr. Liebman will not appear on any of the lists informants have provided. He will pass unnoticed. He will enter the camp with his fortune intact. After that, his safety cannot be assured. Sol Liebman is an old man. Not in years, but in body. His heart is weak so if he is not gassed immediately, he will not survive long. If gassed upon arrival, and this seems likely, the Kommando will sort his clothes and valise. If they find such a cache of wealth, it will disappear never to be seen again. My being with the Kommando will ensure the treasure falls into the right hands. Your hands. And all I ask in return is that his life be spared and that I be removed, alive, from the Kommando after Dr. Liebman arrives."

"You tell a fine tale, Jew 96432," Krueger said. "Why should I believe a word of it?"

"For what other reason would I request joining the Kommando? Of what possible benefit could it be to me? Conversely, how could it harm you to grant my request? If what I say is true, and it is, then the diamonds are yours in exchange for mine and Dr. Liebman's lives. If I am lying, what are the lives of two Jews to you?"

"You present an excellent argument." Krueger's eyes narrowed as he considered. "Very well, I will grant your request. I trust you are aware that the Kommando is gassed every six months."

"I will take the risk."

"You are very brave or very stupid, Jew 96432. Only time will answer."

"What about me, sir," Pietor said, terror in his eyes. "Can I return to the Men's Camp. The Jew Camp is too much for any decent human being."

Krueger stood up and came around his desk. He perched on one corner, towering over Pietor. "Now, now. Your work in the Jew Camp is not finished. Siderman has to be watched. They have accepted you. You will remain there until the threat has been properly assessed."

"Why don't we just send him up the chimney?" Pietor whined.

"These things have to be handled properly. So do as you are told and leave the thinking to me. Is that clear?"

Pietor sulked. "Yes, sir."

"So," Krueger said, bringing his hands together once more. "Return to the Jew Camp. I will send for you when I need you. Enjoy yourselves tonight, though, the pass is only valid until curfew. As a token of my appreciation, I do not expect to learn that it has been passed on. That would be most disrespectful."

Pietor jumped up, both anxious to remove himself from Krueger's presence and eager to get to the brothel. Aaron rose gracefully and joined his companion at the door. They passed into the night.

CHAPTER SEVEN

"**W**hat kind of lunatic are you?" Pietor hissed. They were far from Krueger's ears but it was common knowledge never to raise one's voice outside barracks or risk drawing attention. Especially on the path to the Jewish Camp. "The Kommando?"

"I do not understand your reaction," Aaron said, calmly. "I must make contact with Dr. Liebman. He is not in camp. Therefore my best chance of intercepting him is to work in the Kommando."

"You don't know what you're getting yourself into, comrade. The Kommando is a dirty job."

"I know." Aaron also knew that Krueger did not trust him an inch. The chance he had taken in making his request had gone a lot smoother than he had expected but he knew he would be watched while in the Kommando. This was not a problem for him. What did concern him was the suspicion Krueger no doubt held about how a common Jew could know a particular man would be coming to this camp. A man who could be anywhere in Europe. Or dead for that matter. Aaron was a mystery to the Senior Camp Inmate and mysteries were dangerous to a man in his position.

Pietor noticed Aaron's silence. "Just what have you got up your sleeve? What's you angle? Whatever it is, it won't work. Don't even think of holding out from Krueger."

They stopped at the hill of earth near the main road.

"I'm not. Why did you hold out from me?"

"What?"

"Siderman," Aaron said. "Why didn't you tell me we were working for Krueger in the Jewish Camp?"

"I was told not to," Pietor snapped. "You'd have given us away in a heartbeat. Krueger watches all threats to his authority. Real or imagined. Siderman, well, he's ashes, so why get upset? I'm the one who should be upset. I've got to back in there. The sooner that crazy Jew goes up the chimney, the better. Then I can get back to halfway decent food and my bunk."

"Krueger is a paranoid madman. He'd suspect the sun for shining in his eyes. And he leaves it to you to assess this particular threat. That is interesting."

"Why's that?"

"Another time, Pietor Chekunov. Please do not lie or withhold information from me again."

Aaron strode forward, leaving Pietor to stare after him for a moment, then hurry to catch up. They left the main road and went directly to a low concrete building. There were no windows and a large guard waited outside the door. Pietor hastened his pace, an animal hunger in his eyes. They joined the line. Pietor was relieved to see the guard outside the brothel was one of Krueger's. The customary bribe to gain admittance would not be necessary. It would however be necessary to bribe the SS women who ran the brothel. Nothing could be done about that.

"Do you have any money?" Pietor asked Aaron.

"No."

"Great," Pietor said to himself, "first I'm stuck in the Jew Camp and now I have to pay for this, too."

The line moved steadily and they were soon at the door.

"Pass!" the guard demanded.

They handed them over. Each was scrutinized though Pietor doubted the guard could read. He hoped the guard could read or else the ape might not realize they were from Krueger. Reluctantly, the guard moved to one side and let them through.

The entranceway led to a poorly lit stairway. At the foot of the stairs, a large SS woman stood stock still, a look of disgust and greed on her broad face. Pietor did not speak to the woman, he merely reached into his pocket and withdrew a filthy wad of Reich marks which he handed over, jerking a thumb over his shoulder to indicate the bribe covered Aaron who was studying the transaction with rapt attention.

The marks disappeared into a bulging shirt pocket. Pietor led Aaron up the short flight of stairs. At the top, he slapped Aaron on the back and proceeded down the hall. Moans of ecstasy or anguish could be heard faintly through the closed doors lining the hallway. Pietor listened briefly at each door, then moved on in search of one not in use. He found one at the end of the hall, paused to be sure, then went inside.

Aaron watched all of this with great interest. He had never seen one of these places and the experience intrigued him. He moved slowly away from the closed door, feeling no shame at listening to the sounds coming from the rooms. Pietor had chosen a door on the left and that seemed to be where most of the action was. Halfway down the hall, he stopped at a door on the right. He bent his head slightly, heard nothing, and went inside.

The room contained a chair and a wooden cot. The brief candle perched on the windowsill was adequate lighting to reveal the interior of the tiny cubicle. There was a figure on the bed, face turned away from the door. At the sound of Aaron entering, the figure turned lethargically as if waking from sleep. Seeing Aaron, the woman tossed back the covers and came to her feet.

She wore a loose prison robe draped about her body. For a cruel joke, the tailors had stitched her yellow star of David over her crotch. With eyes staring straight ahead, the woman pulled the robe over her head. It was common practice that the woman present herself to the user for inspection. With medicine scarce, the risk of illness was everywhere so clients had to judge for themselves whether the woman looked healthy enough to risk close contact.

The woman turned slowly for Aaron's inspection. Her hair, though limp and unwashed, was full and dark. The feeble candlelight hid her face in shadow but could not hide the full lips and clear large eyes which seemed all the more alluring set against flaccid cheeks already bearing the first signs of malnutrition. The pale shoulders were thin but broad. High firm breasts hung above the stretch of ribs showing through the dirty skin. Her waist was slim and shapely but soured by protruding hipbones. As she turned, he noticed her pinched buttocks which emphasized the bony hips and thighs. And yet the calves were strong and firm like a dancer's. The woman before him had been attractive once and could be again with a bath and some decent food but it seemed to him that she was like an autumn bloom, beautiful and wilting at the same time.

Hearing no objection, the woman lay down on the cot, knees raised, legs sprawled open, her thin, white hands held to her sides and clenched into tight small fists. She made no sound, just lay there exposed and waiting.

Aaron picked up her robe and tossed it over the pale, waiting form. "Cover yourself."

Her first reaction was abject terror. Woman who failed to stimulate were sent up the chimney. She studied Aaron's movements as he sat in the chair and leaned forward to study her. Sensing that he was not displeased, she placed the robe over her head. One small hand came up to tidy her unkempt hair but the gesture stopped halfway, her eyes riveted to Aaron's face.

"You do not want me? There are others... "

"What is your name?"

Her faced spasmed as if she'd been slapped. "Don't ask me that."

"Why not?"

"I don't have a name. I am yours for these minutes. Isn't that enough?"

"I wish to speak with you. Please tell me your name."

The woman sank back, eyes haunted, fixed on the floor between them. "Ruth." It was a whisper.

"Was that so bad?"

"You don't know, you don't know."

Aaron leaned forward and folded his arms. He cocked his head to one side and regarded the woman.

Ruth made no sound. She sat on the edge of the bed, her hands folded in her lap.

"What were you in life?"

"It doesn't matter."

"Does life mean so little to you?"

"My life ended long ago." Ruth came quickly to her feet. She stared out the narrow window at her own reflection in the soiled glass. "What do you want?"

"I told you. I want to talk."

"Men do not come here to talk."

"I am here with a friend because I did not want to offend Krueger."

She turned and faced him. "Do you have food?"

"Yes." Aaron pulled a small piece of moldy bread from his tunic.

Ruth flung herself at his feet, her faced pressed to his knees.

"Have you words?" he asked.

She raised her head and stared at Aaron. He was an odd one. But the bread! She could get some medicine for her mother-in-law or maybe a bath for the both of them. She released him and returned to the bed. "You want to talk, then talk."

He watched her movements, his eyes missing nothing. "How were you injured?"

She shuddered. "An SS pig."

"Why?"

"He was dissatisfied with my ability. He thought that some time here might teach me something."

"And has it?"

"Yes. It has taught me to hate. I should have cut his prick off ."

"But you did not," Aaron said. "And you are still alive."

"Alive?"

"Is there anyone I can get a message to?"

"No," she lied, turning her face from him. She hung her head and stared at the clenched fists in her lap.

"You are not married?"

She wheeled and flung her head onto the pillow. Her body hitched but no sound escaped her anguished form. Aaron watched her, his brow furrowed in concentration. Abruptly, she sat up, pounded her fists against her thighs and fought the tears.

"Is your husband alive?" Aaron asked. "I can find him for you. It's no trouble."

"Enough, please!" she begged.

He placed the bread on the cot and stood. When he was at the door, he looked back. She was weeping, a small frail form trembling in the weak light. Her sorrows were silent but the tears flowed thick and hot down her pale cheeks. Her lips were drawn back in an expression halfway between sadness and rage. The convulsions of her throat made her head bob up and down in rhythm with her jerking body.

Unsure what to do, Aaron went to her side and reached out a hand. She hesitated, then clutched desperately. She bent forward and leaned her cheek against Aaron's hand. Her tears were burning hot but he did not pull away. From elsewhere came the low cries from the women being used in the other cubicles.

"Our wedding day was so beautiful," Ruth began in a harsh whisper. "A rabbi came from one of the safe houses. My mother-in-law told me how lovely I looked though food had been scarce for many months. The ceremony was short, we feared the SS. My Ely was so tall in his borrowed suit. We had a small reception afterwards. Only four or five people. Friends. Except for Ephrom. When Ely was having a drink with his brother, Ephrom made advances towards me. He promised me safety if I would lay with him. I slapped him. The sound brought Ely running and he and his brother threw the little man into the hallway. It did not spoil the wedding. We did not let it. The SS were seen in the neighborhood and we returned to our hiding places. Naomi, Ely's mother, gave up her bed for us. No man had ever touched me. Naomi had provided us with a thick, woven blanket because the frost was coming. I slid under the blanket while Ely went to the water closet."

Fresh sobs racked her body and Aaron held her tightly.

"Footsteps." She shuddered through her tears. "Boots. They broke in the door, Ephrom leading the way. They took Ely. He struck one but there were too many. Their leader suggested they break in the new bride. Two soldiers held Ely at the foot of the bed. They stuffed a sock into his mouth. Ephrom asked the sergeant if he could forgo the money he was to be paid in exchange for being first. They... They all had me. When I shut my eyes I still see Ephrom's sweating face gloating over me. I can only hope the SS turned on him and he rots in a place like this somewhere."

A thin whine escaped Ruth's clenched lips. She rocked slightly backward and forward, then pitched onto the floor. Her mouth gaped, her stomach clenched but nothing came out. Aaron took her by the arm and raised her up, returning her to the bed. He covered her with the thin, foul blanket and sat by her side. She quieted after a time, bringing her small, child-like hands to her face to swipe away her tears.

"Why did you tell me this?" Aaron asked.

"I... I don't know. It just came out. I have never spoken to anyone about this. You are the first."

"You do not want to die."

"Oh, but I do," she answered matter-of-factly. "Every time one of them touches me."

"Yet you live."

"I exist."

"John tells us a day of reckoning is at hand. Is this what you exist for?"

She sat bolt upright in the bed, her eyes boring into his. "You know of John? He is real?"

"I have listened to him many a night," Aaron replied.

"All the girls speak of him but I did not dare believe. Tell me about him. What is he like?"

"He is a man of vision. That is all I know."

"You... You said earlier that you would help me."

"Yes."

"Take a message to him. Tell him the girls here spread his word to all who come here. Except the SS of course. Tell him, or maybe he knows already, what a comfort his words are."

"I will do as you ask."

There was noise outside and Pietor stuck his head in the door. "Better get moving. There's a troop of SS heading this way. Probably drunk."

Aaron stared into Ruth's eyes as he stood. "Coming," he said over his shoulder.

"Thank you," Ruth said.

"Thank you," Ruth said.

On the stairs, Pietor, his face flushed from exertion, leered at Aaron saying, "Did you hear that bitch? You must have given her something special. Such gratitude."

At the front door, they crouched low and Pietor opened it a crack to look out. He nodded to Aaron and they slipped out. The soldiers were twenty yards away but the moonless night hid Aaron and Pietor as they edged along the wall of the outhouse across from the brothel.

Once clear of the SS, Pietor quickened his pace. His face was ruddy, eyes flashing. Aaron walked steadily behind him. At the turnoff to the Jewish Camp, Pietor continued straight ahead.

"Where are you going?" Aaron asked.

"I've got to see Krueger."

"Now?"

"The bitch I had, she wouldn't shut up about Siderman. I had to break her mouth to keep her quiet. On and on about being triumphant over our enemies, praising God. Really broke my concentration. It seems we've underestimated our Jewish friend's influence. We'll have to move on him a little bit sooner than Krueger planned."

Aaron gave this some thought. "I have another suggestion." He took Pietor's arm and pulled him along the road to the Jewish Camp.

"Let go of me!"

"Listen," Aaron said, tightening his grip. "Siderman is a dreamer but he does no harm."

"Giving people hope when there is none does harm as far as I'm concerned." Pietor yanked his arm free but followed Aaron. "Telling them the future is bright and worth living for leads people to believe that waiting for it isn't enough. Before you know it, they want to help bring it about and that's when things get messy. There can be no rebellion here. All we can do is make the best of it. That's what Krueger has accomplished. I'm no going to sit still and watch it all get torn down by a fanatic!"

"There is another way. Siderman commands respect. He is a man of strong though misguided character. Such men are rare commodities.

Does it not make more sense to turn this resource rather than discard it? Tell me Krueger has no use for someone of Siderman's abilities."

Pietor considered a moment. "You make a good point. But I've seen it before with these zealots. They cannot be turned. They serve their own ideals. It's better for everybody if they go up the chimney."

"A waste."

"Yes, but in the long run we come out ahead."

"We should at least try."

"I told you, talking does no good."

"Then let's try something else."

"Yes. The showers."

"The Prophet."

Pietor was taken aback. "How-- " He recovered himself quickly. "You have a death wish. I'm convinced of that now. The Prophet! Are you out of your mind? Krueger would have both our heads if he caught us listening to that crazy old man."

"He doesn't have to know."

"Krueger knows everything that goes on in camp. I'm not sticking my neck out for Siderman."

"Then let's go. Right now. Krueger thinks we're in the brothel. We can get there and back before anyone even misses us. If the Prophet can scare Siderman off his present course, Krueger gains a valuable tool. If not, we've lost an hour and Siderman is smoke. You recruit for Krueger. Now is your chance to bring in someone he can really make use of."

"Too risky."

"Then I will go myself. All I ask of you is that you delay your report until tomorrow. Can I count on you?"

"You're really serious about this?"

They were at the row of barracks. They turned right and headed down the path to barrack thirteen.

"All right," Pietor said under his breath. They were in earshot of other prisoners taking some air before lights out. "We'll go. I don't know what you've got up your sleeve, but I'll play along. Go and get Siderman. I'll wait here. You're crazy, you know that? You'll get us killed."

"Not I." Aaron moved off into the throng of prisoners. Pietor watched him move through the crowd. He was at least a head taller than most of the inmates and his back was so straight. Pietor leaned up against a wall, suspicion in his gaze. He found himself wondering who was the bigger threat: Siderman or Aaron?

CHAPTER EIGHT

T o the south of the Jewish Camp a stand of trees blocked off a small field from the main body of the camp. The field was a grave for 1100 Polish Jews who had been executed during the expansion of the camp in July 1941.

The action had left a mound of corpses, the disposal of which was an immediate concern. With Crematorium One already overworked, there remained no quick way of removing the decomposing bodies. After more than a week of hot, humid air prevailing, the Kommandant ordered the bodies buried where they lay. Warm temperatures had sped up decomposition, leading the guards to drive the prisoners mercilessly to complete the burial. Rain fell heavily for three days during this time so the guards had the Jews construct a small shack in which they could escape the rain. From here they could oversee the burial as well as rape the Jewish girls away from the lustful eye of the Kommandant.

The graves were dug, the bodies buried. The Kommandant ordered trees planted between the camp and the field to remove this sight from view and deflect the stench. The field and shack were abandoned and it was there the Prophet had been secreted away after having failed a selection in the winter of 1942. Few veterans were aware of the Prophet's existence. A handful of Jews fed him from their rations and cared for him.

Aaron, having told John that someone desperately needed to see him, had led the young man to Pietor who, reluctantly, took them down the path leading to the Prophet. Being close to the barbwire boundary of the camp, they moved cautiously for if the guards spotted them, they might be shot.

There was a route the Prophet's helpers traditionally followed. The latrine for the Jewish Camp was not ten yards from one tip of the crescent-shaped woods. Under cover of darkness, it was relatively easy to cross the open ground and lose oneself in the trees. No guards patrolled the area because the odor of rotting flesh was still prevalent plus the guards were lazy in carrying out their duties, leaving that to the electrified fence bordering the copse. Once in the woods, the three men could slink from tree to tree safely.

Pietor led them quickly, feeling exposed and vulnerable. Aaron took careful note of the route. John simply followed blindly along, trusting his friends to lead him to their destination.

As they neared the edge of the woods, a small rectangular shape became visible through the trees. Weather had warped the wood and stripped paint away, but the structure itself was sound. It had a little pointed roof with one or two shingles still clinging firmly to the boards. There was no light from the single window but the low, distinct sound of whispered chanting could be heard through the broken glass.

"All right," Pietor said, pausing at the door. "Listen carefully. He will not acknowledge you. Also, though he is an old man, he is not deaf so don't shout. You may ask him anything you like. It will be up to you to determine if he has answered. Understood?"

They nodded their understanding.

"And, for your own peace of mind, do not touch him."

"Why not?" John asked.

Pietor laughed but it was a hollow sound. "Ah, they say that if you touch him he will tell your future."

"A prophet indeed," John said.

"It's only camp legend. But it's better not to take chances."

They did not announce their presence. Pietor merely opened the door and stepped in. John pushed past Aaron who stood a moment in the doorway taking in the scene. It was hard to see in the shack for there was no light. A large form seemed to be moving in the center of the room and there was that soft sighing they'd caught from outside. Pietor lit a short candle that cast a dull glow about the room.

There was a tall, cadaverous man with the Prophet, and he demanded to know who they were and why they had come. At the mention of Krueger's name he became more agreeable, though he took the candle from Pietor's hand and held it up to inspect their faces. Satisfied, he handed the candle back and returned to his place near the rocking form in the center. The three men sat on the floor in a half-circle around the dark shape.

The Prophet was a man of indeterminate age. Beneath the coarse blanket around his head, a creased, wrinkled brow like rolling hills cascaded down to eyes so sunken and hidden by horny flesh as to leave nothing but black shadows. The cheeks were concave and yellow, the nose long with a drooping tip. His mouth was an undulating, toothless hole which opened and closed with such rapidity that his face quivered. The flapping, drooling mouth sent drops of saliva flying off his chin onto the soiled pillows in front of him and on the gnarled, twisted hands hanging above his lap. The hands, like the mouth twisted and convulsed as if trying to perform some great work for which they had lost the knowledge. Around the index finger of his right hand a filthy ribbon was knotted in a small bow which bounced and jerked in time with the clutching fingers. The writhing, ceaseless mouth was the source of the soft sighing cacophony of words which poured out filling the room. There was no stove in the room and the thick blankets draped around the man made it impossible to determine his size. Pillows placed on the floor around him gave the impression that they grew from his very person. One could not tell if he sat cross-legged on the dirt floor or if his knees were drawn up to his chest or even if he squatted, so thick were the coverings.

John, seeing this pathetic sight rushed forward. "Dear sir, are you all right?" He extended a sympathetic hand.

"Don't touch him!" Pietor shouted. "You fool! Did you not hear a word I said?"

"You said it was myth," John replied, withdrawing his hand.

"Do you really want to find out?" Pietor cautioned.

John raised an eyebrow at this cryptic reply, then turned to regard the Prophet. "You poor soul. Are you well?"

"...grim is the vision shown to me: the traitor betrayed, the spoiler himself despoiled, the Lord proves men in the furnace of humiliation, wherever I turn men taunt me, and my day is darkened by their sneers, terror upon terror overwhelms me, the poor rise early like the wild ass, they will go in sackcloth, shuddering from head to foot, where sinners gather, the fires break out, retribution blazes up in a rebellious nation, man, the Lord God says: behold the day, the doom is here, it has burst upon them, all the Gentiles will know that there is one who saves and liberates Israel, his heart is firm as a rock, when he raises himself, strong men take flight, the day comes, glowing like a furnace, the light of Israel shall become a fire, who put wisdom in the depths of darkness, look, look, here is what will astonish you and stun you for there is work afoot in your days which you will not believe when it is told you, there is, indeed, a judgment waiting..."

All this the Prophet whispered in his wheezing, breathless voice. So faint was the sound that the men leaned forward, drawn in by the cadence, entranced by the rhythm.

"It is scripture. All jumbled up," John observed. "My God, what have they done to this man?"

"There is a tale," Pietor replied. "It could only be camp talk."

"Does this poor soul have a name?"

"I'm sure I don't know it. Look at his number."

Aaron peered at the blue ink on the man's pale forearm. "So low." He had been discreetly checking the numbers of those he had come in contact with for those with the lowest numbers were veterans and thus knew all the tricks for survival. He had not seen a number this low. The old man must have been on the first transport in 1933.

"He worked in the crematorium, so the story goes," Pietor said. "Four years at the ovens, three before that on grave detail. One day, so they say, while working the ovens, the bodies of his wife and granddaughter came down the chute. He had hidden them away before he'd been arrested and their safety was what carried him through."

John grimaced, torn apart internally by memories too horrible to recall. "What did he do?"

Pietor's eyes flashed angrily. "What do you think? He burned them. He would have been shot if he hadn't. Before he pushed them into the fires, he took a ribbon from his granddaughter. The barbers had taken her hair after she'd been gassed, of course, but the girl had hidden the ribbon in her fist. People from his village said that he used to brush the girl's long hair every morning and he would tie ribbons in it before she went to school. No one knew what happened to the father. He took the ribbon from her dead hand, then stuffed the bodies into his oven. Then he sat down on the pile of corpses around him and began to recite. Three of his comrades helped him up and got him out of there. He whispered to them. They died the next morning. That's the story. Make of it what you will. If you don't believe it, then touch him and see what happens."

John moved half a foot back from the Prophet, but his stare became all the more morose. Aaron however was intrigued by the story and leaned forward as if the truth lay in the twisted features of this unfortunate old man. "How did he come to be here?"

"When the Kapos found out he couldn't work, they sent him to Ka-Be to await the next selection. There some began listening to him. So when the selection came, they put his clothes on a Muselmann and then released him. His followers, if you could call them that, set him up here and take care of him."

"...the righteous perish and no one takes it to heart, men of good faith are swept away and no one cares, the righteous are swept away by the onset of evil, the hair is torn from every head and every beard shaved off, injustice buds, insolence blossoms, violence shoots up into injustice and wickedness, do not sow in the furrows of injustice, my hope of victory vanishes like a cloud, my blackened skin peels off, and my body is scorched by the heat, my mind is distraught, my days are numbered and the grave is waiting for me, if I call the grave my father and the worm my mother, where then will my hope be, time runs on, visions die away.."

"We don't have all night," Pietor said. "If you want to ask him something, get on with it."

Aaron spoke first. "Will I find the man for whom I search?"

"...four kinds of destiny are offered to men: good and evil, life and death, your very rulers are rebels, confederate with thieves, every man of them has accepted bribes to shed blood, evil doers shall be chaff and that day shall set them ablaze, mourn for the dead, for the eclipse of his light..."

"Does that answer your question?" Pietor asked, wryly.

"I am not sure."

"Can we get out of here now?"

"Wait," John pleaded. "There is something I must know."

Pietor glanced around nervously. "Make it quick."

John leaned down and stared into the Prophet's face. "Is salvation at hand?"

"...the Lord God has given me the tongue of a teacher, I offered my back to the lash and let my beard be plucked from my chin, I did not hide my face from spitting and insult, woe is me, I am lost, for in God's sight I am just what you are, I too am a handful of clay, my life is but a breath of wind, the time has come, the day has arrived, the end is not upon you, he is not a man as I am, that I can answer him, he has no equal on earth for he is made quite without fear, hast thou eyes of flesh or dost thou see as mortal man see, are thy days as those of mortal man or thy years as the life of a man, you will be an object of reproach and abuse, a terrible lesson to the nations around you, but the good man, even if he dies an untimely death, will be at rest, comfort, comfort my people, it is the voice of God, speak tenderly to Jerusalem, and tell him she has fulfilled her term of bondage, that her penalty is paid.."

Pietor put a hand on John's shoulder. "We've got to go, now."

"Yes, all right." John stood with Aaron by his side and they left the shack.

Feeling vulnerable outside, Pietor trotted into the woods, pausing long enough to turn and gesture to his comrades to hurry along. They reached the latrine in minutes and set out swiftly along the road running along the barbed wire. Once on the main road, they were in the clear and Pietor relaxed somewhat.

"So, comrades," he said. "Did you find what you were looking for?"

"Indeed I did," John replied. "I must go to him again."

"And you, Aaron?"

"It was interesting. However I must consider what was said this night."

"You do that." Pietor turned to John. "It looks like you missed your meeting. Will the faithful forgive you?"

"That does not concern me," John said, shaking his head. "I will speak no more."

Pietor and Aaron exchanged meaningful glances.

They were almost at the entrance to the Jewish Camp when a door opened ahead, casting a pale light on the mud of the main road. Raucous, drunken laughter shattered the silent twilight. It was the guards leaving the brothel. The three prisoners walked right into them.

Pietor snapped rigidly to attention, whipping his cap from his head. Aaron followed suit a heartbeat behind, both of them trying to disappear into the shadows. John, lost in thought, was slow in assessing the situation. He bumped into one of the guards, then came slowly to attention and forgot to remove his cap.

The guard John had bumped regained his feet and all three regarded the prisoners with bleary eyes. Seeing that John had failed to remove his cap, one guard punched him in the face. John sprawled in the mud, his lip split and bleeding.

"Forgotten your manners, dog?" the guard asked, punctuating the question with a kick to the ribs.

This raised the ire of the other guards and the prisoners could sense the violence about to erupt. It was in the air, palpable. There were three possible courses of action they could take. The most obvious was to fight back, but were they to do so they would be beaten to death. They could run and receive a bullet in the back. Or they could submit and hope they survived the ordeal.

Pietor and Aaron stood numbly by while the guards attacked their comrade. Submission was really the only alternative and they stared straight ahead awaiting their turn. They didn't have to wait long. One of the guards, inspired by his associate's action, kneed Aaron in the groin, then shoved him back into the mud. Pietor was punched in the stomach twice and collapsed atop Aaron. Once down, experienced prisoners knew to cover the face and groin as best they could while the guards had their fun and they both did this. John, however, struggled to rise. For this he was kicked savagely down.

"I think he likes it," one of the guards observed of John's actions.

"Let's not disappoint him, then," said another.

Vicious kicks were delivered to the cowering prisoners. One caught John squarely on the chin, sending him mercifully to oblivion for the duration of the beating. Aaron and Pietor were not so lucky as their attackers sought out their face and kidneys with their rough boots and stamped on fingers. Finally after what seemed an eternity, the attack slackened. The guards panted like racehorses from their exertion.

"I've... an... idea," the leader said. "Get... them... up."

Aaron and Pietor were hauled to their feet. Both bled from a dozen minor wounds and Pietor swayed as he fought to stay erect. The lead guard drew his revolver and gestured with it for his companions to place the prisoners back to back. This was done, the guards linking the prisoner's arms together to keep them standing.

"Mertz told me he finished two with one bullet once," the leader explained.

"Impossible!" the others roared drunkenly. "Show us how it was done."

"Easy." The leader stepped up to Pietor. "Open wide, Jew."

Pietor had no choice but to obey so he opened his mouth wide enough to crack his jaw. He looked like he was screaming but no sound came out. The guard stuck the barrel of his Luger into Pietor's mouth as far as it would go. Pietor gagged, his throat convulsing. With a look of drunken determination on his face, the leader started to squeeze the trigger.

"Wait a minute," he said, relaxing his grip on the gun. "I want three. I want to try three. Get that piece of dog shit up."

The guard dragged the unconscious John up and threw him into

Aaron's arms. With his arms already linked through Pietor's, he could not hold his companion who fell to the ground. The guards tried again but with the same result. The leader, impatient to try his experiment, kept tightening and relaxing his grip on the gun. Tears sprang from Pietor's eyes and left clear tracks in the blood on his face.

Try as they would, they could not get John to stand. In frustration, the leader withdrew the Luger and swung it violently at Pietor's face. Both prisoners fell limply to the ground. The leader stared down at the three motionless prisoners. He put his hands on his knees as he tried to figure out what had happened. His comrades delivered a few more kicks to the still forms but their hearts weren't in it anymore. Satiated in lust and violence, they staggered into the shadows with a parting kick to the prone men.

When the last of their drunken babble and song drifted into the night, Aaron opened his eyes. He raised his head slightly to see if it was clear. Satisfied, he slowly rolled to his knees and examined his comrades.

Aside from various abrasions and a broken nose, Pietor was not seriously injured. Aaron shook his friend to consciousness, then turned his attention to John. The young idealist's face was covered with blood. A quick check of the man's abdomen revealed possibly cracked ribs. John was lucky, he would be off work detail for two weeks. That was if Aaron could get him to Ka-Be before lights out, which was imminent.

Pietor groaned and shook himself awake. He brought a shaking hand to his bleeding nose and groaned again. Aaron, meanwhile, was trying to get John up and moving. If the guards found them outside after lights out, they would be shot on sight. There was a puddle behind Aaron. He grabbed the back of John's head and stuck his face in the puddle. Air bubbles spluttered for several seconds, then John reared back, coughing and spitting.

"We must get moving," Aaron said.

Pietor staggered to his feet, rubbing the places on his body where angry bruises would sprout by morning. He assisted Aaron in dragging John to his feet.

"Goddamn Nazi bastards!" Pietor spat in a spray of blood.

"Do not..." John began, then doubled over. Aaron held him up. "There is an evil on the land."

Pietor turned to Aaron. "I think they've broken his head. Let's get him to Ka-Be."

The prisoners' hospital was a short distance away, but the trip took an eternity. It was almost lights out, and the doctor was tired, so he refused to see them until morning. They would have to get proper authorization from their Kapo before John could be admitted.

Bleeding, sore and battered, they made their way back to the Jewish Camp. They stumbled in just as the prisoners were preparing for lights out. Some were trying to buy buttons for their jackets, others required needles to repairs holes which had been sewn innumerable times. A jacket with a tear or missing button could bring a beating come morning roll call thus the urgency to repair the damage while the light lasted.

Aaron and his companions entered amongst shouts to close the door and pleading for bread from the dying. Jacob met them at the door as if he'd been waiting for their return. Seeing John's condition, he helped him to a spot on the bunks between two of the more skeletal prisoners so John would have more room to spread out.

"He'll be all right," Jacob said after a brief examination.

A form appeared out of the shadows. "Will he speak tonight?"

Pietor snapped his head around to confront the man who spoke. "Of course not, idiot!"

"C-come here," John addressed the man.

The gaunt figure came out of the shadows and knelt beside John. His glowing eyes showed concern, his pasty brow furrowed.

"My friend," John said. "I shall speak no more. The Prophet has told me that our debt is paid. Our liberation is at hand. Soon we will be free."

Before anyone could respond, the Kapo came in for final check before lights out. One look at John slumped in his bunk sent him into a rage. He rushed forward, knocking Aaron, Pietor and the emaciated prisoner aside. He grabbed the front of John's jacket and pulled him off the bunk.

"You preaching again!" It was not a question. "I told you before if you don't stop you'll be ash and I meant it."

The Kapo drove his point home with a meaty fist to John's mouth. John reeled back, cracking his head on the wall behind. He lay there unconscious, blood pouring from his split lip.

"Now shut up, you stinking Jews!" the Kapo said. "Get your beauty rest. You want to look good for the furnace, don't you?"

The Kapo left and the barrack was plunged into darkness.

Aaron took his place on the bunks, lay back and stared at the ceiling.

Tomorrow, Kanada.

CHAPTER NINE

"Kanada, entretien! Transport coming!" shouted the Block Elder, dismissing the messenger who'd brought the news. The messenger disappeared through the open door to alert the next barrack.

The Block Elder's words initiated a flurry of activity. The men leapt from their bunks and raced for the door. Transports meant food, as much as they could eat. But space was limited, the entire Kommando would not be needed to unload the transport. One had to get a good place in line or know the Kapo who did the choosing.

The men lined up, pushing and shoving, but not committing enough of a disturbance to bring the Kapos' axe handles down on their backs. Once in ranks, their names were marked down and they were marched double time to the gates. The men did not mind this exertion, they would have gone faster if not for fear of breaking ranks.

An SS man took careful inventory of who was heading to the ramps. Some were turned roughly back, the others waved ahead five at a time. The chosen marched stiffly, arms at their sides, mouths watering. The pale, winter sun did not blind their eyes. They were sweating, eager for work, desperation the only motive for the task awaiting them.

Marching double time to the ramps they did not notice the armed guards lining both sides of the track. The prisoners took up positions on either side of the triangular, sloping ramps, their shoes kicking up the yellow gravel into clouds of dust. The wind grew stronger, making the trees at the edge of the square sway and stirred up a large cloud of dust which engulfed the guards posted along the rails.

"Fall out!" the Kapo shouted.

The strict ranks dissolved into a chaotic mass as the men slumped thankfully to the ground to await the train. Some leaned against the ramp, others were instantly asleep. Aaron remained standing, gazing intently down the track in the direction the transport would come. For the prisoners this was the hardest part as anticipation gradually gave way to the ever-present fatigue which was their constant nemesis. For Aaron, however, the wait was a time for planning.

For five weeks he had marched with the Kommando, stood in freezing rain and brilliant sun, searching for Sol Liebman. His diligent efforts with the unloading had earned him the praise of the Kapo who had given him a position of note. He was trusted to supervise and coordinate the unloading of the first car of each transport. This was an important responsibility for one had to work under the direct, ever watchful eyes of the SS officers. Everything must go smoothly. At all times. From the end of the ramp, Aaron was able to not only watch who came out of the car he was unloading but also keep an eye down the line as the others cars were emptied, the men and women separated into groups, while the old and sick, children and invalids were herded to one side. Once the separation had been completed, they were marched past Aaron's position for final inspection by the SS before entering the camp. That moment of stillness gave him the chance to look over the new arrivals one last time to see if he missed his quarry.

He knew how he would proceed when he spotted Dr. Liebman. He only needed a second or two to complete his task but he would have to be careful. Any suspicion from the SS would result in not only his death but Liebman's as well, and this he could not allow. He had devoted much time and thought as to the manner in which he would ensure Liebman entered the camp and not the showers and had considered several courses of action though it was impossible to predict which was the best way to proceed given the circumstances.

One idea had been to simply leave the selection to the SS. Workers were needed for every aspect of the German war effort thus a fit, middle-aged man would be a good candidate for work. But Aaron knew he could not take that chance. Krueger's price had been the diamonds Liebman was carrying, treasure destined for the pockets of the SS. Aaron had to contact the doctor before he entered the camp.

Another concern was that he had somehow missed Liebman. The first two weeks of his work in the Sonderkommando, their job had been to hose down the corpses in the shower/gas chamber, making sure no pockets of gas remained trapped beneath the entwined mass of dead. Then, using straps around the wrists, they hauled the corpses to the elevator leading to the crematorium. Aaron had feared that one day he'd be staring into the lifeless face of Dr. Liebman as he picked up each body for burning. This had not been the case though he did not hesitate to have Krueger put him in a better position ostensibly to get the diamonds.

His thoughts were interrupted by the arrival of the SS officers. The prisoners knew that the transport would pull in soon since the officers were always the last to arrive. They did not want to leave their warm, comfortable homes a mile from the camp with their mistresses and whores, but reaping the riches of Europe was too good to miss. They were here to grab the lion's share of the treasure before the Reich. They stepped out of their black staff cars in full uniforms and strutted along the ramp in front of Aaron and the rest of the prisoners. Aaron could hear them sharing a joke, discussing the weather or making plans to dine that evening. When he had first worked the Kommando, he had learned something of how the war was progressing but now, the SS did not speak of it. Instead they removed their briefcases from the cars and tossed platitudes at each other while their eyes held the predatory gleam of greed.

From the direction of the camp, a car motor roared. The Kapo nearest Aaron leapt to his feet on hearing it and cursed and kicked the prisoners to their feet. The Kommandant was coming! Work crews were quickly divided into those who would open the cars and unload the dead and baggage and those who would hand the new arrivals down, separating them into groups by gender for selection. The men staggered, shuffled and ran their way up the ramps and were in place before the Kommandant's car ground to a halt in a spray of yellow gravel.

Kommandant Heydrich Werner stepped from the car resplendent

in full dress uniform as though Himmler himself were here for inspection. He was tall, well-proportioned, a paragon of Aryan purity with stylishly coiffed blond hair and ice-blue eyes. His face was symmetrical perfection, graceful Roman nose, cleft chin and high cheekbones framing a narrow, thin mouth.

His presence was by no means necessary as the processing of the Reich's undesirables was carried out with machine-like precision. However he had not come to oversee the operation. His thirst for women was common knowledge in camp. Rumors told of him once going through twenty-seven in one week. He would choose the ones he wanted and they would be led away to a barrack close to his living quarters where they would wait their turn. He preferred making his choices as they left the train because they still had hair and looked more feminine.

The officers greeted him respectfully, one setting up a lawn chair in the sun for him. The Kommandant took a seat in full view of the ramps. An aid stood on his left with a notepad to record his selections. The expression on his strong features was unreadable. His gaze seemed far away like someone in a trance. He turned and nodded slowly to his aid who'd addressed him, and spoke a word in a barely audible whisper but he gave the impression that he was far away, like a man in a dream, where events progressed but did not affect the dreamer.

"Transport coming!"

All eyes turned in the same direction. A thin distant wisp of black smoke was barely visible on the horizon. Prisoners craned their necks looking for the train. While the talk of food and trade swept over the men, Aaron stood on the railway platform looking at the approaching column of smoke.

Around the bend, one after another, the cattle cars flowed. The conductor blew his whistle, the train shrieked back. The prisoners turned unfeeling, desperate faces to the small barred windows in each car. Pale faces pressed up against the bars, gasping for air. A muffled throbbing moan vibrated along each car.

"Take gold, or anything else besides food and you will be shot for stealing Reich property," an SS major announced as he strolled along the platform. "Verstanden?"

"Jawohl!" the prisoners thundered.

The transport shuddered to a halt with one final ear-piercing shriek. Prisoners took up their positions at the doors like ghosts in the clouds of steam bathing them. Aaron stood back, looking along the length of the train. It was a long transport, perhaps thirty cars.

"Begin!" the major shouted.

The bolts cracked back and the doors banged open, revealing a teeming mass of writhing humanity amongst sacks, suitcases, trunks and corpses. Foul air from the jumble of men and women washed over the prisoners. Gaping like fish, the new arrivals sucked in the cold morning air, the surging pile of people seeking oxygen forced the doors open.

"Attention! Everyone out! Take your luggage with you!" the SS barked. "Pile all your belongings next to the exits!"

A wave of humanity washed over the platform. Men jumped down, then assisted the ladies from the car. Children, pale, frightened, were eased into their mothers waiting arms. The prisoners practically threw the people down in their haste to get at the food hidden in the baggage. As each car was emptied, they jumped in to remove the corpses of those who died en route as well as any luggage left behind. Next to each car, a mountain of food grew. Sausages, bread, jams, were piled next to much larger mound of personal possessions.

As the men and women filed past, the prisoners were asked for water and ignored the pleas. It was strictly forbidden to tell new arrivals what fate lay ahead for them. Calm efficiency had to be maintained throughout the proceedings to prevent panic.

The trucks pulled up to take the luggage to Kanada for sorting and cataloguing. Prisoners rushed to load the baggage as they gnawed at whatever provisions were readily at hand before the lot was taken away. The new arrivals milled about, the prisoners shoving them out of the way as they gazed up at the blinding sun.

"Form up!" the SS man shouted. "Men on the right, woman and children on the left."

Most of the woman and children would be sent directly to the gas chambers, the men were judged according to age and ability to work. The two columns formed up quickly and filed past the SS doctor who picked out invalids and the old and sick from the column of men. Some of the men smiled through toothless gums, trying to curry favor but they were so much cattle to the doctor.

Aaron studied the column. Liebman's features, burned into his mind, provided a recognition pattern. His eyes swept over the young, the beardless and the women.

With the train empty, the people and goods on their way to the camp, the Kapos stepped forward to supervise the cleaning of the cars. Corpses were tossed onto a pile while more trucks arrived to ferry them to the crematorium to be united with their living comrades.

A distant shrill whistle blew from the direction from which the first train approached. Another transport. The Kapos kicked and cuffed the prisoners into action to make way for the next batch, sending some of the men tumbling onto the tracks. Prisoners cursed and leaped after them to pull them clear. A second column of black smoke stained the horizon. The cars from the first train had been cleaned, a river of feces, urine, blood, mud and water ran out of each car, splattering the yellow gravel and seeping into the earth.

The skies darkened as the next train backed in. The prisoners, still swallowing wads of meat and bread from the last transport, clamored once more up the ramps. This second train was smaller, perhaps fifteen cars.

And so it went all through the day. A driving, freezing, numbing rain streaked down all afternoon and well into the night. The trains kept coming. Waves of men and women and children were unloaded, sorted, then condemned to death or a short life of hardship and torture. The spoils of war were gathered, tagged -- to be shipped back to finance the war effort. Men fighting to open umbrellas for their wives against the rain had them ripped from their hands and were roughly separated from their loved ones. Children ran chaotically amongst the prisoners only to be picked up and thrown indiscriminately into the crowds destined for the gas chambers. Some of the parents disowned their children, thinking they would be selected for work if they were childless.

Aaron did not gorge himself on the food and drink left behind. As his comrades stuffed their mouths and washed the wads down with vodka to forget what they were doing, he searched faces. The rain did not distract him, the shouts of the prisoners as they clutched and grabbed at the plenty laid before them did not affect him. His attention did not waver.

When it was full night, the men, exhausted and bloated, collapsed onto the gravel between transports as another train shrieked it's arrival. There can only be so much slaughter before men hardened to emotion and thought succumb to the reality of their actions. The SS officers had long since returned to their warm houses, their cases stuffed with gold, jewels and currency. For them this was treasure enough and there would always be more later. But the prisoners had to herd their comrades to their deaths while growing fat on their belongings. The men's stomachs would ache tomorrow, many would die from furnishing their bodies nourishment it was no longer accustomed to receiving but the true agony ran deeper and could not be assuaged. It was the pain which made them curse the SS guards on the platform, which made them punch and kick the new arrivals from the cars. The bone-deep ache created a panicked urgency to have it over, off the train, into the showers, out of sight, gather up the spoils on the way. Let the ghostly flame from the smokestack be the only light they see, let the demonic roar of the crematorium be the only sound they hear. Better them than me. Stay alive one more hour. Do what you must. Don't think about what chain of events has led to this, why you are here, why the trains will not stop coming. How many can possible be left after so many have turned to smoke? And then the nightmarish thought that it will never end. The transports will never stop. There can never be enough to feed the flames. Even after they themselves have fueled the fires, it will hunger like the stab of famished shame in their bellies.

Through all of this, as the men moved like robots, Aaron kept his solitary vigil. With the rain in his eyes and the dim lights, Aaron suddenly spotted a hunched figure. A soaked felt hat bowed to a wrinkled, high forehead, a sharp nose poked out from the collar of a thick wool coat. A prisoner ripped the suitcase from the figure's hand, a voice of protest, barely audible above the screams.

Aaron had to be sure. There could be no mistake. Moving forward, shoving prisoners out of his way, he moved in for a closer look. He swiped the water out of his eyes with a strong right hand and stared at the figure.

Liebman.

It was time to act. Use the train, use the crowd. With curses and kicks he willed the men to hurry with unloading. This accomplished, the men leapt inside more to be out of the rain rather than to perform their function. Liebman was not far, perhaps fifty meters. A Kapo shoved him roughly into line before the doctor, and the line moved quickly.

Aaron ran forward and jumped into the car. Kicking aside the bloated corpse of a dead infant, he surveyed the scene. The stench hung like a shroud over the piles of excrement and dead. The prisoners struggled with an enormous trunk while others collected the dead children like firewood. The first group got the trunk free from the mud lining the car and began pushing it to the door. Aaron rushed forward.

"Take the bodies first!" he shouted. "The trunk can wait!"

"We've got it, it's coming out!" one of the men said through clenched teeth. "We checked, there's no food."

"Put it down!" Aaron kicked the trunk, sending it and the men into the corpse of a fat man. They toppled over the enormous pile of rotting flesh into a pile of rags soaked with urine and dried blood. Aaron, not giving them a chance to recover, grabbed each one by the collar of his uniform and threw them into the men collecting the corpses.

"The bodies first!" Aaron spat.

No strangers to this type of treatment, the men obeyed. Aaron pulled the fat corpse from its shroud of filth and tossed it at the backs of the men jumping down with the dead children under their arms. Hands clawed at the corpse as they drew it from the car.

Aaron spared a glance in Liebman's direction. Closer now. A Kapo stuck his head into the car, using the collar of his coat to cover his mouth and nose.

"Get that trunk out of there!" He slammed his axe handle down on the floor to emphasize the order.

"Yes, sir," Aaron replied.

He dragged the trunk to the edge of the car when all of the prisoners at the door had moved off with bodies for the trucks. A quick glance in Liebman's direction showed him the top of the man's hat bare meters from where he was standing. Leaping down, Aaron turned and grabbed the thick leather handles of the heavy trunk and heaved it out of the car. With the trunk chest high he backpedaled into the group of new arrivals awaiting inspection. He threw the trunk down, making it look like an accident. He collided with Liebman, using his momentum to take Liebman with him off the platform and beneath the wheels of the train. Recovering first, he took hold of Liebman's coat and ripped the collar off. He crammed the fabric into his mouth and swallowed convulsively. Liebman, seeing what has happening, tried to stop him but it is too late.

Aaron picked Liebman up and drew the man close to whisper to him. "You are forty-two and a carpenter! Tell them! It means your life!"

Before the dazed Liebman could reply, Aaron pitched him up onto the platform, climbing up after him and delivered what appeared to be a vicious kick to Liebman's ribs. He hauled Liebman to his feet and shoved him back in line.

An SS man, drawn by the commotion, came forward, gun drawn. He looked Liebman up and down, then turned his attention to Aaron. "Come here, Jew!"

Aaron whipped off his sodden cap and stood at attention.

"Arms up!" The man brandished the automatic.

Aaron complied, stealing a glance at Liebman who was next in line for the doctor. The guard searched him roughly. Finding nothing, he slapped Aaron, telling him to open his mouth. Aaron complied, his eyes riveted on Liebman. The SS man dug his finger into Aaron's mouth. They tasted like gun oil. He probed under the tongue. Satisfied, he grunted and turned away from Aaron who returned to picking up the corpses. The transport, at last empty, shrieked its departure. A distant shriek echoed its replacement on the way.

Liebman had reached the doctor. Aaron watched as their lips moved and after a moment's hesitation, Liebman was waved to the right, joining the men heading into the camp to work. His face a stony mask, Aaron returned to work. The Kommandant's aid was supervising the proceedings. He stepped from the jutting roof of the station to a waiting car. This was the signal that the arriving transport was the last for the evening. The mouths of the prisoners twitched with the briefest of smiles. The work would soon be ended. Aaron, with one parting glance at Liebman's retreating back, rushed to finish the unloading.

CHAPTER TEN

Kanada awoke to a new world. The temperature had dropped during the night, turning the rain into clinging wet snow. The low morning sun lacked the strength to melt the spongy blanket or the chilled, weary hands of the men as they shuffled and stamped out for morning roll call.

No transports were expected this day so the only work was in sorting baggage collected the night before. Some men were detailed to assist those normally assigned this task. The rest were ordered to the mess hall, then back to barracks, which was welcome news since they had worked the previous day from 6 AM until well after midnight with no rations save those they gathered from the new arrivals. This was a bittersweet moment for the Sonderkommando. As their only function was processing transports, they now possessed the precious gift of leisure time, but having a long stretch where one was not demonstrating one's value to the SS could prompt a selection to thin the ranks and the most likely chosen for the gas chambers would be the ones with nothing but time on their hands.

The order to dismiss was given. Those too sick from yesterday's feasting, staggered to the latrine. The foolish rushed back to barracks to devour more of their spoils. The wise went to the mess hall with their bowls for the morning soup. Last night's bread could be kept for weeks, meat traded for shoes, jam for warm socks. The soup was temporary. If they ate everything now on top of what they'd wolfed down last night there would be nothing but soup when winter came for real. Who knew when the next transport would come?

Aaron made his way to the mess hall but satisfying his hunger was not his objective. Now that he could pay the price for Liebman's safety, it was time to leave Kanada. This was no easy task thus arrangements had to be made.

Bowls at the ready, the men queued up for the morning soup. Aaron took his place in line. The man he sought was near the front of the line though he had arrived at the same time as Aaron who watched the prisoner receive his meager portion and take a seat at the far end of the one-story, brick building. When Aaron's bowl was filled, he slowly made his way over to where his contact sat. It was dangerous to meet amongst the rest of the prisoners as ears were always tuned to such meetings. It was difficult, if not impossible, to make any move, covert or not, without drawing the attention of someone eager to report it to the SS, the SCI or even his block Kapo.

Rubbing his stomach, Aaron took a seat next to his contact. They did not speak. Aaron tasted his soup, wincing as he swallowed. His contact furiously gulped the thin, watery broth. In disgust, Aaron threw his spoon down. This was all his contact needed to see. With spidery, trembling hands, the man pulled Aaron's bowl in front of him and started wolfing down Aaron's portion. Everything in camp had a price and, if Aaron wanted to get in touch with Krueger, the price was the morning's ration to this tiny, pointy-nosed wisp of man. Payment had been made, they could begin now, but cautiously. There was no chance the exchange had gone unobserved. Eyes and ears were opening all along the mess table.

"You are still hungry?" Aaron asked. "Didn't you get enough last night?"

The man did not reply. He had Aaron's bowl tilted up, trying to drain the last dregs of the soup.

"I know I surely did," Aaron went on. "I don't know if I can go back to eating this slop."

"Go ask the Kommandant for a pardon," the contact spoke for the first time, his voice a nasal whine.

"I might just do that."

"You'll need an appointment."

Aaron burst out laughing and slapped the man on the back. His thin, willowy frame shook with the impact. The man laughed as well and the deal was made. Standing, Aaron retrieved his bowl and left the mess hall. He would go back to barracks and wait, word would reach him there.

He used the time to formulate his strategy for handling Krueger. Paying the SCI was easy but he had to try and get the most for the effort. While the prisoners played football or walked in the roll call area, Aaron sat on his bunk, gazing out the tiny upper window. Other prisoners were using these few precious hours between transports to sleep, trying to store up as much rest as they could before more trains rumbled in.

It was late afternoon when Aaron received his reply. A Kapo entered the barracks, calling for him. Aaron leapt gracefully down from his perch, whipping his cap off at the same time. He ran to catch up to the Kapo who had turned and left the barrack after calling out.

The Kapo stopped and turned when they were out of earshot of the rest of the barrack. "Jew 96432?"

"Yes, sir!"

"Block Leader needs men in Kanada," he grunted. "Report to Steinberg."

He grabbed Aaron roughly by the arm and hurled him into a small group up ahead. There were four men, counting Aaron. The Kapo turned on his heel and headed back to his barrack, anxious to get out of the winter chill. Aaron and his new workmates headed for Kanada double-time. Steinberg was a vicious Kapo. If they were slow reporting, they would pay dearly. One thing Aaron noticed about one of his new comrades was that he was a Muselmann. A swarthy political had him by one arm and was pushing/carrying the deranged man forward.

They reported to Steinberg who berated them for their tardiness though they had arrived as quickly as was humanly possible. He did not use his axe handle though. Instead he shouted at them to get to

Sorting Barrack Eleven. They whipped their caps back onto their heads and sped off, the political still carrying the Muselmann.

The sorting area consisted of twelve barracks which divided the property collected from victims so it could be moved to the storage barrack where it would be shipped out. Here were processed trunks and suitcases of every size and shape, parcels and cases as well as items like wheelchairs, artificial limbs, brushes, combs, eyeglasses, skirts, pants, dresses, toys, and the enormous amount of hair collected from the dead women. Shoes were also in abundance and carefully sorted by size and color. The most important barrack, however, dealt with watches, rings and other jewelry collected from the dead, including gold teeth. Even prisoners who possessed gold teeth were registered with the Kanada officials so that before they went up the stack their teeth would be recovered. Any prisoner who removed his own gold teeth to trade for food or clothing would be sent to the Bunker to be tortured.

Aaron and his comrades were detailed to the small area of the clothing barrack reserved for sorting undergarments as well as handkerchiefs and scarves. They would not be used by the Reich in the way they were intended but the material was useful. As night fell, Aaron and the rest were sent to sort an enormous pile close to the door. This was all that remained of yesterday's transports.

As they sorted, the political listed the objects as they were removed from the pile. He made sure the Muselmann worked next to Aaron.

Towards dawn, the men smelled smoke. The political looked up from his notepad directly at Aaron. A pile of rags was smoldering at the man's feet, he made no move to put it out. A tiny flame erupted atop the pile and he nudged it with his foot. The flame grew, in one quick motion, he flipped it with his foot into the substantial mound of clothes the men were working on. Flames began slowly spreading into the pile.

No one moved. Aaron stared at the political, the Muselmann kept working, mumbling to himself. Smoke began filling the room, the political watched the fire for a several seconds, then threw his notepad down.

"Go!" he barked at one of the men. He ran off yelling for help. The political turned his attention back to Aaron. "Strip!"

He leapt forward and grabbed the Muselmann by his shirtfront. He carefully unbuttoned the prisoner's shirt then ripped it off his body. With one vicious tug, he pulled the man's pants down. The Muselmann made no sound even as the political knocked him off his feet so he could get the pants free from around the man's ankles.

Aaron, standing naked, his clothes in his hands, took in the whole scene. With one hand, the political tossed the Muselmann's clothes at Aaron, with the other he tore the bundle Aaron was holding. Aaron dressed quickly in the Muselmann's clothes. The fire was a blaze now, smoke filling the room, roaring up, threatening the wooden roof. Footsteps thundered closer. The cry of 'fire' resounding from every direction.

Both men dressed, the man the political had dispatched returned and he stopped him at the door. "One minute. No more."

He rejoined Aaron and the Muselmann. With a fierce chop to the throat, the political knocked the Muselmann down, then delivered a swift kick to the head, sending him rolling towards the fire.

"Dead?" the last member of the detail asked, coming forward.

"No time to make sure," the political answered.

The two men moved forward, grabbed the inert body and tossed it into the blaze. The body was engulfed immediately, it began to twitch and move but it was impossible to say whether it was simple reflex action of if the man was still alive. The political turned and shoved Aaron ahead of him.

"Let's put it out," he said, calmly.

Men with hoses arrived and they went to meet them. They helped the prisoners with the hoses and within a matter of minutes the fire was out. Smoke filled the room, making the prisoners choke, their eyes water and sting. The Kapo detailed the men to take away the blackened, charred pile when it was cool enough to approach.

The Manpower Utilization Officer entered the sorting area, waving at the thick, black smoke. He listened to a report from the Kapo, then stepped up to the political.

"Anyone hurt?" he asked.

The political whipped off his cap. "Just one, sir. Dieter, 96432.

Dead."

"How?"

"Burned, sir."

"Very well," the MUO said, taking note of the name and number. "Carry on."

To Aaron's surprise, the Kapo dismissed him and his group, leaving others to clean the area. The political led them not to the barracks but to the barbed wire gate separating Kanada from the rest of the camp.

"You are Spiegel, 87661, a Jew," the political told him as they approached the gate. "Remember this if anyone asks."

For the first time Aaron looked down at his new jacket. There was the green triangle of the habitual criminal, overlaid with the yellow for Jew below his new number. The number was lower than the one he'd had previously. That was good. It would give him a certain amount of respect in the Jewish Camp.

A tired SS man checked their numbers against the list he had. The political told him to check with the MUO when he noticed that one of the detail were missing. He did so, then, yawning, waved them through. Pietor was there to meet them as they entered the Jewish Camp.

"Good day, Pietor," Aaron said. "I trust you are well."

Pietor actually stepped forward and shook Aaron's hand. They moved to the roll call area.

"So, Low Number," Pietor began, noticing his comrade's new jacket. "You managed to stay out of the oven even without my help."

What they had accomplished was not lost on Aaron. The Sonderkommando was easy to get into but all but impossible to escape. Krueger had power indeed in camp to be able to pull off such a feat. "That is not all I managed," Aaron replied. "I surmise that Krueger sent you to intercept me."

Pietor looked slightly hurt. "I would have come anyway. But, yes, you are right. We might as well get this over with."

Pietor led Aaron to Krueger's office. He seemed no longer interested in conversation. The sun glowed overhead and the wind whispered winter. Prisoners worked the grounds while others leaned on shovels. Kapos looked from their barrack windows periodically but the chill kept them inside and the SS were nowhere to be seen. Camp veterans saw this as a prime opportunity to rest. There was an odd lethargy to the camp which Aaron found curious after the hectic pace of Kanada.

At the entrance to Krueger's office, they were searched, especially Aaron. Satisfied, one of the Kapos stepped inside to inform Krueger. He returned a moment later and waved them in.

Krueger was at his desk, Aaron could not recall seeing the SCI in any other position. It was as if he grew out of the chair. Pietor fell into the seat across from the desk. Aaron preferred to stand.

"Well, the prodigal son returns," Krueger said, eyeing them. "What say we slaughter the fattened calf, eh, Pietor."

"Let's," he replied, feigning humor at Krueger's joke.

"I would say the calf has been slaughtered already," Aaron said. "Who was that you had tossed in the fire?"

"Does it matter? He is dead, we live. Shed tears for the dead in this place and we would all drown. If it makes you feel better, he was Muselmann and would not have survived the next selection. We did him a favor, ended his misery. Better to die at the hands of brothers, than to me consumed by SS flames."

"You misunderstand my concern," Aaron said. "I only wondered if perhaps he was an enemy you wished to rid yourself of. Perhaps a lesson for a prisoner who has something you covet? The prisoner's worst enemy is the prisoner, no?"

"Have you something I want, Jew 87661?" Krueger asked, his eyes turning to stone.

"Yes. But there are conditions."

"Take care," Krueger warned. "Or you may end up back in Kanada. Not as a worker."

Aaron held up a slender hand. "I assure you, what I ask of you is not threat to your position. My requests are very simple and will go unnoticed in the camp proper."

"Speak."

"First I wish to remain in the Jewish Camp."

Pietor groaned and squirmed in his set. He knew who Krueger

would order to keep watch on him there.

"Done," Krueger barked.

"I wish to have myself and Liebman assigned to Jacob's barrack with access for both of us to the brothel."

"Jacob is dead. You friend John is now Blockaltester. The brothel has been liquidated. Have you grown tired of our friend, Pietor?"

Aaron took the death of his former block elder in stride. "I assumed Pietor's presence alongside me was a given."

Krueger chuckled. "Quite right. Done."

"I would also like our names placed with the Labor Service Officer, ensuring that neither Liebman or myself be transferred to another camp."

"Done!" Krueger's impatience was evident.

"That's all."

Krueger leapt to his feet and slammed his huge hands down on the desk. Pietor flinched, Aaron stood staring straight ahead, hands behind his back. "You waste my time with trifles! Give me what I want!"

Aaron let his hands drop to his sides. With a convulsive constriction of his throat, he brought up that which he had taken from Liebman. The collar of the doctor's coat popped out of his Aaron's mouth. He held it gingerly between his teeth.

Krueger thrust out a large, open hand. Aaron removed the bit of wet cloth from his mouth and set in in the wrinkled palm. The SCI snatched his hand back. His fat thick fingers began massaging the seam in the cloth. There were three large bumps. Dark brown thread ran along a half inch of the seam, the rest was sewn in black. Krueger fell into his seat, one hand clutching the collar, the other fumbling in his desk drawer for the letter opener.

The small blade in hand, he began cutting and tearing at the brown thread. When he had made a small hole, he dug his strong fingers in and widened it. Something glittery, about the size of a raisin fell out onto a stack of papers on the desk and rolled under the uneven pile. Krueger threw the papers to the floor, closing his hand around the prize. He stared dumbly at it resting in his upturned palm, his mouth twitching, then violently shook the collar like a predator

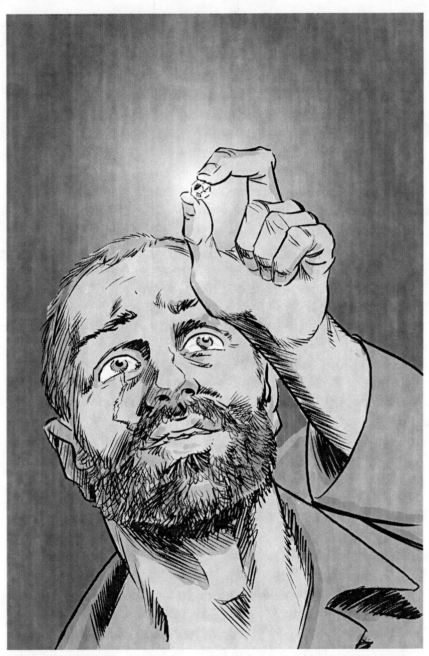

Krueger held up one of the diamonds, letting the light catch each line.

finishing his prey. Two more diamonds of the same dimension as the first fell out. He turned his palm this way and that, his eyes wide and staring. Pietor half leaned, half stood and caught a glimpse of what Krueger held. A whoosh of air escaped his lungs and he fell back into his seat.

"More?" Krueger croaked. "More!"

"That is all there is," Aaron replied, calmly.

"Y-you could buy the camp," Pietor stammered. "A king's ransom."

Krueger held up one of the diamonds, letting the light catch each line. A thin smile cut his features. The diamonds appeared flawless. He turned them so the light could play over them and reveal their secrets. How many karats? Ten? Fourteen? He caught Pietor staring hungrily at the diamonds. The thin smile turned into a snarl.

"What are you looking at, dog?" he bellowed. "Get out of here! Or you'll go up the stack!"

Pietor leapt to his feet and ran for the door. He closed it with a soft click and then got as far away from the office as he could. What Krueger had was a treasure that could kill as well as save. It was a double-edged sword. One could buy one's freedom as well as the freedom of twenty comrades. You could eat like a king for the rest of the war. Or, if the SS got wind of the treasure, you would end up in the stockade being tortured for months until they found your source or collected all that you had. This was danger. Pietor was glad to leave. He felt sorry for Aaron for having been foolish enough to reveal his treasure to Krueger. And then a sudden wave of terror overtook him. They would kill Aaron and Liebman. There was no question about that. He would be eliminated along with them. Not right away though. They would use him first, have him get what he could from Aaron who had been wise to deny the existence of other treasure. Perhaps they could negotiate. He waited outside for Aaron, deep in thought.

If Aaron was thinking along the same lines, his calm features betrayed nothing. The SCI pocketed the stones, then cast a suspicious glance at Aaron. Now that the initial shock had passed, he was thinking clearly, assessing what this Jew was up to.

"What is your game, 87661? For wealth like this you could have bought your freedom or even turned my men against me. And yet you beg trifles for such a prize. There is more here than meets the eye."

Aaron was surprised by Krueger's response. He had assumed a greedy, selfish man like the SCI would be content to line his pockets with a prize unlike anything he was liable to see in camp. "I assure you what I ask is of great importance to me. Wealth such as this is of no use to me here. Where would I hide diamonds for any period of time without them being discovered? I share a barrack with seventy other men. It would only be a matter of time before they were taken from me."

"You'd be dead," Krueger offered.

"I am a practical man. What is of no use to me or Dr. Liebman, is valuable to one of your capabilities and position. Better to trade you two lives for them."

Krueger considered this for a moment. What this Jew said had a logic to it but he always trusted his instincts. Something was not right about the man before him. Anyone foolish enough to part with diamonds for a pittance was either on his way to becoming Muselmann or had another agenda. Time would tell.

"Very well," Krueger said at last. "You and Pietor shall remain in the Jewish Camp. Your Dr. Liebman will join you. I will speak to the LSO to see that you remain there. Take heed, you are still working for me. You and Pietor will continue surveillance on Siderman. There is an uprising in the air. I feel it. It will be stopped before it starts. Understood?"

"Perfectly, sir."

"Go. Pietor knows what to do. Take care, Jew 87661. The future is never certain."

Outside, Aaron looked around for Pietor and saw him leaning against a wall facing the roll call area. Aaron joined him there.

"That was a hell of a chance you took," Pietor said. "I hope you've got more."

"There are no more."

"Then we're dead."

"We?"

"Do you think Krueger will keep me alive now that I know what he has? Why the price the SS would pay for such information..."

"I think you underestimate our leader," Aaron said. "He needs us. We are his eyes and ears and, to a certain extent, he trusts us. We have not yet outlived our usefulness. So, come, the Jewish Camp awaits."

"I can't believe you want to go back there," Pietor said.

"Liebman is there."

"We could have him brought here."

"That is not possible."

"Why not?"

Aaron did not reply. He simply regarded his friend with a look which could pass for amusement. Eventually Pietor gave up waiting for an answer and led them back to the Jewish Camp.

Aaron and Pietor walked through the barbed wire gate into the Jewish Camp under the watchful eyes of the sergeant. This would be there home until the end of the war if Krueger kept his side of the bargain. On their way to Jacob's barrack, they went over their story. Aaron had been outside, in Jenseits these last weeks. A factory making rifle barrels and other iron mongery had been bombed and he'd been volunteered to clear away the rubble and assist in the rebuilding. The factory was now operational and the extra labor was no longer needed so he'd been sent back.

They explained this to John and his associates in the Blockaltester's new quarters upon their return. John accepted their story knowing full well it was a fabrication. His comrades were taken in however and asked questions about the extent of the damage and how long the plant had been out of commission. They knew little of the war effort but the low, distant thunder they heard now at night when the stars shone bright in a clear sky, told them the war was drawing closer to them. Aaron provided details which surprised Pietor though he did not let it show. The men, pleased by what he'd told them, returned to what they'd been doing when the two men had entered.

Aaron was led to Pietor's bunk which was not far from John's. A small group was clustered around the young man who sat silent and staring though his followers implored him to speak.

Aaron moved around the barrack, slowly checking each face. Even those asleep did not escape his notice and he occasionally had to roughly move someone aside to glimpse the face of the man sleeping next to him. This brought a chorus of curses in the dim barrack which he ignored.

Finally at the top corner of the barrack, in the back close to the ceiling, a huddled, sleeping figure shivered in the night. His back was to Aaron but the set of the man's shoulders was unmistakable, the length of frame indisputable. Aaron climbed up, drawing more curses from rudely awakened prisoners, and stood over the sleeping form. So deep was the sleeper's fatigue that the curses hurled up at Aaron did not arouse the man.

"Good evening, Dr. Liebman," Aaron said.

CHAPTER ELEVEN

Morning found Aaron perched on the edge of the bunk Liebman occupied. The first weak light of dawn lit the small windows set near the ceiling of the barrack casting an unearthly glow over the sleeping prisoners. Aaron turned his gaze to the face of the sleeping Liebman. First was the eyes, closed now, beneath a sloping forehead. The head, now bald, was large and almost perfectly round. Only the red, raw skin, remnants of the barber's shears, marred its surface. Similar marks were evident on the cheeks which the night before sprouted a thick beard but were now hairless. Small snorts accompanied Liebman's breathing, the nostrils of the graceful nose flaring with each breath. The thin lips, slightly blue from the morning chill, were pursed just enough to give the impression that Liebman was deep in thought and not exhausted from the ordeal of the train.

A shrill whistle outside the door dared the dead-like prisoners to rise and survive another day. Liebman stirred at the ear-piercing sound but did not awaken. Even amidst the sudden chaos of the men staggering from the bunks, reaching frozen hands for their shirts they were forbidden to wear to sleep. Men cursed as they roughly shoved aside the bodies of two who had hanged themselves in the night. Aaron had heard the noise in the somber shroud of night, had felt the timbers creak and had listened to the small, strangled sound each throat had made as they choked. Now in the morning light, their bodies swung crazily.

He waited until the last possible moment, then gently shoved Liebman awake. The doctor stirred, snorted, but did not awaken. Aaron nudged him again, harder this time. Liebman snapped awake like a man gasping for air. He looked around frantically for a moment, sighed as he realized the last few hours were not the stuff of nightmares.

"You have thirty minutes to dress and get to the mess for morning rations, Aaron said, leaping down from the bunk. "But first you must wash. I will get you a place in line. Hurry or you will get no breakfast."

Aaron was gone before Liebman was able to open his eyes and see who was speaking to him. He finally did roll over and open his eyes and found himself staring into the eyes of one of the hanging dead from the previous night. Instinctively he shrank away from the horror, clinging to the far wall which was freezing against the thin shirt he had unknowingly worn to bed.

Somebody had spoken to him. The voice was familiar somehow. Yes, wash and breakfast. Thirty minutes. He looked around suddenly, the barrack was empty. Only the two dead men swaying gently from their ropes shared the morning with him. Liebman leapt down to the floor in pure panic. "What time is it? Where do I go?"

He reached up, grabbed the small tin bowl they had given him and headed outside. He gasped at the icy air. The barrack was cold but the heat of seventy or so bodies had taken the bite out of it. Outside, however, winter had arrived bringing a fierce wind with the sub-zero winds and a blanket of fresh snow. The scene would have been striking if not for present conditions.

He hugged himself, beating his hands against his sides -- also against regulations. The tin bowl numbed his hands. He had to find the washhouse, get out of the wind. A few prisoners were rushing off to his left. That had to be the direction to go. He followed them. They brought him to a large line formed outside a short, squat building. A prisoner waved for him to join him in line. Liebman hesitated at first but a gust of wind convinced him. He would freeze to death if he stayed outside any longer. Men cursed him as he cut into line.

One large man grabbed his collar and tried to yank him out. Aaron took hold of the man's wrist and squeezed until the men released Liebman's jacket.

Aaron did not acknowledge Liebman as he pushed his way in. He was curious to see how Liebman would respond to the camp. It would give him a good idea of what he could expect from the doctor.

Once the prisoners settled back into their cattle-like patience of waiting their turn, Liebman took a moment to scrutinize his benefactor. There was something familiar about this man. Liebman had seen him before. But with the confusion of the last few days, it was hard to concentrate. Then like a wave it hit him!

"You!" he shouted.

Aaron turned away, looking up to the front of the line.

"Thief! Robber!" All the anger and frustration spawned by what he'd endured since his arrest burst out of him. He clutched Aaron's shirt in his frozen fingers and pulled the taller man around to face him.

A sharp poke from behind made Liebman lose his grip. He whirled around to see a Kapo standing behind him, swinging his axe handle like a pendulum.

"Go on," the Kapo said. "Finish what you started. A cold day like this, I'll work up a sweat beating in that old head of yours."

Liebman stepped back, glaring at the Kapo in disbelief. Aaron appeared to be ignoring the whole scene but missed nothing. The Kapo, seeing that his message had been received, jabbed Liebman in the ribs and moved on.

The line crept slowly forward. Liebman and Aaron did not speak. The doctor began to shake with cold, he swayed slightly as they inched closer. Finally they were in. A stinking room with buckets of cold water set in front of a row of benches. The benches had alternating holes zigzagging their length. A thin wooden divider split the parallel benches which served as a latrine. Liebman almost dropped his bowl in his haste to clamp his hands over his nostrils against the stench of rotting waste. He shook with nausea now. The benches were over a shallow pit that had not been emptied in months. Liebman saw men urinating on their hands to get some warmth in them. Others saw him looking and laughed. He was a newcomer, a High Number, he would learn. The bucket in front of Liebman stood free. He did not notice and was shoved forward by a man behind him. Aaron had taken the bucket next to him and was splashing water on his bare chest and arms. There was no soap.

Liebman dipped his hand into the water. It was ice cold. He drew back but, aware of the cluster of waiting men behind him, whipped off his shirt and set his bowl down. He splashed water on his face, trying not to get any of the ice chunks floating in the bucket. He gasped when the icy needles dug into his cheeks, then plunged his numb hands in again and threw water on his upper body. His eyes blinded by the water, he heard a commotion near him and a grunt of pain. He blinked the water out of his eyes and saw a prisoner lying on the ground, blood trickling from a split lip. Aaron had his left foot planted squarely on the man's outstretched hand which was inches from Liebman's bowl. Aaron released the prisoner's hand and the would-be thief retreated into the crowd, clutching his injured hand to his chest. Aaron picked up Liebman's bowl.

"Never put your bowl down," he said, handing it back. "Never let it out of your sight. No bowl, no ration. That's the rule. Hold your bowl like this when you wash." Aaron shoved the bowl between Liebman's thighs.

The doctor looked around and noticed others protecting their bowls the same way. He turned to thank Aaron but the tall stranger was gone. Liebman finished washing and went outside.

He did not see Aaron. The pale sun was fully up over the soil hill, leaving the camp bathed in light devoid of warmth. Prisoners pushed past on their way to the mess. A dull, hollow rumbling in Liebman's belly guided him in the same direction. Once again the prisoners lined up, each receiving their meager portion of broth and a turnip. Liebman, being new, had to sit in a filthy corner with the Muselmänner apart from the veterans. Here he wolfed down the bitter broth. It was without flavor, but it was warm. He licked his bowl for the last dregs as he saw others doing.

"Do not eat so fast," Aaron said, sitting beside Liebman. He glanced around to make sure they had some measure of privacy.

"You will be ill."

Liebman's tongue darted across his lips at the sight of the warm broth Aaron was spooning past his lips. "Look, you! I don't know what your game is and I don't care. You stole what was mine. Leave me alone!"

"Yes, I did steal from you," Aaron replied in soft tones. "I do not deny it. However, what I obtained for your property is, I trust, of some use to you."

"And what might that be?"

"Your life."

"You expect me to believe you had my best interests at heart when you robbed me?"

"Yes, I do."

Liebman turned away. "Leave me be. Will you?"

"It would have been taken from you anyway," Aaron explained. "Why not have some good come of it?"

"What good has come from your thievery?" Liebman asked.

"Your life has been spared," Aaron replied.

Liebman paused, struck by a sudden thought. "How did you know where to look?"

Aaron set his spoon down, beneath the up-curved side of the bowl where curious fingers couldn't reach it. "There is much about you I know."

"Oh, enlighten me, great oracle," Liebman said, sarcasm dripping from every word.

"As you wish. Your name is Solomon Liebman. You prefer to be called Sol. Date of birth: March 22, 1897. You are a native of Berlin, Germany. Married Esther Elizabeth Klein on September 4, 1943. You were a teacher of Physics at Berlin University until January, 1939, when you and your then-fiancé fled Fascist Germany for Eastern France. Do you wish to hear more?"

Liebman stared in open-mouth wonder at the man sitting next to him. He did not reply to Aaron's question so the young man took that as acquiescence.

"You and your fiancé hid in the small town of Bourgevin near the France-German border. A former pupil of yours, Mr. Helmut

Goetzschoell ran a small printing house specializing in poetry for class study. This was a safe house until Goetzschoell's involvement with the French underground. Using his printing apparatus, he began producing false passports for fleeing Jews. His contacts informed him in October of this year, 1944, that the SS were monitoring his activities. He quickly prepared documentation for you and your wife. The photo in your passport had been smudged during processing and had to be replaced. You insisted your wife leave immediately with your guide, Emile Hillaire, of the underground, who had agreed to conduct you safely to the coast. You would follow after your photo had been replaced. Elizabeth reluctantly agreed and set out. Shortly after, the SS raided the printing facility and you were taken into custody. Goetzschoell was shot as a traitor to the Fatherland. You were shipped out and now you are here."

Liebman was stunned, speechless. There was no way this individual could know the details of his flight and capture. But then again, the world had gone mad and he might as well join in. "You haven't explained how you knew where to look."

"Before you and your wife were separated, she broke apart the necklace her mother had given her as a future wedding present before you fled Berlin. It contained six stones. Three for her, three for you. These were to buy your passage to England and safety."

Liebman found his mind teetering on the brink of madness. This was too much. "How could you possibly know this?" He toyed with the notion that Aaron was a SS spy sent to infiltrate the camp for some nefarious purpose, but that clearly was not the case. Goetzschoell had not been present when he and Elizabeth had divided the stones, or when they parted for the last time. They had been alone. The only way this man could have found this out was if...

"What was the last thing Elizabeth said to me?" he asked, desperately.

"Before she stepped into the truck, she embraced you and whispered in your ear the lines of a poem: 'But if the while I think on thee, dear friend, all losses are restored and sorrows end.'"

Liebman put his head down on his knees. His heart turned to a cold, dead thing in his chest.

"It was from a poem you had given her years before when her family was to vacation in Switzerland and you were to be apart for the summer months. It was the longest separation you had experienced, until now."

Liebman sat motionless, trying to absorb what had just been revealed to him. So it has come to this, he thought. That night, hand in hand, he and Elizabeth, running in terror across the border while the group they were with died at the hands of the patrol which had surprised them in the forest. Guilt! Shame! Joy at seeing two of the group get through with them. Invisible as they dashed through the trees. The tense, hollow look in their eyes above the small fire, hours and miles later. Knowing their eyes were but a refection of their own remorse for living at the cost of others.

Safety. Helmut's charity. A place to hide like fugitives, guilty of no crime. Years spent hiding. Going out by night, cautious of strangers. And amidst the black despair, the joy of love, togetherness. Elizabeth's courage and beauty. The hasty wedding in the glade, speaking aloud that which both hearts had so deeply acknowledged long before.

Separation! Flight! Only memories to light the path ahead. A road paved with corpses leading to the pit itself. His wife's green eyes beacons, sanctuary. All could be endured with that heart waiting for him at journey's end. And now, despair. Elizabeth taken! There was no other way this devil at his side could know lest she had spoken. Tortured and dead! The image of his beautiful Elizabeth bruised and broken swam before his eyes. Rage swelled, seething within him. An overwhelming urge to lash out against this madness, at this man with his calm, unfeeling recitation of events too horrible to comprehend. Better to die now with the sweet, small pride of vengeance, than to slowly waste away.

And then, at the moment of action, resignation. Anger slipped away like water down a drain. He was already dead. Had been so since being crammed into the boxcar with the others. This was the place for the dead. Modern Golgotha with living, breathing skulls spewing terrible truths. Why continue? What possible good could it do to live? Better to make an end of it.

Liebman pounded his forehead against his knees, sobs poured out onto the rough, worn cloth, eyes clenched tight against images beyond imagining.

Aaron, perplexed by Liebman's reaction, watched as the doctor waged an inner battle. This was not the result he had anticipated when he began relaying what he knew. He was unsure how to proceed.

"You do not wish to hear news of your wife?" he asked at last.

"I have no wife," sobbed Liebman, then, as if speaking to some unseen person other than Aaron. "This devil wishes to torment me further. I am beyond his reach!"

"Your wife is safe, Dr. Liebman. Please believe this. She waits for you in England."

Of course! Sweet reunion that will never be! But wait, something this devil said is not right. Liebman raised his head, tears streaming down his cheeks. "How long have you been here?"

"Thirty-eight days."

It was all clear to him now. This was a dream, a nightmare brought about by recent events. How long had he been on the train? Four days? Five. The arrest and separation from Elizabeth no more than a week. And this devil knows of it? Every detail? Impossible! Would the SS send a spy to persecute him? A mere teacher? For what purpose? No, it was madness, all of it. Any minute someone would step on his hand or search his pocket for food and he would awaken in the rolling, clanking grave of the boxcar.

"Understand," Aaron said. "Your wife and child are safe."

Child! Can a dream lie? Elizabeth bore no child. An infection when she was quite young. Her womb barren. At last he had caught the devil.

"A lie!" Liebman shouted, raising his head to face Aaron. "I have no child! Your lies come too quickly."

"In the days preceding your arrest," Aaron resumed, calmly. "Did your wife not complain that she was ill?"

"Yes," Liebman answered. "The cabbage we were forced to eat was not fit for pigs. She..."

Aaron shook his head.

Liebman stared into Aaron's eyes, while his mind played out the last few days with Elizabeth. They had eaten the same refuse and he had not been ill. Her ailment had not been serious, an upset stomach upon waking. He --

"NO! Impossible! She would have told me!"

"And have you worry for two?"

Before Aaron could say another word, Pietor left his vigil to join them. "Bad news. They are liquidating Ka-Be. We must be cautious."

Liebman, his mind reeling, devils and blind panic had hold of him. "What does this mean?"

Aaron knew the implications and explained it to the doctor. When the camp was overcrowded, food was low and the risk of rebellion, to say nothing of epidemic, high. The easiest solution was to reduce the numbers of inmates. First the hospitals were liquidated, then a general selection followed to winnow the ranks. This was the most fearful time in camp for it was difficult even for those well connected to submerge. No one was safe. One's fate rested with luck. Little else could be done to prolong one's life.

"Can Krueger ensure our safety?" Aaron turned to Pietor when his explanation was finished.

"There's no way to be sure," Pietor replied, shaking his head. "I am sure he will do what he can for his people."

"Are you?"

This question went unanswered since the men were heading to the roll call area. Aaron stood and helped Liebman to his feet. Pietor headed for the door, deep in thought. Liebman was overwhelmed by what had just transpired but the crush of prisoners pressed around them with a cacophony of languages. He allowed Aaron to take his arm and guide him from the mess.

The sun was struggling to warm the frozen earth. The prisoners, partly from cold, but mostly in terror of being late, rushed to the open square near the main gate. Hundreds already stood, freezing but immobile in strict ranks, hands at their sides. Aaron, Liebman and Pietor joined the group from their barracks.

A clerk waited with his clipboard. At precisely 7 AM, the roll call was begun. They did not wait for stragglers. The Kapos would deal with the tardy. For forty-five minutes, the entire population of the camp was counted. The prisoners stood motionless in the swirling wind while their numbers were checked off. Some of the ill or weak in the ranks, overcome by the biting cold, fell to the frozen mud. They were carried, dazed and shivering, to the crematorium. The first to go of many when the selection finally came.

At last the order of, "Caps off, Caps on!" was given to the SCI's office. Krueger was not about to stand in the cold.

"Labors details fall in!"

The men scattered to their work assignments as the band struck up a lively tune. A Kapo corralled Aaron, Liebman and Pietor as well as most of Jacob's -- now John's -- barrack to assist in the removal of bodies from Ka-Be. In seconds the details were organized and marching five abreast to the main gate for outside work. Aaron and his comrades joined them since they had to take the main road to get to Ka-Be.

The marching seemed to revive Liebman who was surprised to find a thin clammy sweat on his brow. What he did not know was if it was from exertion of fear. The corpse detail turned left and reached Ka-Be. They were massed outside in ranks of five, some twenty men altogether. The SS doctor came out bundled in a thick coat and spoke briefly to the Kapo. He in turn told the men that they would have to wait as the doctors were not finished with their task.

"Is there an epidemic?" Liebman asked through chattering teeth. "Should we fear infection?"

Two men in front laughed at the High Number's comments. Only the slightest sound. Talking was not allowed in ranks. They hoped Liebman would be caught and punished. Anything to distract them from the seeping cold.

"As Pietor pointed out," Aaron said, speaking out of the side of his mouth, which was the way prisoners talked without the SS hearing, "the camp is overcrowded. The sick receive an injection in the heart. 10cc of Carbolic Acid. Sodium evipan is also used."

Before Liebman could respond to this, the Chief SS Medical Officer came out again to speak to the Kapo. The Camp Medical Officer, a British POW, followed him out. His face was pale as he slowly shook his head from side to side. He was a High Number as well.

The Kapo barked orders and the men went inside two at a time. Their task was a straightforward one. The teams of two would pick up a body from its sick bed and carry it to the flatbed trucks which would carry it to the crematorium. Most of the prisoners relished this duty because they would be inside. Low Numbers knew how to give the appearance of rushing when in fact they were taking their time, trying to soak up as much warmth as possible each time they stepped inside. Also they knew that the SS doctor would soon leave, placing them in the hands of the British POW who, by the look of him, would not care how long the men took. Ka-Be held some six hundred beds. With a little luck, the men could make the work last the entire morning.

Aaron and Liebman formed a team and went inside. The stench of disease filled the low-ceilinged structure. The beds were lined up on either side of a long aisle down the center. At the far end against the wall, some doctors were still administering the poison to the last of the sick. The beds right near the door were already empty so Aaron and Liebman had to make their way farther inside the hospital. It was warm, the heaters going full blast. The prisoners started sweating, but still used every trick they knew to remain as long as possible before going back out into the cold. They did this at the risk of having to pass from extreme heat to extreme cold, potentially leading to sickness and a lethal return visit here.

The two waited, making room for another team to get past with a body, then rushed forward. The first bed they came to held a corpse, pale and emaciated, no more than seventeen, large eyes staring upward from a skeletal face. The mouth was open, black rotten teeth catching the bright lighting. Aaron rushed forward, taking the corpse under the arms. The head lolled sickeningly. Liebman pulled away in revulsion.

"Take the feet!" Aaron hissed. "Now!"

Liebman turned his head to the side and bent down over the bed. His right hand hovered over the thin, filthy feet. He drew back. A rotting odor wafted up from the bed, bringing his soup back into his throat. He gritted his teeth, then lunged for the pencil-thin ankles of the corpse. He expected the body to be cold and was shocked to feel the warmth of living flesh, the boy having died only minutes before.

Liebman heaved, surprised by the lightness of the body. They carried it to the door, the arms stuck out to the side and flapped like a scarecrow. Frigid air stung their faces. They shuffled/ran to the waiting truck and tossed the body onto the growing pile. The cold forced them to double-time back to the warmth of the hospital.

So passed the morning. Just before mid-day break, the Kapo caught them as they were hurrying back inside. They whipped off their caps and awaited orders.

"Come with me!" he barked.

To their surprise, they were led to a small truck. They climbed inside as the Kapo got behind the wheel. No explanation. They did not know where they were going. Liebman's relief at the opportunity to escape the dead was evident, but Aaron knew the danger. Being singled out for special duty was usually a death sentence. They could be heading to the SS hospital for experimentation or maybe to the stockade to be tortured by an SS man with time on his hands. Anything was possible.

The truck rumbled to life. The Kapo put it in gear and they drove off. Aaron's fears were confirmed as through a hole in the canvas in front, he could see they were headed towards the little town constructed for the SS. The truck rumbled and coughed along the main road. Small, quaint houses streaked by on either side. To Liebman's eyes, fresh from the world, it looked like a quiet suburb of Berlin. The very idea of the mill of death they had just left seemed out of place here.

The truck pulled up at a large, two-story house with a turreted bedroom window facing the camp. A long balcony ran the length of the front where one could imagine a family watching the sunset or old men rocking as they discussed simpler times. But this house was home to no such romantic ideas, this was Kommandant Werner's resident. The hulking Mercedes staff car out front was grim testimony to that.

They stopped at the front door. Faint sobbing could be heard off to the left of the house. It was coming from a small tool shed around back. They jumped from the truck. The Kapo did not approach the house to announce their arrival. He simply lit a cigarette and leaned against the door of the truck.

Suddenly a harsh slap came from the partially open window beneath the turret. The sobbing in the tool shed intensified. There was a scream and a loud gunshot. Liebman jumped, started at the sound. Aaron and the Kapo had long since grown accustomed to this noise.

A pale corporal stepped out on the balcony from the front door. Although the air was cold, he dabbed at his forehead with a handkerchief as he waved the men forward. Aaron and Liebman rushed to join him on the balcony. The Kapo stood where he was. Liebman tried to ask Aaron something but was silenced by a short slashing motion of Aaron's hand. One never spoke in the Kommandant's presence, or in the presence of his officers, unless asked a direct question. Silence was always the safest bet. Disappear, attract no attention to yourself. They had already been singled out for special duty, talking without being spoken to would only make things worse.

The corporal ushered them in, waving his handkerchief at the main staircase. It was quiet up there but the memory of the gunshot echoed in their ears.

Aaron took the steps two at a time with Liebman trying to keep up. Both men whipped off their caps as they headed down the long paneled hall to the master bedroom. Before they reached the door, it flew open as Werner staggered nude and blood splattered into the hall waving his pistol.

Seeing them through bleary eyes the Kommandant swept a lose forelock of blond hair out of his face as he stepped back, gesturing angrily with the gun for them to enter. They crossed the threshold and stopped, heads bowed, caps in hand. Do not do anything until you are told was another rule that could save one's life. They did not even look up.

"Get these Jew bitches out of here!" the Kommandant shouted.

"Bring me the next. I want two this time!"

Aaron looked up and took in the scene before him. The bodies of three women sprawled on the bed. Their clothes hung in tatters on bruised, red bodies. The headboard was stained with blood and gray matter. Blood was soaking into the sheets. Their bloody thighs told the story of what had preceded their murder.

As Aaron rushed around the bed, he noticed that another body lay in a pool of blood beneath the window. He made no attempt to pick up this one. The Kommandant, for all he knew, wanted this one left where it was. He was more concerned with Liebman who, after taking in the scene, stopped dead, a trembling hand pressed to his mouth. If the Kommandant had not been fumbling with the fresh bottle of brandy he was trying to open, he would have noticed Liebman's hesitation and most likely shot the doctor for disobeying orders.

Aaron dared not speak to Liebman without rousing the drunken SS officer's attention. Instead he picked up the nearest body and hurled it at Liebman. The body hit him chest high, splattering his face with blood. As he tried to step away, Aaron ran forward, hissing, "Take it!"

Liebman clutched one arm of the corpse, his fingers digging deep into the still soft flesh. Aaron took the feet and, using the body like a battering ram, pushed Liebman backwards towards the door. On the steps Liebman took a quick look at what they carried. He noticed young, pink skin dotted with slight discolorations which had not had time to bruise. He looked away and they staggered down the steps.

Outside the SS man had moved closer to the shed housing the women. The sound of their weeping seemed to excite him for he had a feverish look about him. Aaron and Liebman tossed the lifeless body into the truck then walked quickly to the shed.

"I might have a go at one of these myself," the guard said as Aaron reached for the door. Liebman did not know why the guard talked to them. Perhaps what the guard coveted was so far beyond his reach that expressing the desire would make it more real.

The two prisoners did not answer the guard who stepped away to allow Aaron access to the shed. He threw back the bolt and opened the door. Inside a huddled mass of women cowered and blinked at the harsh sunlight. There were perhaps twenty left of the ones selected from the last transport. They knew what the men were here for. They did not move.

Aaron did not hesitate for to do so would mean his life. He reached forward and grabbed the first girl within reach. The collar of her dress tore as she backed away, terrified at the expressionless prisoner before her. He reached again, grabbing a handful of hair and pulling her forward. She screamed and tried to fight but was no match for Aaron. Her struggle started the rest of the women screaming again. A sound whose pitch increased as the woman was dragged outside.

The guard grabbed a second girl at random. "Patience ladies," he soothed. "You'll get your turn."

Liebman did not help or hinder Aaron. This was all beyond him. Not more than a week ago, on a crisp day such as this, he and Elizabeth would have gone for a long morning walk in the unpatrolled countryside, then sip watery hot chocolate while what birds remained this late in the season serenaded them. And, an eternity ago, he would have rushed home from the university to take his beloved dancing in Berlin. But what struck him the most was that those days so long ago seemed like half-remembered dream and this, this horror was the only true reality. He knew now that if he tried to stop Aaron or protest the inhuman actions before him that both he and Aaron would be killed on the spot. Once this was understood and not simply something to consider, the world shrank to the size of a pinprick. He must not consider anything outside of his survival. He could not afford to. If the task before them was heinous as this, he must trick his conscience into believing that it served a function or, rather, its performance served the function of keeping them alive. Here, nothing else mattered. The dying had begun in his soul. That was the price of bodily life in the camp and that was as it should be for the soul was incorporeal. It could not be bought or sold or eaten or traded, to the camp collective it did not exist. The daily struggle to live was the only thing which mattered. Liebman did not fully comprehend all that this revelation had shown him, that would take time, and, if he ever regained his freedom, he would probably spend what years were left to him trying to find an explanation which allowed him to hold and love his wife without guilt and shame. The rest of the afternoon passed unnoticed to Liebman. He carried out the bodies struck mercilessly down in the bloom of life and dumped them like sods of earth into the truck. The pleading women did not touch his now deaf ears. Machine-like he performed the task before him as quickly and efficiently as he was able.

Werner's thirst for women seemed insatiable. Bottles of brandy rolled and clattered at their feet as they were summoned time and time again to remove the dead. By late afternoon, the Kommandant, his genitals red, raw and flaccid, he continued to rape and thrust, his body performing its function while his brain lurched in an eerie, drunken fog. Only the sharp crack of the revolver punctuated the scene until, finally, the shed was empty. Rage replaced lust as the Kommandant bellowed for more women and brandy. He brandished the Luger, firing at the heavens as if some great injustice had been heaped onto his shoulders. Then he grew quiet, slumping on the front balcony, his gray officer's trousers loose around his ankles. The SS guard who had smoked and napped, cultivating his lusts in mind only, recognized the danger in the Kommandant's mood and ran back to the truck. If Aaron and Liebman had not been standing nearby, caps in hands, they would have been left behind to face the new lust taking over the Kommandant who now gazed into the barrel of his revolver like Oedipus into the pool. Aaron leapt up into the truck as it sped away, pulling Liebman up after him.

Aaron gazed after the Kommandant who was oblivious to their departure. "He knows."

The truck had barely entered the gate when as SS Lieutenant waved them to stop. A Kapo stuck his head into the back and ordered the two prisoners out. No sooner had their shoes touched the frozen mud of the roll call area that the Kapo kicked them into ranks. The roll was underway. A light snow was falling against the last feeble rays of the sun. The wind had picked up. The prisoners shivered in shirtsleeves, every eye focused left. They were to witness punishment before being dispatched to the nightly replaying of the horrors their subconscious had taken careful inventory of.

Aaron and Liebman took their places in the ranks. Three old men, kitchen staff, had been caught eating potatoes by the young boy who carried their chopped buckets to the cooks. The boy received an extra ration, the men would be hanged for their crime not with the merciful snap knot but with an plain rope whose function it was to keep them alive and in agony as long as possible.

The SS man finished his public condemnation of the old men's crime, then turned and nodded to the prisoners standing behind each of the three men. They slipped the coarse rope over their heads. No hoods were provided. The old men were not aware of the rope's presence around their throats.

"Which one'll swing the longest?" one of the men close to Aaron asked.

"I know which one will last the shortest," another said. "Look at the fat one. He's been good at sipping the stew, he'll break the rope."

"I put a bread ration on the last one on the right," the man in front of Liebman said. "He looks younger than the others."

"Look at old Methuselah in the middle. Nothing could finish that bastard. I put a set of shoelaces on him."

The wooden blocks were kicked out from under the feet of the condemned. Feet kicking feebly, they set the gallows creaking in the early winter night. A few strangled grunts reached the ranks of prisoners forced to watch. For Liebman, they seemed to swing for an eternity. Death and he were getting better acquainted but they were not fast friends, yet.

A low, triumphant shout reached his ears. The old man in the middle was still kicking weakly, the other two were still.

"Let's have the bread, comrades," the winning prisoner said, a beaming smile on his face.

"Dear Lord," Liebman whispered. "Where am I?"

CHAPTER TWELVE

With the thin soup (it seemed thinner every day) in their bellies, a faint spark of warmth in their chilled bodies and a day of rest ahead or, at least, a day of inactivity, the prisoners could spend what passed for a pleasant night in camp. The next day being Sunday, there would be no work.

There would be the never-ending battle against cold, hunger, and sickness but there would be no work. The guards could decree a day of 'exercise' for the men which would include hours of deep knee bends or jogging around the camp with no shirts on in the freezing wind. Or then again, they might not -- and rest, the most precious commodity in camp, might be had without consequence.

Some would spend the day in a sleep as black as a moonless night while others would try to organize a pair of socks or a piece of sausage or perhaps another shirt to cut the wind. It was strictly forbidden to wear more than one shirt but if you could organize one several sizes too big, you could put it over the shirt you had and it wouldn't show on your emaciated body. If no one looked closely that is. It was worth the risk for winter was upon them and it would thin the ranks more efficiently than a selection. Liebman slept like the dead while Aaron sat next to him observing the comings and goings of the prisoners.

After supper, John had led a group of his followers, which now comprised about two-thirds of the barrack, to see the Prophet, seeking solace for the liquidation of Ka-Be. Pietor had flashed Aaron a sour look and had gone out with the faithful as per Krueger's orders.

Aaron had led Liebman quickly back to barracks in order to take full advantage of the relative solitude. They were isolated in the back so there was no risk of their conversation being overheard by the few remaining prisoners either collapsed into unconsciousness or staring at nothing from the edge of their bunks.

Liebman cautiously pushed the top layer of soiled straw to one side to reveal the clean underneath before lowering himself onto the pile. He watched Aaron settle down across from him. "How do you know so much about me and my wife?"

"Before I am able to respond to your questions, I must ask several of my own. May I?"

Liebman was not inclined to agree but had no choice in the end. "Ask what you will. Quickly!"

"Do you wish to be conducted safely from this place?"

"Of course! You think I like it here!"

"Do you wish to be reunited with your wife and unborn child?"

"What nonsense is this?" Liebman demanded, grabbing Aaron's arm. "Elizabeth is my life! I cannot go on without her. Now tell me all you know of her!"

Aaron, unmoved, continued, "Do you want my help in conducting you safely from this place to England to be reunited with your wife and unborn child?"

"Yes! Yes! Yes!"

"I am now able to answer your questions."

"Where is my wife? How is she? Tell me!"

"Elizabeth Liebman has reached Paris. She is safely in the hands of the underground who will escort her to a fishing vessel, named Espoire, heading for England in two days."

"Could she really be safe?" Liebman spoke his thoughts aloud. "Is it possible?"

"It is assured."

Liebman met Aaron's gaze. "Nothing is guaranteed. I've learned that much here."

"That is truer than you know," Aaron said. "It is your safety that is of paramount importance right now. This is something that cannot be guaranteed no matter the precautions taken."

"My safety?" Liebman repeated as if conscious of the fact for the first time "Yes, if what you say is true, Elizabeth has fared much better than either of us could have hoped."

"That is so. However, your situation is grave. I have taken steps which should increase the chances of survival. Do you wish a report?"

Liebman paused a moment as the memories of the last few days tumbled past his mind's eye. It seemed he must really be insane. A stranger who knew things he could never have been party to discussing his safety and deliverance from the pit itself. With barbed wire and machine guns, dogs and Kapos, the smoking chimneys, that strange sickly sweet odor of burning rubber and fat, to speak of safety and deliverance. Impossible!

"What do they burn here?" he asked.

"Bodies," Aaron replied. "Prisoners who have died or those deemed non-essential from the transports. New arrivals are gassed and disposed of."

"Dear Lord, can it be true? There were horrid, perverse stories. But we never thought..."

"You saw the smoking chimneys, did you not?"

"Seeing and believing are two very different things in this instance."

"At any rate, do not concern yourself with the crematorium. The Allies will be here before the flames can reach us."

Liebman looked around in dismay. It was strange that after the exposure he'd had that hearing, in cold, emotionless tones, what was being perpetrated here, he could still be horrified. A stony, empty pit opened inside him as he was struck by the full impact of the waking nightmare that imprisoned him. "An ending? Speak not of endings. The Beast is loose and it will take more than a handful of bloody days and thousands of lives to sate it. This war will never end."

"It is impossible to determine how many perished. Best estimates are between 12 and 14 million."

Liebman gasped. The number fell like a great weight. "How can something like this be stopped once it has begun?"

"The end is near," Aaron explained. "Already the Soviets have pushed the Germans back into Poland. The Allies approach from the West. The goal is Berlin. On May 4th of this year, Germany will capitulate."

Liebman placed his hands over his ears. "Please no more! I can't bear it! You know of my wife. I don't know how but you do. You have robbed, then aided me. In some small measure I am grateful. For a while I thought you meant no harm. However I see now that you are demented. Well, no wonder, considering. It will be good to die with someone who knows you. To die alone is to be forgotten."

Aaron paused, assessing his comrade. "I know this must be difficult for you but please try to understand. Elements of the US 761st Armored Battalion will reach this camp in 113 days."

"Yes, yes," Liebman said, soothingly. "Of course."

Aaron drew back. He regarded the new arrival closely, then decided on another line of reasoning.

"I will tell you of the arrangements I have made. Perhaps that will help put your mind at ease. I have aligned with the camp SCI. I have befriended Pietor Chekunov who will prove to be a valuable ally."

A slow, dawning repulsion crept over Liebman's face as Aaron related his actions. "What is this madness?"

"I do not understand."

Liebman leaned forward, clutching Aaron's arm fiercely. "How did you know what was said between Elizabeth and I?"

"Your wife and unborn child are safe. I told you that."

Liebman's reply was a whisper. "My child?"

"Catherine Elizabeth Liebman. Born August 25th, 1945. Yorkshire, England."

"You will drive me mad!" Liebman pulled away but Aaron held him.

"I speak the truth."

"You see the truth of things yet to be," Liebman said, tauntingly. "Are you a seer, then?"

"No. I am from the future."

Liebman closed his eyes and shook his head. "Mad," he hissed.

"Catherine Elizabeth Liebman studied advance physics at Cambridge before moving with her mother, your wife, to the United States in July of 1965 where she continued her studies with applied Chaos Theory. She was awarded the Nobel Prize in 2013. Her theories on time displacement were both radical and innovative, which made funding difficult. Eventually she completed her work. First experiments with time displacement were completed in September of 2027. I was sent through in December of that year to find you."

There was an unsettling glint in Liebman's eyes, he teetered between the rational and insanity. "Was I lost then?"

"No. You were dead," Aaron answered flatly. "You did not survive this camp. Whether you were killed as part of procedure or died during the uprising, no one can say. But dead you were."

Liebman's eyes flashed open for a glimpse at this impossible world. They fixed on Aaron's placid features. He searched the man's face for a hint of reason but saw only cold, set features. He nodded. "Well, better to have a mad companion than none at all."

Aaron studied Liebman as well. He knew this was the hardest part of the mission. If he pushed too hard, the doctor would have nothing to do with him. He chose another angle of approach.

"I have met an acquaintance of yours here."

"Oh, who? Aristotle?"

"John."

"Original."

"He was a student of yours before the war. You and your wife were quite fond of him, I believe."

"John Siderman! He's here?" Liebman sat up, excited at discovering someone sane in this place.

"Yes, I intervened on his behalf before your arrival in the hope that seeing a familiar face might make things more bearable for you."

"Where is he?" Liebman searched the drawn faces of the unconscious men in their bunks. "John? Who would have believed it? What of his father? A more learned man there never lived."

"His father is dead. Gassed and cremated."

"No! More of your torment-- "

"The father is dead. John is Block Leader. He led a small group to see the Prophet after roll call. They should return shortly."

This good news succeeded in chasing away Aaron's mad musing on the future in Liebman's mind. He had to, needed to, see John, speak to him, satisfy himself that something remained of the world he'd been dragged out of. "Can we not go to him?"

"If you wish." Aaron leaped gracefully down from the bunk. "I will show you the way."

On the way through icy rain, he told Liebman the story of the Prophet. As they neared the shack, with its blacked out windows, Liebman found he was as anxious to see this strange old man as he was to see his former pupil.

A wave of heavy, moist air wafted over them as Aaron opened the door. As foul as the air was from the six unwashed bodies sitting cross-legged before the Prophet, the heat was welcome.

Aaron did not have to silence Liebman. The room did that. The muted light and oppressive air moved above the striped backs of the prisoners and around the hulking mass of the Prophet. Liebman was immediately drawn to the sighing, huffing litany seeping from the old man's lips. They would have to wait until the group was ready to leave before introductions could be made. The Prophet could not be interrupted. Liebman lowered himself slowly to the floor, his gaze riveted on the pale oval face in the blankets. Aaron stood by the door.

"...but for the holy ones there shone a great light, be pleased now to send a man whom you trust to go and see the devastation they have brought upon us, do not kindle a sinner's coals for fear of being burnt in the flames of his fire, I shall never again see good days, I am a man of unclean lips but I swear by God, who has denied me justice, and by the Almighty who filled me with bitterness: In the streets the men go clothed in sackcloth, in the cold they have nothing to cover them, the dead are past counting, their bodies lie in heaps..."

Liebman stared at the back of John's head as though willing him to turn around and see his old master. Getting no response, he tried to push closer in his eagerness. This disturbed some of the followers and they glowered at him. Aaron, sensing the mood of the gathered, came forward and put a restraining hand on Liebman's arm, guiding him to sit on a patch of ground behind and to the left of John.

"...great strength is his to exert at any moment and the power of his arm, no man can match, I will unleash my anger upon you, I will call you to account for your doings, so long as there is life left in me and God's breath is in my nostrils, no untrue word shall pass my lips and my tongue shall utter no falsehood, by mere chance were we born and afterwards we shall be as though we had never been, are they ashamed when they practice their abominations, ashamed, not they, therefore they shall fall with a great crash, the man who digs my pit may fall into it..."

The words sent something through John like an electric current, galvanizing him. He tensed, his back rippling as he leaned forward, forearms on his crossed legs, eyes blazing in the weak candlelight.

"...raise thy hand against the heathen, and let them see thy power, who can stand before his wrath, whose injustice dawns as sure as the sunrise, when extortion has done its work and the looting is over, when the heel of the oppressor has vanished from the land, then no child shall ever again die an infant, no old man fail to live out his hundred years, the trumpet has sounded and all is ready, but no one goes out to war, his heart is ashes, his hope worth less than common earth, and his life cheaper than clay, oh, why was I born to see this, the crushing of my people, all alike had their dead past counting, struck down by one common form of death, there were not enough living even to bury the dead, at one stroke, the most precious of their offspring had perished, while they were still mourning, still lamenting their dead, they rushed into another foolish decision and pursued those whom they had begged to leave, God himself has flung me down in the mud, no better than ashes, let us all meet death with a clear conscience, we call Heaven and earth to testify that there is no justice in this slaughter..."

The Prophet's words faltered, his voice barely audible in the close room. One of his caretakers took action at this, snuffing all but one of the candles as he stood, turned to the group and made motions with his hands to depart. John, reluctantly, rose to his feet, pushing past Liebman and Aaron without recognizing either. There was a look of determination in his wide eyes. Aaron and Liebman followed him out.

"You heard the words," John was whispering to his comrades. "You heard them! We are called to action. One is coming. A deliverer! You heard him speak: *'send a man you trust'*, *'great strength is his to exert'*, *'raise thy hand against the heathen'*. And he spoke of justice and the need to show our strength. We must discover the deliverer! Only this way will be free. Only this way -- "

"John?" Liebman said from behind. John turned and glared at him for a moment, recognition slowly dawning. "It is I. Can you not greet an old friend?"

"Professor!" John looked around as if seeing his surroundings for the first time. The others were already clustered together near the stand of trees, anxious to make their way back into the camp before lights out. "Almighty God be praised. Come we must not talk here. I was carried away by the vision shown to me. To the barracks, dear friend. Quickly."

But before they could take a step towards the camp, a low murmur could be heard coming from behind.

"He speaks!" John turned back into the Prophet's hovel. Aaron and Liebman followed on his heels.

"...I have set my face like flint, no insult can wound me, I shall not be put to shame, an end is coming, have firm faith or you will not stand firm, listen, it is the roar of many nations, a day of vengeance to comfort all who mourn, rouse thy wrath, pour out thy fury, all the boots of trampling soldiers and the garments fouled with blood, shall become a burning mass, fuel for fire, but among the waste there is one useless piece, crooked and full of knots, and this he takes and shapes into the image of a human being, declare what will happen hereafter, tell them that you are a sign to warn them, because one who will clear my name is at my side, unleash the fury of thy wrath, loyal men have vanished from the earth, there is not one upright man, let us lift up our hearts, not our hands, to God, all lie in wait to do murder, like collecting stones for your own tomb, wicked men have been set ablaze and neither spares his own brother, the days of punishment are come, the days of vengeance are come, many can

easily be overpowered by a few, yet thou has made him little less than a God, there is no escape for an oppressed people, we look for light but all is darkness, your wounds cannot be assuaged..."

The Prophet trailed off again. They remained clustered around him, waiting, expectant, but the voice did not rise. Finally, they stood and left him. They made their way back to the camp in silence. Aaron watched John as they ran. He moved as though sleepwalking and Aaron could not imagine what effects the Prophet's words had on him.

CHAPTER THIRTEEN

They sat huddled in Aaron's corner of the barracks. Liebman and John were sitting cross-legged facing each other, their heads almost touching. Aaron leaned against the wall and Pietor, who had met them as they returned, sat with his back to them, feet dangling over the edge.

"You can't mean that," Liebman was saying.

"The Prophet has spoken. You heard as well as I. It is almost the end. We can't just sit and wait to be slaughtered. He is coming!"

"If the end is at hand," Aaron said. "Is it not in our best interests to wait for it?"

John pounded a fist on his thigh. "No. NO! They will leave no one alive. Don't you see? We are witnesses to their shame. Silence us, burn the camps to the ground and they can tell whatever story they want. They will cover their escape, destroy evidence. We are evidence. Our turn will come. The deliverer must not find us idle. If we do not prepare he will find only ashes."

"This is dangerous talk," Pietor cautioned, not turning around.

"Every thing and every one is dangerous here," John said. "I say what I say because it is time to live again."

Pietor bowed his head, his voice a soft whisper the others didn't hear. "If one has lived at all."

"What do you propose we do?" Liebman asked.

"We must proceed carefully, cautiously. Here human life is worth a crust of bread and we could be betrayed in a heartbeat. However, we must act quickly. Time is our enemy as well as our salvation. We will seek out those we trust and prepare. Weapons to defend ourselves. Eyes and ears. Organization to prevent chaos. All these we will need. We will be the strong right hand of the deliverer. We will be worthy of his salvation."

Pietor came down off the bunk and stood over them. "Lunatics. You are all as good as dead." And he left them.

"Dr. Liebman, it is almost lights out," Aaron joined in. "You should sleep."

The fatigue was evident in his features but Liebman pressed on. "John, I will help you. Just tell me what you need of me and you will have it. This is a mad house. It must be brought down."

"I don't think you fully know what you are agreeing to," Aaron said, his eyes boring into Liebman's. "Trust my experience in this and stay clear of it."

John glanced at Aaron's number. "What do you know of the camps? You're almost as new as he is. What have you suffered? You know nothing."

"I know how to stay alive here."

"Forget him," Liebman said. "He helped me earlier. Helped me find you. He's harmless though. I suspect slightly mad, as well."

John put his arm on Liebman's. "Do not say that, old friend. His aid probably saved your life. No matter the motive, kindness here is as dangerous as hatred. For when we span the gulf between us to aid another, we risk tumbling off a precipice." He turned to face Aaron. "If you do not wish to help win your freedom, that is your choice. May I beg your silence?"

"I am here to look after Dr. Liebman. That is precisely what I will do."

"Why?"

"I have made my reasons plain to him. If he feels the need to take foolish risks after all I have said, who am I to prevent him? However, I will see to his safety to the best of my abilities."

John smiled. "You are a true friend, then." He turned his gaze to

Liebman whose chin was dropping to his chest in exhaustion. John nudged him gently. "We can accomplish nothing more tonight. Let us rest and begin again tomorrow."

The lights went out as they were climbing into their bunks. By sense of touch, they found their places, and, with one hand continuously on their bowls, slipped out of their jackets, wadding them up for pillows.

Aaron lay down, then heard Liebman's deep sigh as the doctor did likewise. His back to Liebman, Aaron raised his head and spoke over his shoulder. "You are taking a needless risk joining up with John. If I had foreseen your reaction I would have made other arrangements."

"I'm tired. Go to sleep."

"Did nothing I told you earlier mean anything?"

Liebman considered before answering. "Your story has elements which appear incontrovertible. But it's all too fantastic. Put plainly, I can't trust you. If what you say is true, and Elizabeth is with child and away from this madness, then I must act. I must take steps that will bring me to her."

"No. You need do nothing. The Americans will be here in 113 days. Before the camp is evacuated."

"You know this for a fact?"

"Yes."

"Because you are from the future?"

"Yes."

They listened to the low noises around them. Men tumbling into exhausted sleep, whispered prayers, quiet weeping, and the odd shout as the camp followed someone into their dreams.

"How can I believe you?"

"I have furnished enough evidence. How could I have known the words you and Elizabeth exchanged alone together your last night. How?"

"I know." Liebman shifted his position. "Yet it simply cannot be."

"Before you were taken, would you have foreseen such a place as this in your future?"

"No. Never."

"Drink This."

"And you are here. It is a fact. Is what I told you so much harder to fathom?"

"Please let me sleep," Liebman said. "I can't think anymore."

"All right. But before you do." Liebman heard Aaron rustling on the fetid straw. He turned his head, strained to see what was happening in the stygian darkness. There was a noise like someone clearing their throat, followed by a gurgling. Then Aaron turned and handed his bowl to Liebman.

"Drink this," Aaron said.

Gnawing hunger spurred Liebman to action. He fumbled for the bowl pressed against his chest.

"It's soup," Aaron said as if reading Liebman's mind. "Arrangements have been made for you to have an extra ration in this manner. Drink it quickly, quietly."

"How -- "

"Do not question. Do as I say. Quickly."

Blindly, Liebman sniffed, then took a tentative sip. It was soup. His stomach muscles churned hungrily and he clapped his lips around the edge of the bowl. There wasn't much, maybe half a liter, yet it suffused his body with warmth and invigorated him.

He set the bowl down, panting from his efforts to gulp the soup. Realizing the danger of this noise betraying them, he clamped a hand over his mouth and handed the bowl back.

Aaron found it readily in the dark and rolled over again, his back to Liebman.

"How?" the doctor began.

"Sleep now."

Liebman wanted to push the point but the warmth in his body relaxed him and the numbing fatigue returned. He lay back, closed his eyes. There was so much to consider, but he was so tired.

Just before he succumbed to exhaustion, he faintly heard the timbers creak as another prisoner hanged himself. Liebman twitched, then sank into the all-encompassing darkness.

CHAPTER FOURTEEN

For more than a month the camp routine continued inexorably. Through the first snows, a new year -- the last of the war -- and a minor outbreak of typhus, the daily horror swallowed up all humanity, while beneath the surface, change grew like a cancer. The majority of the prisoners were allocated to Jenseits and the munitions plant there. In time, the daily trudge into town became another familiar burden to the inmates.

John plotted rebellion. His every waking thought obsessed with striking back, winning freedom at any cost. His followers grew in number. Gradually. Steadily. Together they formed a network, gathering supplies for the eventual day where they would earn their freedom. First scraps of metal and wood smuggled into camp from the factory in Jenseits. These were sharpened into weapons and hidden until the signal was given. They were a good start, but John wanted guns, gunpowder. He and his followers did not want merely to fight and die. They wanted to vanquish the enemy, destroy them. And to accomplish this they would use the enemy's own weapons. Small amounts of gunpowder made their way into the camp to be stashed in places only known to John and a select few.

Pietor found himself adrift in the early weeks of the new year. Aaron had abandoned him for Liebman and, though his spying on John for Krueger kept him close to the conspirators, he could never feel a part of them due to the motivation for his proximity. He reported regularly to Krueger who seemed less and less interested in camp affairs as time marched on. During these reports, Pietor begged Krueger to get him out of the Jewish Camp before the next selection, but the SCI wouldn't hear of it. His suspicions about John had proved well founded and, if the fool continued sowing the seeds of rebellion, Krueger would have to act. He needed Pietor to keep tabs on things. Something would be done soon was all the assurance he offered Pietor. For now, he was content to let them draw the suspicions of the SS. It kept curious eyes off Krueger who, in these changing times, was making plans of his own.

Aaron cared for Liebman over this time despite the doctor's reticence. And though Liebman asked repeatedly as to the source of the extra ration he received each night, Aaron told him nothing. Many a time Liebman watched Aaron like a hawk in order to learn the secret, never letting Aaron out of his sight. But still it remained a mystery. The extra ration after lights out sustained and fortified him, increasing his chances of surviving until liberation, which Aaron promised him drew closer every day. The incontrovertible fact of the Allies approach kept him constantly after Liebman to stay away from John and his followers. Liebman, for his part, began to recognize the danger of staying in John's inner circle, but felt compelled to do something.

January 19th they heard the distant thunder for the first time. The morning had been cloudy, cold and the sound promised a storm. It was forgotten by the time the work details marched for Jenseits.

However by midday, the skies had cleared and a weak sun made dry mounds of snow by the side of the road glisten under an expanse of blue sky.

And the sound of thunder remained.

Prisoners began to speak aloud what they hadn't dared to dream previously. The sound was not thunder but artillery. The muted roar was the great, beating heart of war pounding against the earth. The Allies were drawing closer. By the end of that day, it was all anyone in camp talked about.

With the joyous news came a great uneasiness. Excited discussions broke out everywhere. In the days that followed, the German civilian workers in the factory at Jenseits were friendlier, more willing to lend a hand or a crust of bread, eager to earn the gratitude of the prisoners, be remembered for an act of kindness. This more than anything demonstrated to the prisoners that change was coming, and as wonderful as freedom was to contemplate, they were not out of the woods yet. If nothing else, their time in camp had taught them that death could come from anywhere, and at any time. One had to be cautious. To die for some foolish error of judgment with the sound of the guns in your ears would be the ultimate tragedy.

In camp, however, John was still able to find all the willing converts he needed. Prisoners expected a miracle at any moment. Prisoners who were spiritualists in life held séances to divine the future, looked for signs that their torment was soon to end. For these individuals desperate to believe, John preached preparation for the deliverer who would lead them to victory. Soon. Watch the dwindling transports for him, John encouraged, search the eyes of the man next to you for the deliverer might already be amongst them, waiting to reveal himself.

And the prisoners could not help but believe. The SS guards seemed less enthusiastic in their punishments as though distracted by the low roar in their ears, the slight vibration in the soles of their feet. For a time the soup was thicker, the bread less moldy. And when the better ration abruptly halted, the prisoners knew it was not some new form of torture, but rather the disruption of supply lines from Allied bombing. This knowledge made the empty space in their bellies a little easier to bear. Just hang on, they told one another. It won't be much longer.

No one understood the need for caution better than Aaron. He explained what steps the SS would take towards the end to Liebman in the hope of impressing on him how vital it was that they recede into the background, distance themselves from John and the others or risk death if the truth came out. Liebman responded to this with further demands to know where the extra soup ration came from every night, accusing Aaron of collaborating with the guards in exchange for information. Aaron dismissed these accusations with a wave of his hand and more warnings that they avoid the various groups positioning themselves to act.

The wisdom of this course of action revealed itself two weeks later in the Jenseits munitions factory. The sound of the approaching front was a constant now, and the townsfolk were terrified over what would happen when the Allies reached them.

To quell this fear, and keep the war effort going, a handful of minor SS officials arrived to inspect the factory. Resplendent in crisp, black uniforms and gleaming skull and crossbones insignia, their presence was meant to re-assure the men and women of Jenseits that the war was running smoothly and that the Fuhrer would repel the invaders from their soil but only through the efforts and sacrifice of the German people.

The inspection consisted of their strutting and preening outside the factory walls, then retreating to the manager's office for good Schnapps and a warm fire until the next performance.

Aaron and Liebman were present that day. John's control had extended to determining who from the Jewish Camp were assigned to outside work details in order to continue stockpiling crude weapons and precious gunpowder. The citizenry's attempts to curry favor with the prisoners included visits from bakers, worker's wives with covered trays and donations from others of hot food and warm clothes, Aaron had asked of John that he and Liebman be placed in one of the work details. In exchange, they would keep their eyes open for anything they could bring into to the camp past the guards. Of course Aaron had no intention of doing so, but John did not need to know this.

At first, Aaron had been concerned with Liebman's stamina, but conditions had so vastly improved in the factory that the work seemed more of a vacation to the low-numbered veterans who had not forgotten the jeers and blows from this self-same townsfolk now doling out sweet meats and warm socks.

As the townsfolk working in the plant consisted of old men, young boys and the wives of servicemen, they were given light assembly line duties, while it fell to the prisoners to stack and transport bombs and ammunition to the loading dock where they would load them on to the rag-tag assembly of trucks to carry the loads West to the ever-growing roar which promised freedom.

The prisoners worked in two-man teams and Aaron and Liebman were stationed at the end of one production line where crates of bullets were being filled. Each team would lift the crate off the line and carry it to a pallet. The crates weighed more than fifty pounds but Aaron was able to take most of the burden on himself, easing the strain on Liebman.

It was shortly after the midday meal and the pallet Aaron and Liebman had been stacking was full and needed to be moved. The line foreman was nowhere to be seen, having taken an opportunity to ingratiate himself with their visiting Nazi masters.

Leaving his post -- an act punishable by death not too long ago -- Aaron went in search of the foreman. Seeing the man's enormous head and salt and pepper walrus mustache through one of the plant manager's office windows fifty yards away, he headed in that direction.

He was almost at the foot of the metal staircase leading up to the office when the door at the top opened and the SS men poured out. Aaron stepped to one side as the men, reeking of Schnapps and cigars, began descending the stairs.

They had taken three steps down when the bomb beneath the staircase went off. A brilliant flash of light and a roaring wall of concussive air hurled Aaron back out of harm's way while a seething, hot mass of exploding gases engulfed the SS men, the plant manager and the line foreman in a fireball which continued up to the dry wooden rafters. The staircase and office walls splintered into a deadly hail of metal and wood shrapnel that shot out in all directions into the two dozen prisoners and townsfolk working close by.

The first reaction in the chaotic seconds following the blast was that Allied bombs had hit the plant. The men and women scrabbled for the exits and the basement bomb shelter until ears ringing from the blast could discern no further explosions and the absence of the distinct hum of aircraft.

Amidst the clatter of falling debris and clouds of roiling black smoke, the agonized wails of the injured could be heard. The office was located a safe distance from the stored munitions and after the terror of the initial blast had passed, it was deemed safe to enter the building. The prisoners and townsfolk returned to the scene of the explosion and began the gristly task of clearing away the debris in search of the dead and wounded.

John and Liebman came running to the carnage with their comrades. Liebman had seen Aaron heading towards the office prior to the blast and was sure his odd benefactor had been killed instantly. All around the burning remains of the office lay bodies no more than blood-sodden heaps of rags shredded by deadly metal and wood fragments.

So close to the flames, they were recruited to help in the bucket brigade fighting to control the small fire while panicked forklift drivers worked feverishly to move explosives stacked, they felt, too close for comfort. After what seemed like hours, the fire was out. John and Liebman, in the reigning confusion, resumed their search for Aaron, first amongst the dead, then the wounded. But there was no sign of him.

Almost overcome by smoke, John stepped outside for some fresh air and to survey the damage, which was considerable though contained. The fire had eaten through a section of roof timbers, redistributing the weight pressing down on the cinder block walls, causing one section to collapse. A work crew was removing the fallen stones by hand.

John saw Aaron with the crew.

Recovering from his initial shock, John headed over to where Aaron was pitching heavy blocks into a wheelbarrow. Aside from the long, narrow tear in his prison jacket and patches of soot, Aaron looked remarkably well.

John reached him, put a hand on his shoulder as Aaron was bent over to pick up a block. "How?" John said. "You were as near as anyone. How could you still be alive?"

Aaron stopped what he was doing and regarded John with his impassive features. "The blast knocked me behind the boiler plate stacked outside the office. This shielded me from the blast. I came out here to get some air and was ordered to help clear away." Concerned for Liebman's safety but unable to leave, he asked. "The fire is under control?"

John nodded dumbly. There was something about Aaron's story that didn't add up. Yes, he recalled seeing thick sections of boilerplate inside but there was more to Aaron's survival than plain luck.

"It-it's a miracle," he said.

"No, it is not." Aaron went back to what he was doing.

The more John thought about it, the surer he was that he had witnessed a miracle. For so long he, and so many, had prayed for a sign, something to show them they were on the right path. Now here it was standing before him, unscathed, while dozens more lay dead and torn. It was a sign from God. And he knew its meaning. He had not authorized any sabotage of the plant. Some impatient fools had taken matters into their own hands. Someone in his group? One of the townspeople? And blood had been spilled. A precursor of what was to come. But God had spared one, a miracle to show that though many would soon die, the chosen would survive, shielded by faith.

He must be here, John mused. Among us this very moment. The deliverer. The transports had dropped to almost nothing because of the bombing. The crematorium reduced the surplus in the camp. Yes, the deliverer was among them. The miracle of Aaron's survival was proof of that. The conviction of the faithful was an impenetrable field. It would shield the deliverer as it had shielded Aaron from the explosion. As it would shield his followers when it was time to strike. And that time was soon. But first he must find the deliverer. Seek his wisdom and blessing.

John stooped to help Aaron clear away the rubble. After a couple of hours, prisoners from inside were detailed to help as all the production lines were shut down for the time being.

Liebman found them and joined them in their work. "My God, you're alive!" he said when he first caught sight of Aaron.

"Yes, it's a miracle from God," John said immediately, his eyes on his work.

"I was fortunate," Aaron corrected.

Liebman was surprised by the relief he felt at seeing Aaron alive and well. Over the weeks, Aaron had been a constant source of irritation with his pacifist mantra, but he had also been a companion, a protector, a teacher, and, much as Liebman hated to admit it, had saved his life. Lord knew that mysterious extra ration had kept him fit for this kind of work. He doubted he'd live long without it.

"Well, miracle or not," he said, "I'm glad you're still around."

"Why, thank you, doctor," Aaron said.

"A miracle," John said with conviction. "The deliverer is among us."

The work continued until sundown, then halted as the blackout was in effect and there were no portable lights to work by even if anyone wished to carry on. Also it had begun to snow heavily and the wind wailed through the power lines.

The men formed ranks and began marching. The guards followed along in trucks as the intense cold, blowing snow and biting wind disinclined them to march alongside their charges.

John's faithful were around him, a protective shield against the elements. He spoke to them from his place of safety. "Heed me! I witnessed a miracle. God wants us to know that the deliverer is among us. We must seek him out. Aid him, until he names the time and date of our retribution. Look for him. It is time we opened our eyes. The hour is almost here."

Aaron and Liebman were some distance away and caught fragments of John's words.

"What is he talking about?" Liebman asked.

"He believes my surviving the explosion heralds the arrival of this deliverer he's been raving about."

"He gives them hope," Liebman said. "You hear the guns. It is safe to hope again."

Aaron went on heedless of what Liebman was saying. "At last he has become dangerous. This is how it begins."

"How what begins?"

"The end."

The march halted abruptly. Prisoners craned their necks to see what was keeping them out in a blizzard. Word finally filtered back to Aaron and Liebman that a large tree heavy with snow had fallen across the road. The front ranks were struggling to move it. The guards were content to wait out the delay in the heated trucks. The prisoners broke but the guards were not concerned. Even in parkas and snow pants, only a fool would think of running off into the storm. And any who tried would have their frozen bodies dug up in the morning.

The prisoners huddled for warmth while a few dozen up front fought to slide the tree off the road. Aaron, seeing Liebman speaking with a group of prisoners they knew, eased out to the side of the road, his back to the forest. His eyes scanned the groups, looking for any curious gazes. The prisoners faced each other as though clustered around campfires to keep the wind on their backs. Aaron stepped back, parallel to one of the trees. Blowing snow and ice pellets obscured his vision, but he was fairly certain no one had seen him separate himself from the others. He took another step and the headlights of a nearby truck came on. He froze. But he needn't have bothered. The guards had put the lights on the prisoners too late to spot him. And he only needed a few seconds.

Turning, he ran twenty yards into the forest and stopped. Over the sound of the engines and the wind he thought he heard footsteps behind him in the deep snow, but when he turned around he saw no one.

With one last glance around, he lifted his shirt, exposing his bare skin to the wind. Metal glinted in his left side, just below his ribs. He took the end of it in two fingers and began sliding it out. The metal was narrow, the grilled tread of the staircase leading to the manager's office pressed into it. Inch after inch it came out of him until a barbed, blunted end was free of the hole in his side. Liquid, black in the penumbra of the truck headlights oozed out. Without giving it a look, Aaron tossed the eight-inch shard into the forest and adjusted his shirt so the hole did not line up with the one in his side. Before he rejoined the others, he stopped by the side of the road and slapped at the thick snow coating his shins.

He returned to the road. The way was clear up ahead and they were forming ranks. He paused at the edge of the forest to swipe at the heavy snow clinging to his pants from ankle to knee. He found Liebman and rejoined the group.

"Where did you get to?" the doctor asked.

"Just went up ahead for a look. The road is clear now."

They returned to the camp and lined up for roll call. The guards, disinterested and freezing, finished in record time.

On the way for the soup ration, Aaron looked around at his fellow prisoners cautiously. Although he was certain no one had seen him slip away, he needed to be sure. With so many groups jockeying for position in these last days, everyone was under suspicion.

Close to one of the barracks, out of the wind, he saw John glaring at him with fiery intensity. He chocked this up to the so-called miracle John was so sure had taken place, and turned away to join Liebman at the door to the mess.

The cluster of followers around John broke at the same instant Aaron turned away and he did not see the thick wet snow coating both shins of John's pants.

CHAPTER FIFTEEN

The attack at the Jenseits munitions plant had profound, far-reaching effects on the camp. For the High Numbers, it was met with pleasure, relief and pride in that whoever was responsible had not only put a crimp in the war effort, but had also granted them temporary freedom from backbreaking labor. The Low Numbers, however, let experience guide their reaction. And this experience told them that the Reich perpetuated their wretched existence as long as they were useful and the closing of the plant effectively put an end to that usefulness. Though they attempted to get this point across to the recent arrivals, their wisdom fell upon deaf ears. But amongst themselves they knew that time had sped up in camp. With the Allies drawing nearer every moment, and no work for the prisoners, the next selection was imminent.

For the first two weeks after the bomb blast, though, the prisoners had much more pressing concerns. The Kommandant had ordered a full investigation, returning conditions in camp to the way they were in 1940.

First a lockdown was initiated. The prisoners were secured in their barracks for seventy-two hours. No food. No water. No access to the lavatory. Guards with machine guns cocked and ready stood at each door with orders to shoot anyone attempting to leave. After twenty-four hours in the close confines of the barracks, the stench of waste and unwashed humanity drove some outside, a brief inhalation of the surprisingly mild air their last breath before being gunned down.

Every barrack was thoroughly searched, every prisoner question-ed. During the process, some tried to boost their spirits by dwelling on the fact that they were at least free from work. There were not even transports to process. Others, knowing their guilt would be uncovered in time, hanged themselves, their bodies added to the fetid pile of old and sick who had succumbed to starvation.

It was very difficult, in some cases impossible, for the barracks to communicate back and forth. The only outside intrusions into the dark, close world were the guards led by an Hauptscharfuehrer making their way through the camp.

John's store of hidden weapons escaped detection thanks only to the half-hearted efforts of the SS noncoms. They, too, had been affected by the rumble of distant guns, and were, in subtle desperation, trying to win favor with the prisoners they had abused and brutalized for so many years by turning a blind eye to the few items they uncovered. Had they found the weapons, things would have been different.

There was much discussion amongst John's people that the time to strike was now while they still possessed the means to fight. They pressed their leader, all but badgered him, but John remained calm, admitting to them in secret that he had seen the deliverer and they had nothing to fear.

Whether by fortune or providence, they were safe. The bombers – POW's with no connection to John -- were turned up in the Men's Camp and led away. They were tortured for seven days. The entire camp was turned out to witness their execution. Even the Kommandant was present, appearing more gaunt and drawn than Aaron remembered seeing him months ago.

While the eight men swung and kicked from their ropes, the Kommandant addressed the prisoners.

"You see the results of treachery. Remember the lesson well." He cocked his head, listening to the approaching front. "You hear it, don't you, scum? Your liberation. Yes? Ridiculous! None of you will ever leave here. We will see to that before the end. Those of you who can still reason might see this as a challenge. My advice to you is to take it up. Yes, I encourage you to revolt. It will make the work that much easier for us."

He withdrew his Luger and stepped up to the closest rank of prisoners. His face a stony mask, he shot the first row one at a time until the gun was empty. He reloaded the weapon, then held it over his head for the thousands of prisoners to see. He threw it down like a gauntlet at the feet of the first rank of prisoners, daring the mass of filthy stick figures to act.

"Come on, then!" he shouted. "What are you waiting for, you stinking vermin! Come on!"

He raised his arms out at his sides and made a slow turn before the tight ranks surrounding him. No one moved. No one breathed. The fresh corpses twitched in the grimy snow, the bodies swayed beneath the gallows.

The Kommandant snorted and returned to his staff car. An SS noncom scurried forward to pick up the discarded Luger. The prisoners had to remain at attention until the car was out of sight. When the Kommandant was gone, fiery gazes began flicking in John's direction, impelling him to give the word. But their leader's gaze was on Aaron standing calmly next to a shivering Liebman.

The prisoners were dismissed. Gratefully they shuffled to their barracks, but suddenly the Kapos appeared, axe handles at the ready, with orders to form work details.

With no work in Jenseits, other work had been found for the prisoners. The prisoners in the Jewish Camp were issued shovels and picks, their destination the mass graves outside the camp.

Aaron, concerned for Liebman's health, went to see John to ensure omission from this gristly detail. It was not only the elements that concerned him, but the threat of disease.

They found John encircled by a group of his lieutenants.

"Do you see?" the frantic followers asked him. "You know what this means! Why do you refuse to act? You say you have seen the deliverer. That was to be the sign. Show him to us and we will strike."

"Comrades." John smiled at all of them. "I understand every word you have spoken. I understand the danger we face. But you must understand, you must see, that we answer now to the deliverer. Only he can give the order." John spotted Aaron at the fringes of the group and gave a slight, respectful nod. "He is among us. He hears your cries. And he knows what must be done."

"Where! Where is he?"

"Patience. He will reveal himself soon. When he does, that will be your battle cry. When he makes himself known to you, strike! Without fear or hesitation."

"Surely we must --- "

"Prepare. We must prepare the way for him as we have been doing. It is almost time. I know it with all my heart."

So great was the respect they had for John that they reluctantly ceased their urging though a few disgruntled members went off to speak in private.

Aaron went to John and asked about Liebman's exemption.

"Of course, or course," John said, the serene smile never leaving his face as he looked at Aaron. "Whatever you wish." With his eyes, he indicated Aaron and Liebman to a nearby Kapo who nodded his understanding.

Liebman thanked him and they turned to go but John put a hand gently on Aaron's arm. "Will it be soon do you think?"

Aaron studied John for a moment before replying. "It would seem so."

"We are ready."

"Yes."

John removed his hand and Aaron and Liebman moved towards their barrack.

"Why is there this cloud over the new detail?" Liebman asked.

"The front is four weeks away," Aaron replied, patiently. "There has been evidence the SS are already destroying files, moving personnel East."

They were at the back inside the relative warmth of the barrack. A few privileged like themselves huddled here and there under blankets. Aaron and Liebman climbed up into their bunk. Liebman dove under the thin, foul blanket, grateful for their corner perch, an arm's length from the rafters, retained some warmth from the body heat rising off those below.

"Why do you think he hesitates? He has spoken so often of retribution and, if what you say is true, the time is now. What is stopping him?"

Aaron took up position a good distance from Liebman and continued his explanation. "Perhaps he is afraid. Talking about a thing and doing it are two very different things."

"That is not the man I know."

"No matter the motivation, he is demonstrating remarkable clair-voyance. The SS garrison, at present, is too strong to be overcome. As we draw closer to liberation, there will be a gradual attrition as men desert to the East. John is right to wait."

"And the deliverer?"

"A delusion. But one which prevents catastrophe."

"You speak of liberation as a terrible thing. Something to be avoided."

Aaron turned his gaze to Liebman. "What will happen is this: The SS garrison are attempting to thin the ranks by exposing the prisoners to the rotting corpses. This will have a two-pronged effect. The first will be to introduce illness into the prison population, the second is to remove evidence of the death squads used in the 1930s. When the Americans arrive they will discover the mass graves but in them will be the victims of typhoid, dysentery, not bullets. The remains of those long murdered will have been burned, the evidence of crimes against humanity, gone. The SS captured by the Allies will later claim that the mass graves were necessary because the crematorium could not work fast enough to curtail the infection."

"But we know different. And we have tongues to speak."

"We will not be here. It is the intention of the SS that we be marched from here before the Americans arrive. The SS will blow up the crematorium, destroy the camp, while we move farther East beyond the reach of liberation. That is their plan but it will not come to pass. A -- "

The sound of someone climbing up to join them reached their

ears. Expecting John, they were surprised to see Pietor's head appear. Once Aaron had found Liebman and John had ascended to Blockaltester, he no longer needed Pietor other than as a tenuous link to Krueger. But the SCI had had little use for them since acquiring Liebman's diamonds. Aaron had kept tabs on Chekunov, however, and knew Pietor was doing the same with John though it had been weeks since Krueger had sent for a report. Aaron had determined from their first meeting that Chekunov was a follower, someone who needed to belong in order to justify his existence. This was something of surprise considering what he knew, but the facts were inescapable. He had exploited Chekunov's weakness after saving the man's life so he could use Krueger to find Liebman. But, now, Pietor, a non-Jew in the Jewish Camp, all but ignored by Aaron and abandoned by Krueger, was adrift, looking to belong again.

Chekunov reached them and perched on the edge, feet dangling.

"You see what's going on outside," he said.

Aaron nodded.

"There will be a selection soon. You know that." He stared at the tips of his worn work boots. "I can't be here when it happens. I'm not a Jew. Krueger has kept me safe so far. At least I think he has. But how can I pass selection? They will see I'm not Jewish and that will be the end."

"What can we do?" Liebman asked.

"It's warm up here," Chekunov observed.

"What do you want?" Aaron asked.

"I-I want to see Krueger. To explain. So he can get me out before it's too late. Could you come with me?"

"Why?"

"Krueger respects you. As much as he respects any man. I saw it. Maybe you could help convince him to get me out."

Aaron considered the proposal. He did need to speak with Krueger, get some accurate intelligence as to the state of the Allied advance so he agreed. Leaving Liebman to sleep in the huddled warmth, Aaron and Chekunov climbed down.

They met John at the hill and he assured them that his Kapos would not try to recruit them into the new work detail. However, they

would be at the mercy of any Kapo not loyal to John and therefore
needed to be careful.

"Or one of you has to anyway," John concluded, cryptically with
another knowing glance at Aaron.

"Do you feel it?" Chekunov asked as they headed up the main
road to the SCI barracks. The air was cold, biting. The snow lined
the road in smooth, speckled rows and filled in the sunken letters
of the tombstones beneath their feet. In the distance, three lorries
rattled and jounced their way up the road leading to Jenseits.

"Could you be more specific?"

"The change. I felt it even before we heard the guns. So long in
camp, it had begun to make sense to me. One does what can. One
continues to think and reason. But life and death are arbitrary. That
is the first lesson. We have no control over either so it is best not to
think of them. Just carry on one moment to the next. Simple. Now
I see there is more. Good and evil. They are interchangeable. I was
not aware of this. We have been victims of terrible evil. The blood
that has been shed... it's staggering." He gripped Aaron's upper arm.
"Listen. Listen to the sound of liberation. Sweet music to our ears
after so much misery. But look to the cause. Bombs. Explosions.
Destruction. Yet it could just as well be birdsong if it meant our
freedom."

"Is this not the goal of all living things? To be free?"

"Certainly." He released Aaron's arm. "Freedom. Freedom to do
what exactly?"

CHAPTER SIXTEEN

They expected to be refused but instead were ordered into the SCI's office four days later. Krueger, his eyes on a trunk sitting open beside his desk, waved them in distractedly. His eyes slid over the contents of the trunk in silent inventory.

"What?" he said.

Pietor cleared his throat, shuffled his feet, his eyes on the floor in front of him. "Sir, it's me, Chekunov. Sorry for the intrusion but I must speak with you."

Krueger closed the trunk, stepped past the two prisoners and went to the door of his office and called for someone named Conrad. Two prisoners instantly appeared in the doorway. The first, Conrad, knew what Krueger needed done and motioned to the other prisoner. They each lifted one side of the trunk and carried it from the office.

While this was going on, Aaron glanced around. The room was all but bare. File cabinets had been removed as were the visitor chairs. The desktop was also free of reports or files. And time had worked on Krueger. Though still massive through the arms and chest, he appeared somehow shrunken in his crisp prison grays. Deep lines were etched in his pale face, running into the tangle of beard shot with white and ragged.

Krueger watched the men leave, then returned to his desk, leaning one set of hairy knuckles on the dark wood and staring at Aaron and

Pietor. "Does this concern John?"

Pietor shook his head.

"Then what is the reason for this intrusion? Quickly! I have more pressing concerns."

Pietor rapidly related his predicament. As a non-Jew in the Jewish Camp, his identity would be instantly discovered in the next selection and there would be many questions about his presence there. And lingering, painful death at the end of the ordeal.

When he was finished, Krueger laughed, his whole body shook.

"My boy," he said. "You trouble me with such trifles. Lucky for you I am in a good mood."

Pietor couldn't comprehend his master's reaction. "Sir, if I am made to answer, the SS would learn it was you who sent me to the Jewish Camp."

Krueger's smile vanished. His brow clouded and he glared at Chekunov, his eyes smoldering coals. "You dare threaten me!"

"Oh, no, sir. Never." Pietor took a step back. "But if I am taken, how could I prevent their learning the truth?"

"You would throw yourself on the wire before they came for you. Simple enough."

Pietor swallowed. "Yes, sir. Is it not possible for me to return to the Men's Camp and avoid the situation altogether?"

"No."

"Sir?"

Krueger went around his desk and sat down. He raised his thick arms and indicated the all but empty office and bare walls. "The SS came for it two days ago. Files. Camp records. All of it. It was no matter to me. They are welcome to it." He leaned forward, his elbows on the desk. "The war is over. Therefore this camp no longer exists. I am looking forward and have much to prepare. Camp business is of little interest to me."

Pietor looked dumbly at Aaron who studied the Senior Camp Inmate before speaking. "Sir, there will be a selection and -- "

"Sooner than you think. I welcome it. War is an excellent means of forging the future." Krueger stared off past their shoulders. "It was foolish to hope all the kindling would burn before the war ended.

However, there has been progress. We've thinned the ranks, left those fit to survive for the most part. The world of tomorrow will be a better place because of it."

His gaze found them again. "Peace will be dangerous. We have been tossed up into the air like autumn leaves and as we settle to earth once more there will be opportunity and peril. Man has lost his tie with the Old World. All is in upheaval. During such times, even a fortunate fool can be heard while the wise and crafty step back into shadow to watch and wait.

Pietor chewed his lower lip. "Sir, what has this to do with -- "

Krueger slammed his fist down on the desk. "Nothing can interfere! Are you blind as well as stupid?"

"I understand you, sir," Aaron spoke for the first time. "You must ensure your future in a time without assurances. The coming peace will be a chaotic jumble where even the most careful planning might come undone despite preparations for every contingency."

"Well said, Jew. Truth from the grave itself." Krueger smiled.

Chekunov grew even more agitated. "I don't understand. I want to understand."

"Very well," Krueger said, nodding eagerly. "I will make myself plain. John and his rabble continue to be a threat though they keep the SS occupied. A threat I have taken steps to deal with. You must remain my eyes and ears because that is precisely what I need you to be. You will do as I say without question. If there is even a hint you have been discovered, you will silence yourself for my benefit. Is that clear enough?" His tone darkened. "Remember, no one is beyond my reach. Not John, and certainly not the likes of you. Now, is there anything else?"

Aaron stepped forward. "A question, if I may?"

Krueger held up a meaty finger. "One."

"Is today February 25th, 1945?"

The question puzzled Krueger for a moment. He tried to read meaning into the way Aaron stood, the tone of voice in which the question had been asked. He could find nothing significant. He nodded slowly.

"Thank you, sir."

"Is today February 25th, 1945?"

THE LIGHT OF MEN

He studied Aaron a moment longer, then seemed to shake off the presence of the two prisoners. He opened a drawer and began placing small, tightly wrapped bundles into an olive green duffle bag with US ARMY stenciled on the side. From deep within the offices they heard scraping and banging as Krueger's people cleaned out other sections. Aaron turned to leave, Pietor reluctantly followed.

Outside the wind had stilled and Krueger's guards were not in their usual places. Even the birds were silent and not so much as a rat scurried over the gray/white snow. The only sounds were the roar of the crematorium and the ever-present thunder of war.

Pietor did not speak until they were back on the tombstone road leading into the camp. "So it has come to this. I am cast aside. The faithful servant receives his reward."

"Krueger says he needs you. And he's right. You've heard the talk from John's followers. Their patience wears thin. The fuse has been lit."

Pietor shook his head angrily. "No. It is not that at all. You heard him say John is taken care of. If he says it, it is a fact. He has cut me loose. He has finished with me. He wants me to die here. He wants me silenced for I have seen such things..." He threw his head back. "Sacred mother! What am I to do?"

Aaron didn't say anything. He watched as Pietor took a stumbling step towards the electrified barbwire flanking the road. In the moment between one step and the next, Pietor's instinct for self-preservation overrode everything else and he fell back into step with Aaron.

"There is still time," he said. "That is all I need. I can organize something before the next selection."

They entered the Jewish Camp. The work details were still at the mass graves, which made avoiding detection by Kapos John did not control all the more difficult. The weather worked in their favor however. It was so cold that the Kapos were indoors huddled over tiny cast iron stoves, trying to stay warm and the only SS they saw were blowing on their numb hands up in the guard towers.

Aaron registered these things as he played over the current state of affairs in his mind. His estimate of the date was accurate, and seeing Krueger's early preparations for flight meant the historical timeline did not appear to have been greatly affected by Aaron's presence. It was interesting to see Krueger and the SS trying to subtly prepare their getaway without arousing the attention of the prisoners and bringing about a riot. They acted on the intelligence they received, the timetable was set in their minds. However they were in for a surprise. It would not be long now.

Pietor continued to mutter, but Aaron paid him no mind. He could have told Pietor that he had sixteen days before the next selection, but the fate of Pietor Chekunov, though it had become suddenly clearer, was not his concern.

All his attention was on ensuring that Liebman pass the selection. Aaron had done what he could to maintain the doctor's fitness level. The water in the soup swelled the ankles and hollows of the eyes and Liebman's appearance had changed dramatically since his admittance. He was much thinner of course. This was no pressing matter, as he resembled any other inmate now. The elimination of the excess water strained the kidneys and the lack of anything even approaching balanced nutrition had caused Liebman to move like an old man after a long day's labor. When pressed though, Liebman showed remarkable tenacity and his performance at the coming selection would be satisfactory under normal circumstances.

But the coming selection, the last in Gutundbose, would test every prisoner's limits of endurance. The SS would be looking for any display of weakness to send a prisoner to the crematorium. One slip meant certain death. He would have to step up his measures with Liebman. And he had to see to his own concerns as well. The mission was almost over. He must not let anything interfere.

That night, Liebman, well rested from a day of what passed for restful sleep grumbled and groused when Aaron had him perform some limbering exercises much to the delight of the other prisoners. Beforehand he had explained to the doctor about the coming selection, which was an exceptional motivational tool. After lights out, Liebman readily accepted Aaron's bowl of soup though he did not suck it down so greedily as in the past.

Liebman sputtered through the first sip. "Ack! What are they putting in here?" Hunger surged in him at that first swallow and he made quick work of it. He felt oddly invigorated as he handed the bowl back to Aaron. This he chocked up to the full day of inactivity. The energy improved his mood and for the first time in awhile he did not pester Aaron as to the mysterious source of the extra ration.

"The soup was different tonight," he said. "Tasted like medicine."

Aaron made no comment.

Later, just before dawn, Aaron crept down to the bucket used as a toilet at night. This was for the use of every prisoner in the barracks and the prisoner who topped it off had the duty of emptying it at the latrine in the middle of the night. This duty usually fell to the High Numbers as the veterans had long learned to judge by the echo in the bucket when it was safe to go down and relieve oneself. Aaron pulled down the front of his pants and urinated against the side of the bucket so the sound wouldn't carry. The bucket looked to be about half full in the pale moonlight so he quickly filled it, then showing the night-guard he was wearing the mandatory night uniform (shirt and pants) he took the bucket outside.

The night was bitterly cold, the snow crunched under his feet. All was still in the camp. The guards dozed in the watchtowers, the wind hissed through the barbed wire in grim harmony to the whine of the electrical current. The front sounded nearer, almost outside the wire. He knew this was not the case but the noise served as a reminder that change would come.

The bucket swayed in his fist and he held it out to the side so it wouldn't bang against his leg and splash the foul mess on his shoes. He dumped it and headed back.

CHAPTER SEVENTEEN

S election.

The word had sparked a change in camp routine days before it took place. Krueger's people in the Men's Camp had learned of the selection and word had spread from the lowest numbered veteran to the highest numbered new arrival. The word reached the Jewish Camp through John's people in Camp Headquarters and Ka-Be.

The actual date was uncertain at first, but rumor had it that it would be soon. The first sign of change occurred in the latrines and washrooms. The men, naked following their meager ablutions, showed each other their chests, buttocks and thighs, reassuring each other: "You are all right," they said. "It will certainly not be your turn this time."

Aaron, witnessing his first and last, selection noticed a peculiar partisanship which developed amongst the prisoners. The young prisoners became certain that only the old would be chosen. The healthy and strong were certain only the sick would go. And there were further delineations expressed in absolutes: German Jews would be excluded. Specialists needed in Jenseits, for the factory had re-opened, would be excluded. All the Low Numbers would be excluded. It was all speculation Aaron knew but the overriding theme was: "You will be chosen. I will not."

The Low Numbers knew best how to prepare. Once everyone knew the day, they organized a shave to improve their appearance for the doctor. Others tried to time a trip to Ka-Be with a minor injury so as to be out of barracks when the time came.

As for Pietor, his situation had improved dramatically from his last meeting with Krueger. At first he'd struggled to organize a way out of the Jewish Camp but no one in a position to help dared risk exposing themselves at this sensitive time. The only one who listened was John who welcomed Pietor into his group. Aaron watched with fascination how Pietor threw himself into John's rebellion plans, giving freely what he'd learned of camp procedure in the years he'd belonged to Krueger. The Russian had clearly severed all ties to the SCI. John repaid Pietor's allegiance by helping him submerge, hiding him in a crawlspace barely two feet high under Ka-Be.

For Liebman it was a time of great excitement and numbing fear. After more than two weeks of Aaron's exercises, he felt limber and assumed the extra soup ration, despite it's increasingly brackish taste, was working. He felt the strongest he'd ever been in camp. His ribs still protruded from the pale, dry skin of his torso and his hands were calloused from hard work, but the isometric and stretching exercises had kept his joints and ligaments pliable and he walked with an almost normal gate. Aaron had warned him not to show off his state of health lest envious prisoners accuse him of hording or collaborating.

Physically he was fairly certain he could pass the selection. But, like everything else in camp, he knew whether he lived or died was completely arbitrary. He'd listened with growing dread to Aaron's recounting of the selection process from historical records. How if a man stumbled on the way in it could mean instant condemnation and a trip to the crematorium. Or how the SS doctor, bored with the process, could decide to choose the next ten prisoners, sight unseen, just to move things along. A thousand different things could happen. This terrified him though Aaron reassured him that the SS were looking for prisoners still economically useful to the war effort.

What added to Liebman's list of worries was his growing concern for Aaron. He was sure his strange benefactor was ill. Every night Aaron was down at the latrine bucket urinating endlessly. There was that barely discernable gash all but healed in his side that he would not speak of. Also Aaron appeared more gaunt and drawn than Liebman remembered seeing him. In fact, Aaron had shown little of the normal deterioration camp life inflicted which made his suddenly sickly appearance all the more shocking. Aaron's energy seemed boundless as usual and he reassured Liebman there was nothing wrong.

Liebman found he really didn't want any harm to come to Aaron and this concern had nothing to do with the extra soup ration every night. True, he was still half certain his benefactor's story of being from the future was nonsense. But it was a blessing to have someone looking out for him in camp where a prisoner's worst enemy was his fellow prisoner, and death lurked in every corner. Aaron's selfless regard for Liebman's well-being was a balm to the wounds, physical and spiritual, inflicted on him by the camp. He could not be certain of Aaron's sanity but he was absolutely certain now that his benefactor was utterly dedicated to seeing him safely out of the camp and back with Elizabeth and his unborn child.

Aaron's impossible knowledge of the camp and uncanny precision when it came to dates and times still pricked at Liebman's reasoning. The only explanation that made sense was exactly what Aaron had told him. The whole thing was too fantastic to be believed, but the facts remained. Well, there was something different about Aaron. That much was certain. He promised himself he would delve deeper into the mystery provided he passed the selection. Until such time, all his energy was directed to surviving the coming hours.

When the bell sounded in the afternoon it was time for blocksperre -- lockdown. The Blockaltester for each barracks made sure every prisoner was accounted for, then issued each inmate their card containing number, name, profession, age and nationality. Aaron was reminded that his name for the past four months had been Spiegel.

After the cards had been distributed, the prisoners were ordered to undress. The did so quickly and efficiently, placing their clothes neatly on top of their beds along with bowls and spoons. Under normal conditions this would be a sure way to have them instantly stolen, but there would be no one in barracks to take them during the selection.

This flurry of activity was followed by a prolonged period of tense waiting, the naked inmates standing beside their beds. There was no way to know how long it would take for the SS to reach them so the prisoners climbed under their blankets to keep warm. No one slept except the Muselmänner long since oblivious to what was going on around them. For the rest an all-consuming terror lurked behind their yellow eyes.

Aaron sat on the edge of his bunk, Liebman lying next to him, shivering slightly.

"Remember what I told you," Aaron said in low tones. "It is imperative you convey an aura of health and vitality. We have taken steps to improve your fitness level but you must pass before the inspector as if you had energy to spare. Summon every ounce of remaining strength. There will be time to rest afterwards."

"Hey! You up there!"

Aaron looked down at an angular face glaring up at him. The prisoner was lying on his back, his head hanging out over the edge of the bunk, eyes desperate with fear.

"We are not your concern," Aaron said.

"How did you get so fat?" the prisoner continued. "Look at him! All of you! Look!"

Amidst some grumbling to shut up from the others, the prisoner continued. "Look at him, I say. Getting fat while we starve. He's getting extra rations for informing. He's collaborating. Look at him!"

The Kapo, summoned by the shouting, entered, cudgel raised. He threatened the prisoner with a beating, which was all it took to silence him. Bruises or cut lips could mean certain death in the selection.

Aaron glanced around in the silence. There were still a few envious, curious eyes fixed on him. He made a note of each prisoner's face so he could watch them in future. Then his gaze found John who smiled back at him, his eyes shining. It was not the first time Aaron had noticed John watching him. John seemed obsessed with Aaron since the explosion at the factory and it was beginning to cost him favor with his followers eager to strike. It was a situation which could not endure much longer.

Barked orders shocked the prisoners out of wherever their minds had retreated to in order to escape the present. The Blockaltester shouted commands and everyone leaped off their bunks to be herded into the tagesraum or Quartermaster's office. This was a cramped room and close, the prisoners' naked bodies pressed tightly against each other. It was from here they would go to be inspected and in minutes the air was saturated with the stench of body odor, expelled carbon dioxide and fear.

Ten minutes later the Blockaltester opened the door leading outside where the SS doctor and a subaltern waited at the foot of the hill. This struck the Low Numbers as odd for, with freezing temperatures, it made sense for the inspector to want to remain indoors. This was not normal procedure and the veterans did not know what to make of it. The Blockaltester nodded to someone the prisoners could not see and one by one the prisoners ran to the inspector.

Liebman sweated in the close confines while an icy chill raced up and down his backbone. He gripped his card fiercely in his slick palms as he replayed what Aaron had told him about the procedure: Each inmate had to run up the SS doctor and subaltern, hand over his identification card, then run back. This allowed the doctor a chance to see the prisoner, front and back, then make his determination. This would be illustrated by two piles of cards in front of him. One meant life, the other death. Prisoners would try to see onto which pile their card was placed though there was no way to know which pile was the correct one until afterwards.

They had decided that Aaron would go first to observe the process with Liebman hanging back until a few others had gone in between. The strategy was that Aaron, though sickly in Liebman's eyes, appeared young and robust compared to most of the others, Liebman included. And to have the middle-aged doctor follow in Aaron's footsteps would cast Liebman in an unflattering light by comparison.

It was almost Aaron's turn. At the door, he turned and spoke to Liebman.

"Be strong. This is the last test you will face. Think of Elizabeth."

Then he disappeared through the door.

Adrenalin raced so hard through Liebman's system his body trembled. He flexed his arms and legs, breathed deeply to expand his chest and hopped in place, urging blood into his muscles, staining his cheeks red and ruddy as Aaron had instructed.

Aaron returned, jaw set, expression relaxed. He was not even breathing hard from the sprint.

Liebman continued his exercises while the next few inmates dashed out. As the third returned with wobbling gait, Liebman knew it was time. Life and death hung on the passage of a few seconds running. He'd used to love to run as a boy through the streets of Berlin with his schoolmates, and on the soccer field. Now his very existence depended on how well he ran at this moment decades later.

He felt a slight nudge in his back from Aaron. This was his cue. He shot out of the doorway, moving as Aaron had instructed him with brisk, elastic steps, head high, chest out, muscles contracted. He felt the strain after only a half-dozen steps but terror pushed more adrenalin into his system. The subaltern was seated directly ahead, his back to one of the barracks. The doctor stood next to him, flanked by the Blockaltester on the left and the Quartermaster on the right.

Liebman tried to keep his eyes fixed straight ahead but the ground was uneven, hard in some places, soft in others from all the coming and going. Puddles, their icy surfaces cracked by running feet, splashed freezing water onto his bare feet and legs. He felt his left heel slide as it hit the edge of one puddle and for an instant lost his equilibrium and he was sure he would pitch headlong at the subaltern's boots. But he somehow kept his balance, the falter unnoticed, he hoped, by his potential executioner.

He came to a full, steady stop, his breathing controlled, the muscles of his torso tensed and tight to mask the pounding of his heart. The subaltern stared through him at a space three feet behind where he stood. The doctor barely glanced at him. With as much military precision as he could muster, he handed the card to the Quartermaster, who passed it to the subaltern, who, without so much as glancing at it, extended it to the doctor. The SS doctor turned bored eyes once more on Liebman then placed the card on one of the piles in front of him.

Liebman was in the process of turning smartly as this took place and thought he saw the card go atop the pile on the right. Then his back was to the inspector and he was sprinting to the Quartermaster's office, now free to watch where he placed his feet. An odd emptiness settled over him. His fate had been decided in a heartbeat, and he'd had no say in the matter, and yet, despite his pounding heart, he felt nothing.

At the door to the Quartermaster's office, he saw Aaron watching his return. Had he been there the entire time?

Liebman all but dove into the fetid mass wedged into the office, the oppressive heat welcome after the brief exposure outside.

"You performed flawlessly," Aaron said. "The selection is over for us. Do not worry."

"I hope John will fare as well," Liebman said, still trembling from the cold and shock which was beginning to set in. "And poor Pietor. He must be frozen."

"Both will be fine."

"You say that with such certainty."

"You know why I say it."

Because you're from the future, Liebman wanted to say but didn't dare. Although he had to admit that Aaron was too calm under these horrific conditions for it to be the product of a simple delusion. Liebman was already beginning to shake uncontrollably as the adrenalin worked its way out of his system. Aaron, however, was aloof, stoic, exactly the kind of reaction one would expect from one who viewed what was happening as history. And yet, he had kept watch at the door when it was Liebman's turn. Why? If all this was the distant past to him, then why?

When the last of the prisoners returned, the veterans began pushing their way to the inner door so they could be first back in barracks to dress and get under their tattered blankets. This movement alerted the others that the selection was over. Those destined for the crematorium would be collected later.

While this was going on, the Blockaltester appeared in the doorway,

THE LIGHT OF MEN

a fistful of cards in his hands. He began rattling off numbers. This froze everyone where they stood. Even the Low Numbers didn't know what to make of it.

The first few numbers reported to the Blockaltester and were roughly shoved outside without a word of explanation.

Aaron heard his number and shot a look at Liebman. It was clear to the doctor that his benefactor had no idea what was happening. There was nothing else to do but come forward, so Aaron stepped outside with the others. Liebman joined him moments later and John shortly after that.

"You claim to know everything," Liebman said past chattering teeth. "What is this about?"

"I don't know." Aaron glanced around at the Kapos and SS guards appearing like minutes on a clock face around the huddled prisoners. "It looks like recreation, but I cannot be sure."

"What's on the agenda, a soccer match?" Someone near them said.

Aaron bent close to Liebman, grasped his arm and whispered into his ear. "Recreation means we will be run around the camp, continuously, until we drop from exhaustion."

"Then we are dead. This has all been for nothing."

Aaron tugged fiercely on Liebman's arm. "Look around. There are no Muselmänner here, no sick or old. We have not been selected. What pile was your card placed on?"

"The right."

"As was mine. That clinches it."

"We are doomed."

"No. Recreation is a means of thinning ranks. Those left inside have been selected for the crematorium. We are the healthy. The SS want to thin our numbers as well. Therefore this recreation will be a test of endurance, not merely a run to the death. If they wanted us all dead, why bother with a selection at all? Why not proceed directly with recreation? We will survive this."

"Speak for yourself. I'm frozen."

"Listen to me! When we are ordered to run, pace yourself and remain in the center of the group. The Kapos and SS will beat us, trip us up, weaken us. In the center, you will be spared most of this. Stay away from the edges of the group."

"All right! Run you mongrels!" the SS sergeant shouted, swinging his club. "Nice day for a jog, I think."

The prisoners moved forward in a stumbling mass. The high-stepping poise they'd demonstrated earlier had exhausted many of them as it came on the tail end of intense anxiety leading up to the selection. The cold did its deadly work as well. Once clear of the barracks and out in the roll call area, the wind swirled and gusted around the sweating, naked bodies of the prisoners, leeching heat and stiffening muscles.

The first victims fell there, pawing at the frozen mud with their hands, kicking furrows with their blue feet, mouths gasping to suck cold air into their constricted lungs.

Aaron guided Liebman with nudges of his shoulders into the denser parts of the group. Liebman was sweating, he saw, but his teeth were also clicking together uncontrollably.

More prisoners fell as they passed Ka-Be and headed towards the gates. Aaron could see Krueger watching from his office window, steaming mug in hand, sipping as the prisoners turned at the barbed wire between them. A couple knowing they were almost spent, hurled themselves onto the electrified wire, robbing the SS of the pleasure of killing them.

The Kapos and SS did their parts. Grunts and screams sounded as axe handles and lathes smacked against the backs of the prisoners' thighs and into the base of their spines.

Liebman faltered and Aaron steadied him. One of the Kapos saw this and landed a vicious blow to Aaron's left shoulder. The blow knocked him forward but he held onto Liebman.

They made another circuit. And another, stepping over and around the fallen. The pace was weakening Liebman, who could barely catch his breath. Aaron seeing this, said, "Not much longer! Hold on! For Elizabeth! For your daughter! It can't last much longer! Hold on!"

What he did not tell the doctor was that he saw the reason for the culling. While the SS doled out punishment to the closest victim, the Kapos were concentrating their attention on John and his group, many of whom had already fallen. John himself was bloodied and covered in dark red patches where blows had been struck. He kept on though, running as fast as he could twenty feet in front of Aaron. This attention, plus Krueger's interest, told Aaron that the SCI had decided to remove the threat John posed once and for all.

But this was not his concern. Aaron saw the light dimming in Liebman's eyes. His lips were blue, his cheeks white and hard. Liebman was freezing to death.

"Come close to me!" Aaron urged. "Almost touching, slightly behind."

Liebman made no reply but did as he was told and they ran in step their bodies so close they rubbed together at times.

Aaron glanced around, saw the SS had retreated to their heated quarters and most of the Kapos, breathing hard from their exertions, had also returned indoors or stood catching their breath. The beatings were over. They had only to run now.

Judging it safe to do so, he dropped back out of what was left of the group. Liebman followed dumbly until they were free of the others, four or five feet behind.

Liebman plodded on, his feet moving mechanically, his mind shut off. The cold probed with a million sharp fingers into his skin, his veins, damming up the blue tide slowing within. Eyes closed, forehead lowered until it brushed Aaron's shoulder blade, he pressed on.

After several moments of this proximity, he felt heat, steadily growing in intensity. It penetrated, warmed his white, lifeless skin, radiated around him. The cold was still there, pressing, searching, biting, but the heat was stronger. It was like sitting at a camp fire on a winter's day. His front warm, his back cold.

The heat revived him, cleared the ice out of his thoughts. Where was it coming from? Was it a fever dream? An hallucination? Was he really lying on the cold ground at this very instant, his life ebbing away? He wanted to ask Aaron but needed to conserve every ounce of strength. His thoughts still hazy, he had a waking dream that he was back in barracks, under the covers, savoring this same pervasive heat he'd enjoyed so often in the past...

His eyes flung open, inches from Aaron's shoulder. It wasn't just warm, he realized, it was hot -- as if running past a burning building. Where was the heat coming from? He knew there was only one explanation but it was impossible. He reached out tentatively to touch Aaron's arm but his benefactor suddenly increased his pace to rejoin the group, Liebman's fingers a hair's breadth from making contact.

Replenished by the warmth, Liebman used his last reserve of strength to keep pace and rejoin the group. The moment he did so the order came to halt and return to barracks.

As they made their way, two men supporting John, Liebman made a point of brushing Aaron's shoulder but the young man's skin was just slightly warm, no more so than any of the others who dripped with sweat after so long a run. Yet there was something different about him.

Inside, the prisoners threw their clothes on and dove under the blankets or fought for space close to the small, inadequate stove. The barracks was cold, the men slick with sweat. Pneumonia was a real threat. Those of John's followers who survived the ordeal, placed their leader on his bunk and threw their own blankets around him while they shivered. John was a mass of red welts and blood flowed with the rivulets of sweat down his arms and sides. How he had survived the beating was a miracle.

Those still able to move clustered around the sick or Muselmänner, who had been spared the recreation, to find out which pile their cards had been placed in. Those not singled out for recreation had all had their cards placed on the left pile whereas the frozen runners had comprised the pile on the right. This settled the matter and confirmed Aaron's theory that only those not chosen to die during the selection had been subjected to recreation. Those still alive would remain so for the time being. The selection, for them, was truly over.

This was confirmed a short time afterwards when the bell rang a second time, signaling the end of the selection. The Blockaltester, with armed SS, came in and collected those whose cards had gone on the left pile. To them would fall the duty of carting the frozen bodies to the crematorium, then joining their fallen comrades in the flames.

Liebman regarded Aaron critically as he attempted to sponge the sweat from his body with his outer jacket before putting it on. He was confused by what had happened outside, all but convinced it had been an hallucination. The heat which had saved his life had come from within, he was sure. Perhaps fuelled by his love for Elizabeth. Glancing around seemed to confirm this. No one else was looking at Aaron. If his benefactor had turned himself into a human radiator, surely they would have felt it as well. But they were all swiping at the sheen of sweat and shivering while Aaron, dressed, sat on the edge of the bunk, surveying the scene.

Liebman crawled under the blanket fully clothed and felt exhaustion creeping over him like a sheet of lead, pressing him down into the hard slats beneath him. He was still sweating slightly, but it was comfortable under the blanket. As sleep pulled like a shroud over his thoughts, the something odd about Aaron he'd sensed earlier became instantly clear in his mind.

Aaron hadn't been sweating when they'd returned to barracks. The others, himself included, had been dripping. How...

Then the thought was gone as he tumbled into a black pit.

CHAPTER EIGHTEEN

L iebman awoke to darkness. For a moment he didn't know where he was but the breathing of the other prisoners and the smell were all the reminders he needed. He sat up, his eyes drawn to the moonlight coming through the small window overhead. Beneath the window, his back against the wall, watching him, sat Aaron.

Liebman cleared his throat before speaking. "How long was I asleep?"

"It is after midnight."

Dear Lord, Liebman thought, the selection had taken place immediately after the midday meal. He took stock of his body. He had more than his share of aches and pains and his legs throbbed and tingled. It was agony to move them. There was no work on a selection day and he was grateful for that. It was doubtful he could have risen from his bunk, let alone put in a day of back breaking labor. Aside from the pain, he felt rested and managed a weak smile at Aaron. There was something about his comrade. It had come to him before sleep overtook him. Well, it was gone, whatever it was.

"Are you hungry?" Aaron asked. "I saved your ration."

The thought of food put a thick gurgle in his empty stomach, but after what he'd been through earlier, he wanted real food. Not the barely flavored hot water he'd had for too long now.

"In a minute," he said, shifting on the sharp straw beneath him. "Did everyone make it through?"

"John is still with us. Pietor returned undetected. Many were chosen. I sent two to Ka-Be personally for trying to steal our things.

More will go when sickness comes from exposure. As no new inmates will arrive, conditions will improve."

"What happened?" Liebman asked, regarding Aaron intently. "You claimed to know precisely what would transpire. It was all the past to you. Why didn't you mention the recreation?"

"I didn't know. It was not normal procedure."

"How could you not know, future man?"

"I have been analyzing that very thing."

Aaron's somber tone took some of the mocking ire out of Liebman's reply. "And what have you come up with?"

"There are only two conclusions. The first is incomplete knowledge in the historical record. The second is that my presence here has subtly altered the timeline. This is not unexpected."

Liebman groaned up into a sitting position. "What does that mean?"

"It means the events of the next few days cannot be predicted with a high degree of accuracy."

"What's going to happen in the next few days?"

"Much."

Liebman's stomach rumbled. Aaron heard it from where he sat and uncovered the bowl of soup next to him. He handed it over.

"Damn the soup," Liebman said, pushing the bowl away. "What were you saying?"

Aaron set the bowl down. "As it is almost the end, I will tell you what I know." Liebman, despite Aaron's words, pulled the bowl to him after a few moments and began eating so fixated on Aaron that he did not notice how hot the soup was. "Today is March 17th, 1945. The US Third Army crossed the Rhine on the 5th. The SS know this and have estimated they have roughly three weeks before the camp is taken."

Liebman's eyes widened in surprise, the pale whites shone in the moonlight. Liberation. For so long a dream, now almost a reality. He put a hand on Aaron's knee, gave it a heartfelt squeeze. He was smiling and the pull on his facial muscles felt strange.

"Have you forgotten so soon?" Aaron watched the smile fade from Liebman's lips and the doctor went back to eating, his eyes never leaving his benefactor. "The SS will evacuate the camp at the last possible moment. They will attempt to destroy whatever documents remain. They will destroy the crematorium and gas chamber, burn the camp. Every prisoner alive at that time will be marched deeper into Germany. Most will die en route. Those who survive will be absorbed by camps still in operation. We are North of Frankfurt. Camp Buchenwald is closest. Flossenburg a little farther to the South. Dora-Nordhausen is also a possibility though unlikely. Buchenwald will be liberated by the US Army on April 11th. It is doubtful anyone from here would still be alive by that date."

"What do you mean doubtful? Don't you know? Isn't that what happened? What will happen, I mean."

"No. It is not. As I said, the SS believe they have until the first week of April to evacuate. That assessment is essentially correct. The main body of the US 3rd Army will arrive here on April 4th. However, what the SS do not know is that elements of the 761st Tank Battalion and the 183rd Engineer Combat Battalion have already broken through at Koblenz, ahead of the main body, and are speeding their way in this direction. They will be here on April 1st."

"It can't be true," Liebman gasped. "We are saved!"

"Keep your voice down. Things are not so simple. Much will happen between now and then."

"Bah! What can the SS do to us? They have no idea our liberators are due to arrive."

"What happens here over the next 96 hours has nothing to do with the SS."

"Speak plain, man. No more cryptic announcements."

"No. That is enough for now. If you knew more you would speak of it to others and it is vital we make every attempt to preserve as much of the timeline as possible."

"Preserve?"

Aaron shook his head. "No more. This information is potentially catastrophic. For this reason, I was not told how my being here was accomplished for fear the SS might somehow get it out of me. I have only the historical record and whatever your wife conveyed to your daughter about your life before the war and your time in hiding. The less you know about time travel, the better. Besides, you should try to sleep. There will be an air raid in eighty-one minutes."

"What!"

"Quiet!" Aaron hissed. "Do not awaken the others. The raid will not come near the barracks. Only the SS quarters will be hit."

Liebman threw back his blanket, tried to sit up. "You don't know that. You said so yourself. This timeline of yours -- "

Good God he was believing Aaron's story! Was desperate to believe it in fact. Liberation mere days away. It was too much to hope for.

Aaron put his hands on Liebman's shoulders and forced the doctor down. "Lay back. The raid will be a small one, the damage minimal in the short term. It will have far reaching effects however."

"You can't be sure -- "

"You must trust me. The raid should do no direct damage. It will awaken the entire camp though so you should try to sleep while you can."

Liebman did as he was told. He closed his eyes, tried to relax. He was bone tired but his mind raced. Minutes ticked by in the darkness. He couldn't keep track and was certain he heard the bombers droning overhead every few seconds. The tension built and he found himself fidgeting under his blanket. Aaron lay beside him, his broad back to Liebman.

"You are awake," Aaron said. It was not a question.

"Of course," Liebman grumbled. "Only a dead man could sleep under these conditions. How much longer, do you think?"

"Twenty-nine minutes."

Did his benefactor have a clock in his head? Certainly no one in camp possessed a pocket watch. Time was the first thing the SS stole from them.

"As long as you are awake, would you like your extra ration?"

Liebman's mouth watered at the thought. He already needed to urinate and, if a raid was imminent, he would have to climb down soon and relieve himself.

"I'd better not."

"It would be prudent to reconsider. The raid will disrupt camp routine. There will be no morning meal and no chance of organizing rations for many hours. This is your last opportunity to eat for some time."

Liebman's stomach clenched tighter. He couldn't remember ever feeling this empty. "All right, then."

Liebman waited in complete darkness. The moon was obscured now by cloud and he could barely discern Aaron's back six inches in front of him. He felt Aaron hitch slightly. Then again. At the third hitch the drone of bombers swelled suddenly around them as if materializing out of thin air. The SS in the guard towers began cranking the alarm siren.

"Looks like they're early," Liebman said, his light tone masking his terror.

Aaron did not reply. His body spasmed again.

The doctor put a hand on Aaron's shoulder and tried to roll him over to see what was wrong. Aaron resisted, his upper body immovable as stone.

"We've got to turn out. The siren." Liebman clambered over the inert form as the bombs began raining down. The first explosion was close, seemingly lifting the barracks and dropping it down again. The prisoners jounced wildly in their bunks. Liebman was tossed up and over Aaron so that he sprawled atop him, his face inches from Aaron's.

The next bomb hit with a blinding flash, illuminating the pitch-black barracks.

Liebman saw Aaron's face lit as though by a spotlight and recoiled in horror, tumbling over Aaron's hips and legs and coming to rest at the edge of the bunk, perilously close to falling over the side. He saw soup dribbling out of Aaron's open mouth poised over the bowl. Aaron's throat worked, his eyes wide and staring at Liebman blankly.

"In the name of all that's holy -- " Liebman began as the barracks was plunged once again into darkness. Over the explosions, the wail of the sirens and the sounds of the prisoners launching themselves out of their bunks, he heard Aaron coming towards him. He shrieked and reared back, felt his balance go and a wave of vertigo as he went over the side. His fall was halted by a strong grip on the front of his jacket. Terrified, he beat at the hand that had saved him as he was drawn back from the edge.

The bombs thundered down as the prisoners dressed and automatically made their beds. The explosions were smaller now, distant, tapering off when the Blockaltester entered barking commands over the siren. Torch beams lanced through the darkness, dancing crazily. One backlit Liebman and caught Aaron full in the face. He looked the way Liebman had always seen him. No change whatsoever. But he could not forget the sight of that cascade of soup down his chin. His stomach heaved at the image in his mind but there was nothing inside to come up.

Aaron released him as a Kapo came to stand below them. "Get down from there, arseholes! Right now! If I have to come up there I'll be tossing down corpses. Move!"

The discipline of camp routine came to Liebman's rescue. He all but hurled himself down and joined the other prisoners. Aaron rushed to catch up but the doctor did not look back. His one desire was to get as far away from Aaron as possible.

Outside, the prisoners were organized into details and marched over to the SS barracks. Liebman looked around for John in order to plead for protection against the monster he'd bunked with but the charismatic leader was nowhere to be found. This was strange, especially since a number of John's surviving followers were also unaccounted for and the Kapo did not seem concerned by their absence.

Liebman was thankful that Aaron had wound up in a separate detail. He wasn't sure exactly what he'd seen back in barracks. Didn't want to believe it, rather. But before he returned to his bunk, he had to find John. The connection to his benefactor was over. He knew that much.

There was no more time to think of Aaron when they reached the SS compound. The raid had been brief, but effective. Many of the buildings were burning piles of rubble. Half-dressed SS men ran in all directions, shouting orders and questions. For most this was their first taste of combat and the bombs had momentarily knocked the discipline out of them.

The prisoners were put to work on bucket brigade. Liebman took his place and was soon soaked to the skin by splashed water. Luckily the heat from the fires had warmed the surrounding area. In seconds he was sweating and the work became routine. He made the mistake of staring into the first bucket and the black, shining water reminded him of what he'd seen coming out of Aaron's mouth and his gorge rose. He passed the following buckets with his eyes staring straight ahead.

It was a small storeroom ablaze and they had the fire down to a smolder in short order. Liebman and his brigade was moved over to the SS divisional replacement depot where a variety of weapons were kept. The structure had been hit only a glancing blow but one side had collapsed and was burning fiercely. The prisoners worked to extinguish the fire while the SS, armed now, kept a watchful distance.

Liebman found out why moments later when he overheard other prisoners talking. Rifles, carbines, pistols, hand grenades and ammunition were stored here and if the flames got to the live rounds...

He found himself at the front of the line, the heat so intense it singed the hair on his hands and eyebrows. He threw bucket after bucket, but all seemed lost as the fire swelled and roared with demonic fury. The instinct to run was almost overpowering. Only the fact that he'd be shot in the attempt kept him rooted to the spot.

His salvation came in the form of a fire wagon which pulled up behind the line, the horses whinnying at the intense heat as the hoses were brought to bear on the blaze. While all attention was on the wagon, Liebman turned to throw his last bucket and caught a glimpse, or at least thought he caught a glimpse, of figures moving inside the building behind the flames and billowing smoke. For some reason, his first thought was that it must be Aaron, but he'd seen his former benefactor in a bucket brigade working on the SS quarters. Before he could peer deeper into the burning ruin, he was pushed aside by the men working the hoses.

It took more than two hours to extinguish the fires. The emergency over, the prisoners were used to clean up the debris, which took until dawn while the fire brigade made sure the fires were completely out. Most of the SS quarters lay in ruins. The offices had been marginally hit however. Details were formed to remove the dead and injured SS. Prisoners overcome by smoke, heat, exhaustion (or all three) lay were they'd fallen.

In the first gray light of morning, the prisoners were marched back to camp. With every step, Liebman felt a growing dread which was confirmed when he learned there was to be a roll call and that they would not be returning to barracks. Just as Aaron had predicted.

As there had not been a transport in a month and the ranks had been culled by the selection, Liebman hoped the roll call would proceed quickly. This was not to be the case. The SS took painstaking measures to account for every prisoner, living and dead, as if trying to re-assert their control over the finite universe of the camp in the wake of the bombing. The dead had to be carried back and lined up their numbers checked and re-checked as dawn gave way to morning.

Every few seconds a prisoner would spasm, his cheeks momentarily inflating as he stifled a cough. The prisoners were forbidden to make any sound during roll call other than to acknowledge their number. There was muted conversation in sneering whispers out of one side of the mouth, which was common.

One reason for the delay was that not all of the details had returned at the same time and the early arrivals, Liebman among them, had to stand in place while the stragglers took their positions in ranks.

By the start of the third count, it looked as if all the prisoners had returned, but one detail was not accounted for. John and a handful of his associates had not returned.

Kapos loyal to Krueger exchanged glances. A runner was called forward and stood ready. For the SS the discrepancy was cause for alarm. The danger of an escape attempt in the confusion was a very real one. During a raid, the guard towers stood empty and the fence current was turned off for safety. The guards were ordered to shoot anyone they found outside the gates on sight afterwards.

The count was performed again with no response from the

missing detail. The RCO was called forward and given a dressing down. Both the SS and Krueger's men were about to dispatch their runners when the sound of marching feet could be heard.

All eyes turned to the front gates but this was not the source of the sound. As it drew near, they determined the direction and the prisoners and SS watched as John's detail rounded a corner, marching with strict military precision: eyes straight ahead, soot-blackened faces set, arms like poles at their sides, their hands black as pitch, to join ranks.

The Kapos loyal to John stepped up to the RCO and explained the delay. This was accepted with a curt nod, leading Liebman to believe that the roll call officer was partly under John's influence. With the missing detail back in ranks, the count was taken twice more to the satisfaction of the SS. Liebman heaved a sigh of relief not only because the roll would soon be finished, but also for John's safe return. He was going to seek John out the instant they were dismissed. What struck him as odd though was that Krueger's Kapo sent the runner he had waiting. What could there possibly be to report to the SCI?

The order finally came and the prisoners broke ranks and all but ran to the soup pots that had been wheeled into place during the long count. Liebman had been sure he would never be able to eat again after the incident with Aaron. However the gnawing in his stomach was more intense than usual and he found himself eagerly joining the line.

He saw Aaron standing off to one side, out of line, his gaze fixed in Liebman's direction. The doctor looked away, seeking John and saw him coming to join the line.

"May I speak with you?" he asked, as John, flanked by his followers, Pietor amongst them, came up to him.

"Of course, Doctor." John seemed very pleased with himself, almost buoyant after so many hours of hard labor and no breakfast. "Today is an important day. For all of us."

"You mean the bombing?" Liebman still could not believe that during the raid and battling the fires after, he had been gripped with joy not terror. And at no time had he feared for his life. The sounds

of the explosions and the hissing roar of the flames had been music
to his ears. "Yes, it is encouraging."

"It is more than that, I'm sure."

Liebman leaned forward, speaking so low he was almost inaudible.
"I seek your protection. I offer all that I am in return."

John's expression grew worried. "Protection? From whom? You
are my dear comrade. This is known in camp. Who would dare?"

Liebman considered what he was about to say. As much as he
wanted to be free of his benefactor, he was well aware that his next
words could cost the man, if man he was, his life. This close to
liberation, it was a risk he had to take. "Aaron," he said.

John's eyebrows shot up in surprise. Liebman watched, confused,
as John's expression softened and his eyes gentled, went almost
glassy. "You are mistaken."

"I tell you-- "

"We have nothing to fear from that one," John stressed. "You must
trust me. Trust him." He paused and sniffed the air. "Do you smell
it? Spring. The first hint of it. Isn't it marvelous?"

"I am asking for your help," Liebman repeated. "Will you deny
me your protection?"

"Never, my dear comrade. Never." John put a hand on Liebman's
arm and smiled. "You ask it of me, I grant it without reservation. I
simply want you to understand that Aaron poses no threat. Quite the
reverse in fact."

"What do you mean?"

"That is not for me to say."

"Yes, well, thank you at any rate."

"You are most welcome." It was almost their turn to be served.
"Let us eat. We will need our strength. Now more than ever."

CHAPTER NINETEEN

"We are armed," Pietor said the moment he joined Aaron on his bunk.

"I know," Aaron replied. "They were obtained three days ago after the raid of the burning SS divisional replacement depot by John and a handful of his followers."

There had only been light work in the morning, loading trucks for the SS. In the two days since the bombing, camp routine had eroded -- another sign that the end was near. Aaron had spent the time watching, waiting, while seeking an opportunity to speak with Liebman.

"How could you know?" Pietor was stunned. "Who has spoken of it?"

"How I know does not matter now." Aaron turned his head to look at his former comrade. "I know that John and his followers removed weapons and concealed the arms in the woods near the Prophet and behind hastily re-plastered walls."

Pietor leaned back in shocked silence, then said, "You will inform on us?"

"Why would I do that?"

"For what happened with Liebman."

This was meaningless conversation to Aaron. "Why have you come to me?"

Pietor watched Aaron closely, like an astronomer peering at a distant star. "If you know our secret, then you must also be aware that the time to act is almost upon us."

"Why come to me?" Aaron repeated.

"It is time to make a choice. All of us must choose. There can be no exceptions."

"Why, Pietor Chekunov?"

"I might say for what has passed between us months ago. You saved my life. We were comrades once though, like Krueger, you tired of my presence. I might say that or I might say I thought your life worth saving and wanted to offer you the chance to strike with us. I could say these things but, in truth, John wishes to speak with you and sent me."

Aaron stared up at the ceiling, considering. "Interesting. The second most powerful inmate in camp wishes to speak to me and sends an envoy to ask permission. Does that not strike you as strange?"

"I do not question my betters. John's will is poised to assert itself over the camp. I am an instrument of that will. He awaits your answer."

"I will come, of course."

They climbed down and moved between the tiered bunks. The soup was more water than anything else and the strength of the prisoners was waning. Most lay gasping in their bunks, eyes wide and staring, silently praying they could last until liberation. The relentless sound of the approaching guns, the bombing of Jenseits and the SS preparations for flight had all strengthened their resolve. However these invigorating elements battled with the food reduction and the closing of Ka-Be in a lethal tug of war. Every strand of the camp was drawn tight.

"He agreed," Pietor announced as they approached John in the Quartermaster's office, which had been donated by that officer who was now loyal to their cause.

Aaron stepped in, saw Liebman amongst several of John's lieutenants. The doctor did not return his glance.

John's face lit up at the sight of Aaron and he begged permission to speak with him alone. Liebman and the others complied at once and soon John and Aaron had the room to themselves.

"You wished to see me," Aaron said.

"Did Pietor explain to you where we stand?"

Aaron saw no reason to go into how the information was exchanged so he simply nodded.

"Good, good." John's eyes darted around the room nervously. He tapped a finger on the tabletop.

"What did you want to see me about?" Aaron prompted.

John did not appear to hear the question. "One would think death held no more surprises for us. After what we have seen. Yes?" He closed his eyes against a flood of memories. "All we have seen. Death has been our close companion, ready to strike at a moment's notice from the instant we bow our heads and enter the camp. So how can death terrify me now?"

"I cannot answer you. I know what is coming. That is plain."

"Yes, of course you do. That is why I sent for you."

"To answer this question?"

"No, no."

John got up and moved around the room, pacing like a caged animal. "I don't know how to say this. I guess the direct approach is best. Do you wish to lead the revolt? I can be your eyes and ears, if you think me worthy."

Aaron was confused. "You want me to join you?"

"Not at all. Dear God, no! We are ready. The others grow impatient. I have told them we must wait for the chosen one to give the word. You have revealed yourself to me." John came and stood before Aaron. "Please forgive my impertinence but I must ask, why do you delay showing yourself to the others? I have thought long and hard, trying to understand your wisdom. At first I thought it was the lack of weapons to ensure at least a chance of success. Now that obstacle has been overcome. Then I thought there was some aspect of our plan I had overlooked. Some detail that would finish us. But I do not know what it could be. And we must act. The food is running out. There is no medicine. The SS have all but forgotten us and they will murder us all to ensure our silence before we can be liberated. The time is now."

Aaron was well aware of conditions in camp. "You will do what you feel is right. What does my opinion matter?"

"Please, no more of that. There is no more time for concealment. I know who and what you are. I have known for a while and have kept your secret. I was blessed to see you in the forest after the explosion at Jenseits. The miracle I witnessed that night was all the evidence I needed. You are the chosen one foretold by the Prophet: *'great strength is his to exert at any moment and the power of his arm, no man can match.'* Remember? You were there. *'Raise thy hand against the heathen, and let them see thy power, who can stand before his wrath.'* *'The days of vengeance are come, many can easily be overpowered by a few, yet thou has made him little less than a God.'"*

John stepped back in awe of Aaron and sat down again. "I knew then that I must wait for the deliverer. Then you survived the blast at the factory and pulled the metal shaft from you body. And I knew. Do not stand before me and deny it, please. I have been your faithful servant."

Aaron listened to all of this in silence, then said, "Believe what you want. It changes nothing."

John hung his head. "I am unworthy then. You seek another to carry out your will."

"My will is my concern. And mine alone. Your course cannot be altered by me or anyone. It is immutable."

John's expression brightened. "Then we have your blessing? Though you will not lead."

"Nothing I say or do must interfere with what is to come."

John's body sagged. He exhaled in a long, drawn out sigh. "Thank you, deliverer. I sought your blessing, prayed you would assist us, feared you would choose to lead and find me wanting. Your way is best. We must earn a place at your side and we will accomplish this. Thank you, chosen one."

"I am not -- " Aaron began, but saw the glassy look coming over John's eyes. He'd been concerned at John's revelation that he had witnessed what had happened in the forest. However, he doubted now that John would be believed if he spoke of it. The resistance

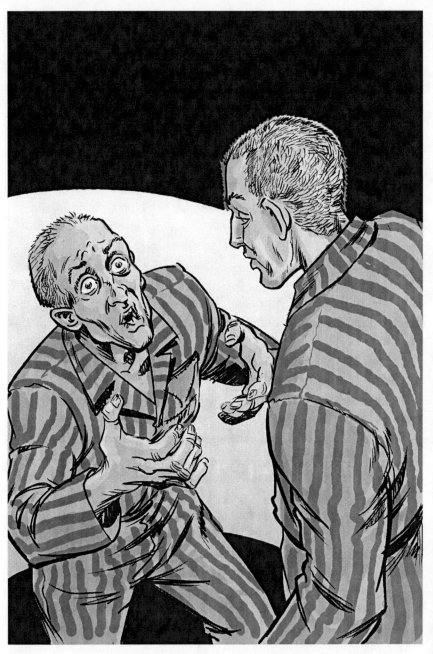

"You are the chosen one foretold by the prophet..."

leader's mind was clearly unbalanced. There was no danger here though he had to speak with Liebman.

John did not seem poised to say anything further so Aaron turned for the door.

"I know what it is I fear," John said suddenly. "It is not death, as I believed. It is choice. Living so long without it in camp, we have forgotten its power. Choosing a course of action is terrifying."

Aaron stopped and faced John. "Only if it is the wrong path you choose."

"How is one to know?"

"The individual cannot know. History forges truth."

John nodded weakly. "May I go to the Prophet, deliverer?"

Aaron saw an opportunity to get Liebman alone so he said, "If you desire his counsel, seek it out."

Aaron watched from his bunk as John and his followers gathered to go see the Prophet. With subdued reverence, they left the barracks. No one spoke, heads held high, eyes focused on a future only they could see, they made their way. Their departure left an indolence which fell over the remaining prisoners. Hungry, sick, worked past all limits of human endurance, they could only wait.

Aaron gave the others time to enter the woods surrounding the Prophet's hole then climbed down and followed. The night held a slight chill but, being late March, spring would not be denied and the gentle evening breeze was without rancor. Discipline was lax in these last few hours of the camp and John's group did not need to conceal their actions. Aaron fell back so as not to give away his presence.

They solemnly entered the Prophet's hovel, Liebman last of all. Aaron crept silently forward. He was five feet away when the door suddenly opened and he caught the Prophet's wheeze carried on the wind.

"...destroy the adversaries, wipe out the enemy, let fiery anger devour the survivors and let the oppressors of thy people be doomed, but this man's purpose is lawless, lawless are the plans in his mind..."

Liebman and John were talking quietly. John held the door open but was preventing the doctor from leaving. He was speaking earnestly to Liebman who shook his head slowly and left the shack. John went back inside. Aaron let Liebman take a few aimless steps away from the door before he came up behind him and clamped a hand over Liebman's mouth.

"It is I," he whispered into the doctor's ear.

Liebman stiffened at the sound of the all-too familiar voice, then relaxed. Aaron released him and they faced each other.

"I want nothing to do with you," Liebman said. "I thought I made that clear."

"You were allowed to seek out John because he offered sound protection. Also, allowing you to forgo the extra ration was an acceptable risk this close to liberation."

Liebman made a disgusted sound in his throat and moved to re-enter the shack. Aaron restrained him.

"Let me go," Liebman hissed. "I came out here to escape all this talk of the future and now you are here with more of the same."

He struggled to free himself but Aaron's grip was like a vise.

"Listen to me, doctor," Aaron said. "There is no longer time to permit you to elude my protection. I am not your enemy."

"Permit me!" Liebman fought with what remained of his strength but could not free himself from Aaron's grasp. He ceased struggling. "I don't know what you are. But I know what I saw. As God is my witness, I know what I saw. Leave me be."

Aaron looked off into the woods for a moment, then pulled Liebman forward away from the Prophet.

"Release me, I say! I will call the others."

"I offer you the truth," Aaron said. "Will you not hear it?"

"Traveler from the future, I have heard your truth and I do not believe a word of it."

"Really? Your wife? Your unborn child? These mean nothing to you? If you do not listen to me, you will never see them again."

"You threaten -- "

"No. I state the simple truth. It will not be by my hand that you are prevented from leaving here. I merely state that if you do not do as I say, you will die here. Soon."

Liebman sagged against Aaron. He gazed up at the sky and ran a shaking hand over his features. "Dear Lord, what am I to do?"

"I am an android," Aaron said.

"What?"

"I am an android. An artificial being."

Liebman lowered his hands from his face and turned his gaze to his former benefactor. "I don't understand."

"Robot," Aaron said. "For lack of a better term. Automaton."

"As in the play by the Czech writer? You are a machine?"

"Highly sophisticated, but yes, a mechanism. An artificial person."

Liebman reared back. "No. More lies! You were ill before the selection. I heard you using the latrine bucket. You certainly kept me up half the night with your coming and going. That makes you human my friend. Deranged, of course, but human still."

"I was removing fluid from my organic tissue. As I knew we would be nude during the selection process, I did not want to appear too healthy before the others lest I be accused of collaborating. I purged myself of water to project a more gaunt appearance. I was almost found out regardless if you recall."

Liebman put his hands over his ears and closed his eyes tight. "I won't listen to this. You are insane!"

Aaron pulled one of Liebman's hands from his ear. "Feel my pulse," he said, extending his left hand. He placed Liebman's hand on his wrist. Feel it!"

With his hand pressed down over the spot, Liebman couldn't help but detect the strong, firm beat of Aaron's pulse.

"I have it," he said. "And it confirms what I already know -- "

The pulse stopped.

Confused, Liebman slid his fingers over the dry skin, searching for the artery. He had it, he was sure, but there was no pulse to detect. He dug his fingers in as hard as he could. Aaron stood there impassively.

"Your daughter told me once you enjoyed the William Tell Overture as a child. She learned this from your wife. Is this correct?"

Liebman nodded mutely, his fingers still fumbling for a pulse.

Suddenly his fingers found it, racing at an incredible rate. He was about to declare his triumph, when something odd about the beats drew his attention. Aaron's pulse was not throbbing with the steady pound of exertion, rather it was drumming with a staccato, undeniable rhythm like a horse a full gallop with two-beat pauses. That rhythm --

He released Aaron's arm as though he were holding a poisonous snake and stepped back, his eyes wide with horror. What he'd felt had been the William Tell Overture played out through Aaron's pulse with percussive force. "How can this be?"

"Your daughter is a Nobel Prize winning scientist in advanced robotics. She went on to construct the first artificial intelligence. Me. When her colleagues wanted to prove they had breached the time continuum in 2027, she offered myself as their test subject so that I might save the life of the father she never knew."

Liebman leaned against a tree and stared off into the shadows.

"Sending a human being to such a place as this was not practical as he or she would be susceptible to the same dangers the prisoners faced. Disease, malnutrition, starvation, broken bones, bullets and the crematorium. An android was the only logical choice. Surely you can see that?"

Aaron waited for some reaction from Liebman. He could see the doctor's gaze turn inward, his reason digesting what he'd learned.

"The night of the bombing," he said. "What happened?"

"I do not require food," Aaron replied calmly. "Therefore I was outfitted with an internal, sanitized receptacle to hold my ration of soup. To which I added a nutrient compound stored in my chest cavity. The mixture was geared to extend your health and ensure your survival. These measures had to be concealed. The SS are extremely thorough as you well know. I regurgitated the soup/compound mixture for your consumption. I generated heat to keep you warm -- "

Aaron paused when Liebman's face went ashen. The doctor's gorge rose for a moment. He fought back the urge to vomit. He had to admit that he had always felt invigorated after that extra ration and now he knew why. Or did he?

"It's all too fantastic," he said.

"In the year 1945, perhaps. But in 2027 there have been advances in every aspect of daily life that are beyond your imagination."

"You do not need to eat or drink?"

"No."

"You don't breathe? Or have a pulse?"

Aaron shook his head.

"And your intellect, you say it is mechanical?"

"Correct."

"Then you won't feel this!" Liebman drew his foot back and kicked Aaron's shin with all his strength. Aaron swayed a little with the impact but that was all.

Liebman stood there, stunned. "It must be true. There is no other explanation."

"I told you I offered the truth."

"You cannot be hurt? Injured?"

"I am not invulnerable. However I was constructed to withstand whatever tortures were commonplace in a camp of this kind. I was damaged in the bomb blast at Jenseits. Fortunately it was not serious. The wound you questioned me about. There were repercussions however."

"What do you mean?"

"On the march back to camp, it was necessary to make repairs. I removed a length of shrapnel from my side. When I did so, I thought I was unobserved but John witnessed the action and learned I had survived an injury no human being could overcome. This has convinced him that I am the deliverer he keeps talking about."

"Oh, my Lord!" Liebman stepped forward and gripped Aaron's forearms. "John means to rebel tomorrow night. He sought the Prophet's blessing."

"And mine."

"You did not give it!"

"No. I cannot commit either way," Aaron spoke calmly. "My mission is to see to your safety. I cannot interfere in what is to come."

"And what will happen?"

"It is better if I do not tell you. You do not comprehend the dangers. Removing you safely from the camp alters the timeline. You'll recall the bombing was earlier than I predicted. The time of the raid was gleaned from surviving SS records. It was stated precisely at 4:51:48 AM, March 17th, 1945. The date was correct but the bombing took place at 4:30:19 AM. Now perhaps the log entry was faulty or a correcting document was lost after liberation. That is one alternative. The other is that the timeline has been compromised. For this reason, I must do nothing during what is to come."

"If it is so fragile, why save me?"

"This was deemed an acceptable risk. My presence here has splintered the timeline, created a parallel stream, an alternate reality for lack of a better term. Your daughter and her colleagues hoped that Quantum Theory's hypothesis that the divergent time lines will collapse into a single reality will follow this limited interference. If you imagine a stream flowing around a boulder you will understand the concept. The end result will be a timeline that is a hybrid of the two realities that varies only subtly from the original -- one of those variations being your continued existence. As I am the first to make such a journey, there is no way to be certain. What I have stated is mere theory even in the year 2027."

Liebman took a moment to absorb this, then he said, "What about John and the others? They will revolt tomorrow night. If you know something -- "

"I cannot interfere. Have I not stated this plainly enough? My presence here has already splintered the time line. Saving your life will widen the gap. I must take no further action in the hope that the divergent streams will become merged."

"You would let them die?"

"They are already dead. Please understand. As real as this time is to you, it is merely a footnote in the history of human civilization. A few abandoned camps remain standing in the year 2027. Tangible symbols of a bygone time. However what transpired here, the war and genocide is but one of many. Before and since."

"Then we learned nothing? All of this has no meaning?"

"It has brought about some changes in international relations.

There is a United Nations Council which investigates and condemns crimes against humanity. This Holocaust did not put an end to such atrocity the same way the xenophobic tendencies of the preceding generations did not forestall this one."

"Tell me at least the madmen behind it will be punished."

"Some were executed. Some served prison terms and were released. Many were never found. All are dead in 2027."

Liebman shook his head. It couldn't be possible that the terror and sacrifice accomplished so little. How could the world let the perpetrators go free? Was there no justice?

"Couldn't you stop it? You can't be hurt like the rest of us. Why don't you help John? With you we can seize control with a minimum of bloodshed. Think of the lives we could save."

"I cannot intervene. I will save you and only you. That is interference enough. In 60 hours this camp will be liberated. Everything must unfold as it did. To change things would be like tossing a pebble into calm water, ripples would extend in all directions, changing everything. I am here to observe, record and see to your safety. Those are my mission parameters."

Liebman made a disgusted sound in his throat and turned away from Aaron. "Then those who sent you are short-sighted fools."

"Your daughter sent me."

"As you say." Liebman looked back in the direction of the Prophet's shack. "I must be getting back. The others will wonder."

"I will go with you. This Prophet intrigues me."

"If you must. Just so we are clear, I have pledged myself to John and his cause. I will not abandon him when the time comes."

"You will not have to. Believe me."

Liebman was put off by Aaron's cryptic tone, but said nothing. They stepped inside and joined the circle around the swaying, jabbering hulk in the center of the room. John saw Aaron and smiled, his body swaying in syncopation to the Prophet's cadence. Pietor did not acknowledge their arrival. He stared raptly at the Prophet who spoke:

"...though they escape the fire, fire shall burn them up, what use is an idol when its maker has shaped it, it is only an image, a source *of lies, wisdom and knowledge are the mainstay of salvation, clench your fists for the land is full of bloodshed, one man shall look aghast at another and their faces will burn with shame, captives of unending night, they all grow feverish, hot as an oven, and devour the rulers, after two days he will revive us, on the third day, he will restore us, his Holy One shall become a flame, which in one day shall burn up and consume, throw down the wicked where they stand and shroud them in an unknown grave, they walked in the heat of the fire praising God, because he did not recognize by whom he himself was molded, your own right hand can save you..."*

CHAPTER TWENTY

The spring rains came while the camp simmered. A ceaseless, murderous torrent, it beat on the roofs of the barracks, streaked windows, made search lights sizzle, bowed every budding branch and transformed every open area of the earth in the camp into lakes of deep mud.

For the prisoners, when they were called out for roll call, the rain would represent cloying damp, chills and the risk of disease. In Krueger's world the downpour was excellent cover for his continuing plans, which would culminate in his imminent departure. The rain meant water for the day's soup and mold for the warehouse managers. Down the wide chimneys of the crematorium, the rain raised ash clouds laced with wisps of smoke though the fires had been extinguished for several days. It scrubbed the air of the stench of rotting corpses, washed dried blood, urine and feces off the gallows to mix with the mud and drowned the stubby flowers just starting to open. It thundered down like steel rods right through the dawn and had not diminished when the morning bell sounded.

The prisoners leapt from their bunks, dropped their feet into icy puddles that had formed overnight on the dirt floor of the barracks. The prisoners dressed, bunks were made -- slightly more lax than the day before and the day previous to that. Discipline was bleeding out of the camp like blood from a severed artery. John and his people welcomed this but not the rain for it caused them to reconsider their plans. The heavy cloud cover smothered the sun, footing was nonexistent and moving about undetected seemed aided by the low visibility but really was hampered by it because anyone outside in the deluge would draw the attention of the guards in the absence of other prisoners.

John's followers stood in the rain, debating out of the sides of their mouths as the roll call dragged on. It had been decided they would attack today. The question of when had yet to be determined. John looked to Aaron for guidance, but none was forthcoming so he made it clear that the rebellion would begin when the rain ceased and that all should be ready when the time came.

The rain seemed satisfied to torment them. As the day wore on, it gained strength rather than diminishing. The prisoners were put to work outside draining standing pools of water, fixing roof leaks and collecting the bodies of dead rats unable to reach higher ground.

The SS had no intention of venturing out to supervise this work, leaving the task exclusively to the Kapos -- half of whom were loyal to John, the other half belonging to Krueger.

John and most of his lieutenants, including Pietor, made up the roof Kommando and, out of earshot of the Kapos below in the mud, discussed freely the plan of attack.

Aaron and Liebman were in the Kommando draining standing water around the storehouses. Liebman, still in awe of what had been revealed to him the night before, kept stealing glances at Aaron as they worked. Whereas Liebman was soaked to the skin, his feet sunk deep in the brown mud, Aaron seemed unfazed by the external conditions. Water poured from the top of his smooth scalp in tiny rivulets and splashed high as the heavy drops struck the top of his head, yet he handled his bucket with dexterous ease with each oiled thrust of his torso. And his arms did not tremble as Liebman's did. The doctor couldn't feel his hands or feet. Twisting to upend his bucket over the empty barrels atop the low wagons was agony and his arms shook from fatigue as well as cold. Aaron's movements were, he understood now, machine-like. Precise. Unhindered. As a scientist of sorts himself, Liebman was fascinated by the robot, or what was the word it (and Aaron was an 'it' he told himself) had used? Android-- that was it. He was amazed by the android's ability to appear utterly human. The prisoners around them did not seem to notice anything different about Aaron yet everything about his benefactor seemed strange and alien to Liebman. Even the name: android. He preferred robot. The word was Czech, derived from Robota, which was the word for laborer in that language. Appropriate given their situation.

"Stay close to me today," Aaron said, "And do precisely what I say."

"Do the Americans arrive today?"

"No. There are still fifty-three hours. Dangerous hours."

"John will give the order today. Is that what you are saying?"

"Yes."

"Then why must we wait for the Americans? The rebellion -- "

"There will be no rebellion today." Aaron scooped up a bucket of filthy water and dumped it into the full barrel. The prisoners attending the wagon dragged it off to be dumped in the trenches in front of the electrified fence. As a new wagon was wheeled into position Liebman took advantage of the distance of listening ears.

"What are you saying? John and the others are ready. When he gives the word -- "

"He will give the word."

"Then what is to stop -- "

"But there will be no rebellion today."

Liebman shot a glance at the approaching wagon. "Speak plainly! If you know something, then say it. If there is no attack, then what is the danger?"

"Stay close to me," Aaron said, then returned to filling his bucket.

As the day wore on, Liebman felt the tension building. His body numbed by the chilling rain, his senses heightened -- seeking input beyond the nerve endings beneath his frozen skin. Krueger's runners dashed this way and that, gray ghosts in the gloom. John's moved with grim determination to knots of working prisoners. Kapos huddled over open braziers talked amongst themselves. Prisoners, here and there, left their work details and were swallowed up by the rain.

Every time something out of the ordinary took place, he would look over at Aaron who was watching as well and demand to know what was happening. Each time he received no answer.

Until an old truck appeared at the top of the hill near barrack 18, which John, Pietor and others were patching. The truck, a rusted hulk, was back end to the slope, perched precariously at the top like a child's toboggan about to plunge, it's rear wheels plowing the mud. Liebman watched, curious to determine what was the driver's intention in placing the truck there. The back of the truck was empty, there was nothing on the hill or near it for loading and the prisoners couldn't be expected to push full rain barrels up the thirty foot rise -- not without spilling the contents and what would be the point of that?

Unable to fathom what the truck was doing there and convinced it was yet another example of the senseless routine of the camp, Liebman turned to resume work, and saw Aaron standing stock still, staring at the truck.

"What is it?" he asked.

"The end," Aaron replied.

As if on cue, the Kapos broke from their group around the fire and moved amongst the nearest work Kommandos shouting orders punctuated by clouds of rainwater spewing from their lips.

The prisoners were kicked and herded into ranks. John and his followers climbed down from the roof and, led by Pietor, took their places. Aaron, guiding Liebman, made sure they were well clear of them when they came to attention in ranks.

"Because it's such a gorgeous day!" the head Kapo announced. "We're going to do our exercises. We'll start by running in place. Begin!"

The prisoners followed the order. Dozens of feet splashed and cratered the oozing mud. After a minute, clouds of breath plumed out of their mouths.

"Face down, you scum!" the Kapo spat.

The prisoners threw themselves down in to the mud, their noses and lips in the sodden earth.

"Now up! Down! Up! Down! Up! Down!"

The breath of the prisoners was a fog now around them from the exertion. A couple of inmates slow to rise when ordered were beaten to death by the other Kapos whose leader jerked the prisoners up and down like yo-yos with his words.

"Let's have some deep knee bends," he said. "Begin!"

He had them continue this exercise for five uninterrupted minutes, keeping the rhythm of his commands to piston-like precision. The prisoners fought exhaustion to obey, ignoring the deep burning in their lungs and thighs. Some toppled over and got the same treatment as their comrades had received earlier.

"All right, we're going to run!" the Kapo ordered.

The prisoners could not coordinate their exhausted, blood-engorged thighs and barely managed a halted, staggering shuffle.

"That's it! Faster now. And... Down!"

The prisoners hurled themselves face first into the mud. They were all covered head to toe now, one indistinguishable from the other as they were ordered to run, then throw themselves down again and again. The effort of raising their bodies up time after time sapped their remaining strength. The Kapo, well aware of this fact, increased the frequency of his commands until the prisoners were barely able to stand. Then he ordered them down and left them there, panting and gasping in the mud while the rain drummed on their backs.

"You dogs really take to the water," he observed, pleasantly, walking between the supine ranks. "Like a flock of ducks, aren't you?" He put his hands on his hips and studied the sprawled inmates. "Well, if you want to be ducks, then walk like ducks. Up on your haunches, ducks! Let's see you waddle!"

Summoning last reserves of strength, the prisoners rose, hunkered down and began duck-walking, using their arms as pendulums.

"That's not waddling," the Kapo said. "You ever see a duck swing his wings like that? Get those arms straight out in front of you. Straight now. Like Frankenstein from the cinema."

The prisoners complied though they could not hold the posture long. A few did something unheard of a month ago, they spoke out, indicating the front which was almost upon them and threatening retribution. These were silenced with swift, merciless blows from axe handles wielded by the Kapos. The other prisoners began toppling over, gasping up into the relentless rain, the last sound reaching them before the Kapos descended on them was the throb of guns in their ears and vibrating through the ground. The noise was so loud it all but drown out the roar of blood in their ears.

The Kapo was losing his audience for what was to follow, and seeing as it had been John's lieutenants who had received most of the beatings and lay dead or dying in the mud according to plan, he put a stop to the squat-walking and resumed the running in place with the occasional drop into the icy mud.

He seemed to gauge exactly when the prisoners could stand no more and ordered them to double-time it up the hill and form ranks trailing down on either side of the idling truck's rear end at the summit.

Aaron held Liebman up halfway down the hill. The doctor was panting and ashen despite the aid Aaron had managed whenever the opportunity presented itself. Aaron, thinking only of the doctor's fragile health, was momentarily not breathing, but this went unnoticed amidst the plumes of breath from the others.

"The worst is over," he said to Liebman. "For us. It's over. Just hold on a little longer."

"Quite the bunch of athletes here," the Kapo was saying. "Maybe we should hold an Olympics."

Aaron heard the sound coming from behind them a second before Liebman and put a restraining hand on the doctor's wrist as he started to turn. Liebman saw the look of closed terror come over the face of the prisoners lined up across from him and the Kapos holding rifles, coming up behind them -- a mirror image of what was happening behind the rank he and Aaron were in.

Moving only his eyes, Aaron surveyed first the rank of prisoners opposite him, then his own rank. The Kapos had preformed their task skillfully. John was near the top and most, if not all, of his followers lay dead or dying behind them in the mud. The run up the hill had churned the soaked, earthen slope into a quagmire. And armed Kapos meant only one thing: Krueger. The trap had sprung, the prey inside.

"Who will be our fist athlete?" The Kapo made a show of looking around but it was clear to Aaron who would be selected.

The Kapo came and stood before John. "You! Step forward!"

John was in the rank across from where Aaron and Liebman stood. Before he stepped forward, his eyes slid past the prisoners until they found Aaron's. Eyes calm, yet expectant, he stared at Aaron who gazed back placidly.

"What is to happen?" Liebman implored in a harsh whisper. "What do we do?"

"Nothing, Doctor," Aaron replied. He dropped his voice so only Liebman could hear. "This has already happened. Stay close to me."

The instant John locked eyes with Aaron seemed to drag on interminably. His lieutenants dead, Pietor frozen with fear, his deliverer unable, or unwilling, to come to his aid, John's gaze turned inward and he stepped forward.

The Kapo hauled him out of ranks and made him stand in front of the truck. Its rear end was above him atop the hill, John's eyes even with the mud-caked rear axle. The truck's twin exhausts snorted out clouds of black smoke like a bull preparing to charge.

When John was in place, the Kapo dropped all pretense and nodded curtly to the driver who had his head out the window, craned back to watch the spectacle going on behind him. He put the truck in reverse and it eased back towards John who stood facing it, feet consumed by the thick, cold mud.

It only took a tap on the gas pedal to upset the fragile balance and the truck's rear wheels burrowed counterclockwise into the mud as it began to inch down the hill.

Gravity took over and the driver put the truck in neutral. The angle being gradual, the truck came at John in slow motion. Flanked by Kapos with rifles, John had no choice but to set his feet firmly in the mud and raise his arms to stop the truck's descent.

"Kamaraden, ich bin der letzte!" he cried out with all the force he could muster. *'Comrades, I am the last one!'*

He lunged forward to meet the truck. His palms slapped the wide
rear bumper and his whole body shook with the impact which slid
him back six inches. The truck's momentum was halted for the
moment, halted as long as John's strength held out.

Head down, body trembling with the strain, his lips pulled back
from his clenched, yellow teeth in a hideous rictus, he thrust against
the unstoppable weight. Agonized seconds ground by while the other
prisoners watched in mute horror.

"Stop this!" Liebman spat at Aaron. "For God's sake, how can you
stand there?"

Aaron did not look at Liebman. "Stay where you are. Do
nothing."

"No! That time has passed. Never again!"

Liebman dove forward. Aaron reached out and took hold of the
doctor's sleeve but the seam of the worn garment gave way and the
sleeve ripped free from the shoulder. Liebman stumbled and sluiced
up the hill and joined John at the rear of the truck. Together they
strained against the inexorable weight.

The Kapos rushed forward, guns ready to prevent Liebman
from helping but their leader held up a hand to halt their approach.
Watching two succumb was better than watching one.

Aaron hesitated a fraction of a second as his motivational
subroutines sorted themselves out. His mission was to save
Liebman's life and see him safely from the camp with a minimum of
interference. To do so now, he would have to directly affect what had
originally transpired and that risk fell outside his safe margin. The
alternative, however, was Liebman's death and an unsuccessful end
to the mission. He could not allow that to happen.

He dashed forward and joined them. John was in the center,
Liebman on his left, Aaron at the end. He seized the bumper, his
grip crimping the thick steel. Survivors afterwards would testify
that they saw the rear wheels of the truck lifted clear out of the mud.
The truck's descent was instantly halted.

"I have it," Aaron said, no stress in his voice. "Jump clear."

"I knew you'd come," Liebman said past clenched teeth, a hint of
a smile on his compressed lips. "John! You first!"

But before any of them could move, Aaron's footing gave out beneath him. The wheels thudded down into the mud as Aaron twisted and fell to one side. The bumper slammed into John and Liebman, knocking them down the hill. Aaron dug in his heels and pushed harder but inertia took over and the truck seemed to gain weight by the second, sliding Aaron backwards down the hill to where John and Liebman sprawled.

Aaron had no choice but to attempt to throw the truck clear. As his arms extended to do this, his heels came up against a large boulder beneath the mud and the weight of the truck tipped him over. His back slapped the mud. He heard screams. Then the rear wheel slammed into his chest. Wedged against the rock by the wheel he heard part of his torso crumple as the screams were cut short. The wheel rolled over him, up his side to his shoulder and the left side of his face. His re-enforced skeleton absorbed most of the impact but systems winked out one after the other inside him. There was a crushing weight against his left cheek and eye, then everything went dark.

CHAPTER TWENTY-ONE

I nput.

"Come on, Jew! Wake up!"

Aaron opened his eyes. The tint and focus were off giving his view a red-tinged, washed out appearance. An internal diagnostic was still cycling so no adjustments to his visual imaging system were possible. Aaron was unaware of the two guards. His thought processes were limited to random spurts of data. His autonomic functions had not been severely damaged by the truck so he kept blinking, his pulse beat, and his chest rose and fell in a semblance of breathing. The data bursts came from all of his motivational subroutines. One moment it was data on his torture, the next how to trade a shoe lace and come out ahead in the bargain, then it was the list of Red Cross stations in the area he was to contact after the camp was liberated, followed by the vitamin ratio for Liebman's soup. On and on these stray kernels flashed through his mind like shooting stars. He could not put them together into coherent thought.

He was bound, hands behind his back, palms together. And he was suspended off the ground, hanging by his wrists, the arms pulled up at an unnatural angle. A stray spurt of data told him that this hanging was a form of torture and punishment, the idea being to leave the victim suspended this way until their own body weight dislocated their shoulders. The pain was said to be agonizing in the interim. Aaron felt nothing of course.

"He is still alive, Schiller," one of the two SS men was saying. "I thought you'd finished him."

The two guards were atop the gallows platform eight feet off the ground. Aaron hung from a cross beam adjacent to the platform at eye level to where the men stood. Aaron's unstaring eyes were fixed on their muddy boots. The guards had their tunics open, still damp from the rain which had ceased for the moment. They smoked and drank from brandy bottles clenched in their fists. The two guards and Aaron were the only people about in the punishment square. As explosions trembled the ground beneath them, the roar was mingled with the sounds of activity: metal doors slamming, the growl of engines, barked commands in German.

"I think I brought him to life," Schiller said, turning his head to one side and staring at Aaron. "That's the first time he's moved since we hung him."

The other guard, whose name was Faust, took a long pull on his bottle and grimaced as the liquor burned a track down his throat. "Maybe we should just finish him and get back to the others. Listen to those guns! The damn Americans are almost on top of us."

"Ah, what are you worried about," Schiller said, casually though fear lurked behind his eyes. "I've got a friend close to the Kommandant. He says we've got two, three days at least. We'll be long gone before they get here. So let's have some fun."

He pulled a leather thong from around his neck, stepped closer to Aaron and placed the thong around Aaron's neck, then proceeded to throttle him. Aaron did not react, his eyes staring through the man's chest inches away.

"Don't do that, Schiller," Faust said. "Let me get my licks in first."

Schiller grunted and stepped back, too drunk to notice the lack of reaction in Aaron. "Well, hurry up, then."

Faust carefully placed his bottle on the wood floor and came forward. With practiced grace, he began throwing punches with everything he had. Aaron swung like a pendulum. One blow dug into Aaron's midsection and Faust cried out.

"Damn, it's like hitting a tank."

"Let me try." Schiller shoved Faust aside and began beating Aaron. He lacked Faust's trained motion but he was the larger of the two and his fists smacked wetly against Aaron's flesh. "You're right," he said, pausing to catch his breath. "What's this Jew made of?" He felt Aaron's left side, where the truck had gone over, give a little under his hand. "Feels like a couple of ribs have gone." He threw some jabs into the area, then lost his balance, toppled off the platform and fell into the mud. This brought a laugh from Faust who then tried the same spot on Aaron his sprawled companion had showed him.

Schiller and Faust beat him another hour or so, switching to clubs when their fists grew sore. Bottles finally empty, they spat and urinated on him then staggered off in the direction of the engine noises.

Aaron swung, unmoving and alone. The wind picked up, drying his bare chest and rippling the waters in the mud hollows. The sun was setting and a thick bank of clouds was overtaking it, extinguishing the light prematurely. Aaron's arc grew smaller and smaller as time passed and he came to a stop, turned slightly by the wind.

When a deep, shadowless twilight had settled over the square, footsteps approached from beneath the gallows platform. The figure emerged and stood looking up at Aaron. He saw Aaron's chest rise and fall, saw him blink.

"I do not believe it." It was Pietor Chekunov's voice. "After two days, you still live." He stared up at Aaron a moment longer until a memory made him drop his gaze. "I do not have your courage." He slid a long knife from his sleeve and showed it to Aaron. "I came to kill you. If I found you still alive, and I hoped not to find you so. For mercy's sake. Krueger told me many times that there was no place for soft feelings in camp. And he is right. Or partially so. 'The prisoner's worst enemy is the prisoner.' Remember? Look out for one's self. Use anything and anyone to survive."

He returned the knife to his sleeve. "Yet here I am taking a terrible risk to do something for a fellow prisoner, a comrade. And the irony is my courage has brought me this far and I can go no farther."

He strained to see Aaron's face in the deepening gloom and his eyes softened. "You must be in terrible pain. Terrible." His body trembled as he fought against his fear, then he stepped forward. "I must!"

Desperately he climbed up the stairs to the gallows and went to stand beside Aaron. He pulled the knife from his sleeve and stabbed it into Aaron's midsection to the hilt. "Forgive me," he said. He'd closed his eyes as he thrust, but now that the deed was done, he opened them and stared into Aaron's eyes. His brow furrowed as there was no reaction. Frightened, Pietor let go of the knife and stepped back. Aaron swayed gently, the knife protruding from his stomach. There was no blood, no spasms of pain. Pietor saw his comrade's eyes open, staring past him.

"This cannot be," he said. Gingerly he eased closer to Aaron. With an uneasy hand he withdrew the knife and threw it away as though it were hot to the touch. He peered at the wound, which was slowly sealing before his eyes. "Can it be true? John told me about you the night before he was killed on the hill. I did not believe it. When I saw you seize the truck as if it were a hay bale, I did not want to believe. When it rolled over you and you were not crushed, I did not want to believe. Now, what choice have I?" He moved back and ran a hand over his features, considering the irrefutable evidence in front of him. "John said your presence here was a sign that we had not been forgotten, that our cause was just and right. John -- "

Pietor bowed his head and sobbed. Tears fell from his cheeks and splashed in the puddles at his feet. "I stood there and watched him die. As I had done for so many others here in this place. Only this time it was different. Before I could remain where I was, not lift a finger, because I was relieved it was someone else dying and not me. No, that is only partially true. I stayed where I was because I was certain nothing mattered. To live or die. Myself or another. What difference did it make? Yet, when I watched John with the truck, I wished it was me in his place. And I wanted to come forward as you and Liebman did. But I was afraid. I couldn't move. And it was not because I did not want to lay down my life. I was paralyzed because I was terrified that he might be right. Terrified that if a deliverer had been sent to us, that there were things worth dying for, then a life spent convinced there was nothing greater in the world than what you could wrest from the hands of others would be the lie. If I went to John on that hill, his truth would reveal itself to me and my existence would be meaningless. And I ran away in the confusion."

He pawed at his eyes and looked again at Aaron. "These last two days I have thought about my cowardice while everything John fought to build teetered on the brink."

Pietor's words reached Aaron as though from a great distance. Each one shot an image through his fractured awareness: John, kill, courage, Liebman, deliverer, truth and so on, each carrying a prompt guiding the data shooting through his mind. The gallows reminded him of the first day, when he watched the woman being hanged. The image replayed in his thoughts as the word prompts flashed.

"Revenge," he whispered.

Pietor consumed with self-loathing did not hear him. "I would destroy the world right now if I could!" He raised his fists, clenched so tight his arms shook. "Rage! At myself. At Krueger and the SS who murder us. Even at John for revealing to me that which I could not bear to see. And you!" He reached out and seized Aaron by the shoulder. "Deliverer. Truth to my lie. You have opened a dam in me and I cannot stop what is pouring out."

"Revenge," Aaron whispered again caught in a prompt loop.

"You speak?" Pietor leaned closer, their heads inches apart.

"Revenge."

Pietor's eyes opened wide at hearing the spoken word. He released Aaron and looked down at his balled fists. "Yes!" He ground his fists together. The desperate need to obliterate not only himself but the witnesses to his wasted life consumed him. "Yes! I will destroy this world. Tonight! I will be the spark to the fuse."

He ran down the gallows steps and stood beneath Aaron. He placed his hands on Aaron's feet dangling before his face. "Listen for it. Soon you will hear it. Everything consumed."

He turned and walked away, tall and straight, no longer using the gallows for cover. He stopped and turned.

"Listen for it," he said. "Listen."

CHAPTER TWENTY-TWO

INPUT

MISSION PARAMETERS:

1. *Infiltrate camp*
2. *Observe/Follow Routine*
3. *Secure the target*
4. *Protect the target*
5. *Liberate the target*

(Revenge)

SUB-HEADINGS

1. *Camp Gutundbose, 48°9'0", 11°34'59"*

(The prisoner's worst enemy is the prisoner)

2. *(a) Pietor Chekunov*

-right hand SCI Hans Krueger

-Revolt leader

   (b) John Siderman

-associate target Solomon Liebman

(Target Terminated)

3. *Doctor Solomon Liebman DOB 3/22/97 Berlin, Germany*

-Spouse: Elizabeth Liebman DOB 11/22/10 Berlin, Germany

4. *(a) Allied Chekunov/ Krueger*   *(b) Augmented ration*

   (c) Maintained health of target

(Target Terminated)

(Target Terminated)

(Target Terminated)

   (d) Secured target admittance

   (e) Arranged soft labor

   (f) Passed selection

   (g) --

(Target Terminated)

5. Liberation 361st Battalion

- 133 days from entry

-CURRENT ETA 1 hr, 9 min, 51 sec

(The prisoner's worst enemy --

9. (a) Red Cross Station Alpha

-Treat target health

-Doctor Solomon Liebman

-First med evac

-destination Munich

-Transport to Ivory Coast

(Revenge)

-Port Coast

-Transport England

-Transfer New York Harbor, USA

SUMMARY (1)

4. Protect target

2. Observe...

1. Infiltrate --

2. Observe/ Follow routine

5. Liberate target

ERROR

RECONFIGURE

2. Observe --

1. Infiltrate target

5. --

5.

5.

5. Revenge --

ERROR

RECONFIGURE
1. Terminate
ERROR
RECONFIGURE
5. Terminate target
-Target Terminated
2. Observe/ Follow routine
4. Revenge the target
5. Liberate --
ERROR
RECONFIGURE
RECONFIGURE
RE-
Observe worst prisoner's prisoner *Infiltrate* enemy target
ERROR
RECONFIGURE
RE-
(Revenge)
RE-
(-venge)
SUMMARY (2)
1. Infiltrate Camp
ACCOMPLISHED
2. Observe/ Follow routine
ACCOMPLISHED
3. Secure the target
ACCOMPLISHED
4. Protect the target
ACCOMPLISHED
-Target Terminated
(?)
*4. Protect **(Revenge)** Target*
-Target Terminated
ERROR
RE-
(- venge)

ERROR
SUMMARY (3)
4. Protect the target
-Target terminated
ACCOMPLISHED
-Target terminated
ACCOMPLISHED
ACC-
Terminate
(Revenge)
4. ***Revenge*** *the target*
-Terminate -
ERROR
RE-
(- venge)
4. ***RE-*** *venge -*
4. ***REvenge***
ACC-
-Target terminated
A-
(Terminated)
A-
(Terminated)
A-
(- venge)
4. ***A-venge*** *the target*
ACCOMPLISHED
(?)
ERROR
RECONFIGURE
SUMMARY (4)
1. Infiltrate the camp: ACCOMPLISHED
2. Observe/ Follow Routine: ACCOMPLISHED
3. Secure the target: ACCOMPLISHED
4. Avenge the target: PENDING
5. Liberate the target: PENDING

361st: CURRENT ETA 1 hour, 3 minutes, 12 seconds
(The prisoner's worst enemy is the prisoner)
PRISONERS:
1. Solomon Liebman: TERMINATED
2. John Siderman : TERMINATED
3. Hans Krueger: SCI
4. Pietor Chekunov: Revolt Leader
(The prisoner's worst enemy is the prisoner)
VIABLE TARGETS(?)
Hans Krueger/Pietor Chekunov
TARGET - *Doctor Solomon Liebman:* TERMINATED
4. *Avenge the target:* PENDING
361st CURRENT ETA 1 hour, 1 minute, 1 second
SUMMARY (5)
4. *Avenge* the target:

IMMEDIATE IMPLEMENTATION

FINAL

Faust and Schiller returned just before dawn. They'd been up all night drinking as had most of the SS still in camp. Bonfires raged all over as files and records were destroyed. Others were loaded on trucks for the coming evacuation, which would begin at first light. As the rain thundered down once more in the early hours before dawn, there was still much activity going on in camp. Discipline and routine had been consigned to the flames. Prisoners and SS moved about, both hoping to achieve the same objective though by different means.

Faust and Schiller stood looking up at Aaron hanging motionless in the rain. Eyes glassy and no motion in Aaron's chest led them to believe he was finally dead. Feeling cheated, Schiller jumped up and hung from Aaron's legs in the hope of yanking the prisoner's arms from their sockets. This did not happen and Schiller dangled for a moment then dropped to the ground.

"He's a tough bastard," Schiller said, giving Aaron's foot a shove.

"...a raging fireball (made) Aaron appear
to be floating free of the earth."

"I'll give him that."

"I think he's dead. Look, he's not breathing."

"Do you have shit in your ears? Listen! You can hear him mumbling."

"What's he saying?"

Schiller grabbed hold of Faust and jerked him forward so they both stood directly under Aaron. "Listen for yourself."

Faust cocked his head drunkenly to one side to hear over the roar of the rain and distant explosions.

"One - Accomplished," Aaron whispered. "Two - Accomplished. Three- Accomplished. Four - Pending. Four - Immediate Implementation. Final!"

As Schiller and Faust turned to look stupidly at each other, Aaron was suddenly moving. Startled they stepped back and stared up at the prisoner. Aaron's arms, extended rigidly behind him at an unnatural angle, tensed, and his body rose as he pulled down with his shoulders.

"There's still some fight in him!" Schiller shouted, triumphantly. "Now we'll have our fun. Grab hold!"

They each grabbed hold of Aaron's legs and bounced, waiting for the wet pop of the prisoner's shoulders dislocating. Instead they were raised upwards as Aaron's arms continued in their downward arc until his fists were beneath his buttocks.

Stunned by this inhuman display of strength, the two guards let go and fell sprawling, staring up at Aaron in mute horror. They heard a wet, shredding sound and saw, for a fraction of a second, Aaron's arms extended out at his sides, strands of rope hanging from his wrists. At that same instant the SS divisional replacement depot went up in a raging fireball behind Aaron making him appear to be floating free of the earth.

Schiller and Faust turned to flee, slipping and sliding in the thick mud. They heard Aaron's boots plunge into the mud behind them and froze. Faust cowered, but Schiller, brave with brandy, turned to confront the prisoner.

What he saw when he swung his head around were the tips of the prisoner's fingers lancing towards him as Aaron extended his arm, the hand flat like the tip of a spear. The fingers struck Schiller in the forehead with such force that they broke the skin, shattered his skull and burrowed deep into his brain. He twitched and flopped at the end of Aaron's arm, his blood mixing with the rain.

Faust screamed in terror, got his feet under him and tried to run. Aaron wanted to give chase but he was hindered by Schiller's corpse entrapping his hand. With his free hand, he tore the metal canteen from Schiller's belt and with deadly accuracy launched it at the back of Faust's head. It hit dead center with a hollow thud. The impact propelled Faust forward, but it had also caved in the man's skull and his lifeless body slid face down in the mud.

Aaron freed his hand from Schiller's corpse and surveyed the scene. Gunfire from the left indicated that the prisoners had recovered their weapons. Chaotic shouts coming from the direction of the SS barracks told him there was time to fulfill his mission objective before organized opposition stood in his way. He would find Krueger. The SCI had been the one who had set up John's and ultimately TARGET: SOLOMON LIEBMAN'S murders.

A second explosion ripped through the camp. The pop and hiss of gunfire increased all around him and Aaron saw shadowed figures running in all directions.

This time the nearest guard tower had been hit and it burned lustily. Aaron detected the sickly sweet odor of burning human flesh as strode past the inferno and it called up his data of the time he spent in the Sonderkommando.

He made his way up the main road, sure-footed on the slick tombstones. Trucks roared out of the main gate up ahead, the SS standing in the back covering their escape with bursts of machine gun fire. Some fled on foot, unarmed and desperate for the dark embrace of the forest.

Aaron met no opposition as he passed through the open gate and continued along the wire towards Krueger's quarters. The odd bullet whined past him, one grazed his forearm just above the wrist as his arm swung out. The shouts waxed and waned in the darkness, one minute seeming right next to him, the other as if coming from deep inside the camp.

The rate of gunfire increased to a staccato roar as he neared his destination. Some of the SS caught by surprise had regrouped and were fighting back while their comrades made good their escape.

Two prisoners clutching rifles stood at either side of Krueger's door. They gazed into the distant fires, expecting attack to come from inside the camp and so did not see Aaron until he was almost upon them.

The man on the right spat a surprised oath and raised his rifle. Before he could aim and fire, Aaron leapt forward and smacked the weapon out of the man's hands. He seized the front of the man's tunic and thrust backwards sending the man through the stout wooden door.

The second guard watched this in shocked immobility, then swung his rifle up and fired without aiming. The bullet struck Aaron in the lower chest and he swayed back with the impact. His progress was halted for only a moment, however, and he grabbed the man's left arm, the hand of which supported the barrel of the rifle and twisted savagely. The bone snapped and the man howled. Aaron ripped the rifle from the man's hands, reversed it, and drove it through the man's midsection. The man tumbled off the porch and Aaron turned to enter Krueger's quarters.

He stepped over the body of the man he had propelled through the door and headed straight for the Senior Camp Inmate's office. But the SCI was not there. He fine-tuned his hearing and detected noise coming from the rear of the building. Voices.

Two barn-like doors made up the rear wall of the building and they were swung open. A truck had been backed in close to the opening and Krueger was handing suitcases across to men in the back of the covered truck.

Free of his burden, Krueger whirled and, unaware of Aaron's presence in the shadows, strode through the door of a small storage room between Aaron and himself. Aaron caught the look of intense concentration on the face of the massive man. The power was out and the short corridor was as black as the inside of the truck. Aaron moved forward and entered the storeroom undetected.

The room was a miniature of the enormous storerooms used for the belongings gleaned from gassed victims. Fur coats hung along one wall, the rest of the room piled high with suitcases with a narrow walkway bisecting the room.

Krueger was hunched down, spinning the tumbler of a squat, heavy safe surrounded by bulging cases. Sensing a presence, Krueger spun, gun in hand, rising to his feet all in one motion.

"So, you have come this far," Krueger observed, then fired twice into Aaron's stomach.

The bullets knocked Aaron back, destroyed a few of his subsystems but did no permanent damage. The densely packed bags served to muffle the gun's retort and the men frantically loading the truck heard nothing. Aaron did not give Krueger the chance to fire again. He swatted the gun aside and seized the SCI by the throat, forcing him back against the wall.

Krueger got over his shock of seeing Aaron unfazed by the bullets in his stomach. "So," he hissed through clenched teeth, his hands digging futilely at Aaron's fingers around his throat. "The deliverer. John was many things, but not a liar it seems."

"John Siderman is dead," Aaron said.

"Of course," Krueger said. His gaze flickered to the sounds of battle faintly audible in the close confines of the storeroom. "This is no time for fools. It is time for straight thinking and action. What are your plans?"

"A-venge the TARGET. Final! I will kill you."

"To what end?"

"A-venge the TARGET. Final!"

Krueger smiled. "Vengeance? Ah! You truly are the deliverer these fools spoke of. Whom do you avenge?"

"TARGET: Solomon Liebman."

"Him alone? And whom would you kill?"

"You are responsible."

"Only me? Did I arrest Liebman? Did I bring him here to this place? How did I place him in danger?"

Aaron's damaged logic directives slowly absorbed Krueger's queries and formulated a response. "The truck -- "

"Was for John," Krueger said quickly. "And John alone. Liebman chose to interfere. It was not my doing."

Aaron's grip slackened slightly as he processed this information. Krueger slid down the wall until his feet touched the floor.

"I have observed and recorded," Aaron said at last. "The strong rule the weak. The oppressor oppresses."

"You speak the truth," Krueger agreed, eagerly.

"This place is... unnatural. The balance has been upset. TARGET: Solomon Liebman has been terminated. Final! I must... see to those responsible."

"Yes, deliverer, yes." Krueger managed a nod. "However, you must expand your vision. Strike down the guilty. It was the SS who seized Liebman, humiliated him, brought him here to the crucible. The SS are your enemy. Not I. I am a prisoner like yourself. I was seized against my will, brought here. The same as Liebman. As you yourself came to be here."

"You... exploit. Oppress. Unnatural."

"To survive only. No different from you. As everyone does here against their will. The state imposed this environment. Survival necessitates narrow focus."

"Whatever lives, obeys."

"Precisely. Those who created these imposed conditions are our mutual enemies. If you wish to restore balance, avenge Liebman, then our mutual enemy must be destroyed."

Aaron's logic centers recorded and analyzed.

Krueger, sensing an advantage, pressed it home. "We must destroy our enemy. Take action. But not just here. Wherever the enemy resides. The imbalance is not only in this place. You must avenge the oppressed everywhere in the world."

To Aaron's damaged brain, the logic was inescapable. His mission directive was clear: avenge TARGET: Solomon Liebman. Final? His confusion stemmed from implementation. Killing Krueger seemed the immediate objective, but this was not so. The jailors were equally to blame. Those who created the environment of oppression were to blame. For the former could not exist without the latter. To avenge: TARGET: Solomon Liebman, the unnatural had to be made natural. The balance had to be restored.

"Which is stronger?" Aaron asked, data files from an earlier meeting with Krueger kept flashing through his awareness. "The will of the state, or the will of the individual?"

"This is what we will determine here tonight," Krueger replied, a predatory glint in his eyes.

Aaron's entire body went still. He retained his grip on Krueger while he processed the new data with the old and amended his mission parameters. He would destroy the camp. Destroy all those who oppress. Then, and only then could humanity live free of imposed restriction. The implementation of an unnatural environment creates unnatural behavior. Remove the imposed conditions and all can live in balance and harmony. Without warning, his body stiffened and his eyes locked on Krueger's. "Surrender to the state is contrary to human nature."

His newfound directives in place, Aaron released Krueger and turned. Krueger took an instant to inhale lustily, then pulled a small hatchet from his belt and imbedded it deep in Aaron's neck where it met the shoulder.

Blood and lubricant geysered out, staining the walls of leather suitcases rust red. Krueger tired to free the axe but could not and backed himself against the wall, steeled for battle.

Aaron, aware now that imposed conditions dictated behavior, acted accordingly. He curled his hand into a fist and drove it into Krueger's body with short, lethal piston-like jabs.

Krueger's whole body trembled with each impact, then his knees gave out and he crumpled. He sprawled at Aaron's feet, smiling up at him through bloody, broken teeth.

"Yes, deliver us from evil," he said derisively. "Free the oppressed. See what good it will do."

Aaron reached down and picked up the iron safe Krueger had been trying to open and raised it over his head.

Krueger laughed, then spat a gob of blood at Aaron's feet. "The prisoner's worst enemy -- "

"Is the prisoner," Aaron finished, then brought the safe down on Krueger's head.

CHAPTER TWENTY-THREE

Aaron left the storeroom and headed for the truck. The men were halfway out, coming to see what was holding up their lord and master. They saw Aaron and reached for sidearms. Aaron leapt into the back of the truck, gripping the two men by the throat and smashing their heads together, then dropped them and tore through the canvas covering on the driver's side.

Startled by the commotion, the driver started the engine and was fumbling with the gearshift when Aaron grabbed him by the collar and hauled him through the open window. With a sharp twist, Aaron broke the man's neck.

The dead driver had a bandolier of grenades across his chest and a second lay on the passenger seat with two .45s and a Colt revolver. Aaron took the grenades and headed for the SS quarters.

He reached the kitchen first, pulled the pins on two of the grenades, and tossed them in. The wooden structure exploded behind him. Next was the SS Infirmary. This was constructed of brick and the two grenades Aaron threw in blew out the windows and sent thick coils of black smoke up into the false dawn.

The explosions took the fight out of the SS. Pressed on one side by the erratic though determined resistance of the prisoners with explosions in the rear proved too much for them and they scattered. The prisoners let out a roar and charged forward. Some were cut down but the others pushed on. It was every man for himself now as the SS retreated to their compound where Aaron was still methodically dismantling the area, one explosion at a time.

He was almost at the Armory when he spotted Pietor Chekunov, bleeding from his left shoulder and leading a group of men armed with rifles in that direction. Well aware of the Armory's strategic importance, the SS had beaten the prisoners there and were entrenched, prepared to defend it to the last. Chekunov and his followers fired on the defenders but ammunition was scarce and they could not do any significant damage.

Aaron accessed his fragmented historical data. Despite the gaps he extrapolated that this is where Chekunov fell, killed by an SS bullet, and that a small memorial plaque had been erected on the spot in the 1960s that still stood in his time. Perhaps he could remove the need for the plaque.

With Chekunov and the others crouched behind a burning staff car, Aaron removed three grenades from the second bandolier and walked towards the Armory.

The SS saw him and began firing. Most of the shots missed, but a few found the mark, staggering him.

Chekunov peered around the dented front fender of the car and watched in awe as Aaron seemed to absorb bullets. Aaron stopped a dozen yards from the building, armed the grenades and tossed them in, then turned to face the prisoners.

The defenders, as dumbstruck as Chekunov, shouted in terror and leapt through the shot out windows. Chekunov rallied his men and they charged towards the fleeing SS. The building went up in a fireball which shook the earth beneath their feet. The running SS were thrown forward as was Aaron. Chekunov and the others were blown onto their backs. A gout of flame shot up into the sky.

Aaron was the first one to regain his feet. Chekunov's men sprawled inches away and he stood over them. They all had shrapnel wounds of varying severity from the exploded window frames. Aaron was aware of sixteen shards embedded in his back from the explosion. The others rolled around, moaning in the mud. Except Chekunov. A section of broken glass had been launched through the air by the explosion, spinning like the blade of a circular saw and had neatly sheared off the top of the resistance leader's head. Blood and gray matter ran out into the mud. His eyes were open, fixed on Aaron and his mouth worked like a fish out of water, but no sound came out. Then the eyes went glassy and the mouth fell open.

Aaron's logic centers tried to process what had happened but he could not grasp the full meaning of how Chekunov died after he had altered the means of death. Had he been human he might have believed fate had played a hand. Aaron made a record of what had happened and, with grenades in hand, turned and walked away.

For the next hour the fighting continued as Aaron systematically eradicated the camp. He found the Kommandant on the porch of his lavish quarters, dead from a self-inflicted bullet through the temple. The house was wood so he used one grenade. Next went a conference room, the motor pool, the Administration building.

The prisoners were encountering only sporadic resistance at this point. As the first rays of dawn found their harried, mud-splattered faces, the camp was theirs. Most had looted food from the SS barracks prior to Aaron's destruction of the buildings and wolfed it down as they ran in all directions in search of the enemy. Others, the last of their strength gone, collapsed, breathing their first lungfuls of air as free men from their backs on the cold, wet mud.

Fires raged everywhere. Only the prisoner barracks were still standing. Even the crematorium was a burning pile of rubble. The surviving SS fled into the forest while feeble shouts sounded here and there.

Aaron, his grenades used up, left the celebrating prisoners struggling to comprehend the finality of what they had achieved, still unable to believe, after so many years of torture, that they were free. Aaron knew that one more surprise awaited them. Or thought he did. Chekunov's death, despite Aaron's direct, deliberate action to alter the past, still had him confused. He required further data if he was going to carry out his mission. If his historical records of the coming months and years could no longer be relied upon due to his participation in the revolt altering the timeline, how could he safely predict what lay ahead? There was only one place he could think of to get the information he needed.

Returning to the camp, past clusters of prisoners in the roll call area eating, drinking, or merely holding onto each other to keep from falling down Aaron headed for the dwelling place of the Prophet.

With everyone involved in the fighting, the Prophet's caretakers were nowhere to be seen. The Prophet sat alone, babbling his litany to an empty room.

Aaron took a seat and listened.

"... *grief dims my eyes, they are worn out with all my woes, why should the sufferer be born to see the light? prisoners of darkness, wrapped in a murky pall of smoke, the land is scorched by the fury, why is life given to those who find it so bitter? justice is far away from us, a throne shall be set up and on it there shall sit a true judge, what is a man and what use is he? you try to think the thoughts of a god, come, O wind, from every quarter and breathe into these slain, that they may come to life, who was it that inspired him with an active soul and breathed into him the breath of life, what do your evil deeds signify? your wickedness shall never be purged until you die, be gone, this is no resting place for you, it was not I who gave you life and breath and set in motion your bodily frame...*"

Aaron recalled the warning that to touch the Prophet was to learn the future. He clasped the Prophet's thin, wasted wrist and held on.

"...*have the gates of death been revealed to you? for his thought is only to destroy and to wipe out nation after nation, how fierce he is when he is aroused, he hunted and tracked down the lawless, he has shattered the yoke that burdened us, have you seen the door-keepers of the place of darkness? it makes no difference to Heaven to save by many or few, he will turn darkness into light, he has saved us from the furnace of burning flame, I will pour out my wrath upon you, I will breathe out my blazing wrath over you, have you comprehended the vast expanse of the world? these heathen men imagined they could lord it over the people, Man learns his lesson on a bed of pain, he will lay waste to mountains, he will be judge between nations, what deliverance have you brought to the world? those who suffer he rescues through suffering and teaches them by the discipline of affliction, you are sprung from nothing, your works are rotten, the idol made by human hands is accursed..."*

Aaron released the Prophet's wrist and sat back, considered what he'd heard, but could make no sense of it. Concluding the Prophet's ability to divine the future was a myth, he pulled back the covering from the door. The glow from the distant fires bathed the Prophet's face in red and ochre. Aaron stepped through the doorway, closed the door behind him, shutting out the light.

The first rays of the rising sun replaced the glow of flames as Aaron returned to the prisoner barracks. It would soon be time to leave the camp, but first he wanted to be sure he had exorcised evil from the place. He heard the roar of diesel engines in the distance.

The time for action was passed, now he would observe.

The liberators were here.

CHAPTER TWENTY-FOUR

D awn recon had gotten better with the arrival of spring, but as far as First-Lieutenant Luther Moses was concerned, it had a long way to go to beat a Saturday night at the Savoy.

The tall trees flanking the narrow road his column of M18 tanks clattered along cut the wind and the sun was warm on his broad, brown face. The leather headset he wore was added protection, the goggles on top like a second set of eyes reflecting the rising sun.

He served with the 761st Tank Battalion, the best Negro division in the United States Army. Since hitting Omaha beach in October, the Black Panther Tank Battalion had served with distinction in France, Belgium and now Germany. 146 straight days of combat in some of the worst winter weather any of the locals could remember.

As a segregated unit, the men of the 761st had had to prove themselves every step of the way as part of Patton's 3rd Army. Now every infantry division slogging through the mud wanted "Eleanor Roosevelt's Niggers" running support. Currently they were supporting the 71st infantry after serving with the 103rd with whom they'd had the honor of being one of the first units through Germany's impregnable Siegfried Line. Not that anyone back home knew of this accomplishment. The reporters from Stars and Stripes had flat-out ignored the 761st by the time the scribblers had caught up to the advance. This was nothing new to Moses. Alabama born and raised, racism was a way of life. Why he thought the Army would be any different, he didn't know. From Camp Hood, Texas to Camp Claiborne, Louisiana, it had been the same old, same old. It was only when the bullets started flying that everyone went color blind.

Moses scanned the area and gave instructions to his driver. The road forked up ahead, but from his vantage point, he'd seen thin wisps of smoke rising from the left. The sound of gunfire an hour before had drawn their attention to this area. There was nothing on any of the maps, except some town called Jenseits and the Air Force had pounded it good. Moses knew that dense forest bounced sounds around so the shots they'd heard could have been coming from anywhere.

When the tank rounded the corner and Moses gazed out at the open field spreading before him, he was sure they were chasing an echo. Then through a break in the timberline he saw the tendrils of smoke again, rising up the road and, as they drew closer, spotted a high fence stretching off on either side of the road and a big gate dead ahead with wrought iron writing over it. Pointed roofs poked out of the tree cover.

Moses ordered a halt and the tank behind him slewed to a stop on the train tracks, motors growling.

In the relative quiet, he detected faint, distant voices and the crackle of flames. Well, he concluded, that barb wire gate was protecting something. Better have a look.

He grabbed the mike on his chest and spoke to the driver. "Knock that gate down. Let's see what's what."

The gate sent up little geysers of mud as Moses's tank rammed it down. The soldiers hitching a ride behind the turrets tensed, the barrels of their carbines bristling out from the body of the tank, aimed at the surrounding forest. Moses had the tanks reduce speed and some of the soldiers dropped off to slog along behind.

There was a clearing up ahead, the roofs he had seen earlier now clearly visible through the clouds of smoke sailing past. The crackle of burning wood could be heard all around but the smell was unlike anything they'd experienced.

Then they were through the smoke and the camp stretched out before them.

The tanks ground to a halt in the roll call area. Moses stared open-mouthed at the emaciated prisoners sprawled in the compound. They didn't look human and he was reminded of the skeleton in Doc Gardner's office back home.

The infantry fanned out from behind the tanks. Rifles dangling limply in their hands, the black soldiers glanced around, their eyes wide and staring. Sweat ran down from their close-cropped hair. The few who had remained seated behind the turrets stood up, mouths open.

"Looks like the land of the living dead," one of the men behind Moses said. "What is this place?"

Moses, somewhat recovered from the initial shock, ordered the tanks forward until they were in the center of the roll call area. The men spread out, unsure how to approach the clusters of living and dead around them. The fires were almost exhausted and the wind had picked up, shifting most of the smoke from their position.

One of the men had exchanged a word or two with a prisoner who lay on the ground, too weak to stand. He put a comforting hand on the prisoner's arm, then rushed over to Moses. "They say this is a concentration camp."

The words sent a cold shiver down Moses' spine. They'd heard rumors but no one had believed them. Just propaganda, they'd all thought.

By this time many of the soldiers were shuffling past mounds of corpses and clusters of the dying. Some were sick to their stomachs, most just looked around in shocked disbelief, tears running down their cheeks.

Moses climbed down, his gut heaving from the stench.

Three prisoners with rifles pointed at the ground approached tentatively. An armed group stood some distance away, watching the others draw near.

"You American?" one of the prisoners asked in broken English.

"Yeah," Moses whispered, his eyes sliding over the scene around him. He shook his head and focused on the man. "Yeah," he said again, more forcefully this time. "We're Americans."

The shoulders of the three wretched prisoners shifted as if an invisible weight had fallen off. Their eyes filled with tears and they dropped their weapons. One came forward, embraced Moses and kissed him. Moses put a hand on the bony back, felt the vertebrae sharply defined through the soiled, torn shirt and could no longer contain his emotions.

Tears spilling from his large, almond-shaped eyes, he said, "We're here to help. It'll be all right now."

The prisoners and soldiers began mixing freely. Most of the infantry carried food on their backs because food kitchens couldn't keep up with their advance. They began passing the rations out to the prisoners who, sobbing, could do little else but wrap their harried minds around the fact that the liberators had come.

Swiping at his eyes, Moses climbed back up to the turret and asked for the hand radio. He cleared his throat and paused before speaking. "Recon to base," he said. "All clear. No sign of the enemy."

He moved the mike away from his mouth and fought back another wave of emotion.

"It's worse than Tillet," a man said, referring to the counter action they'd been in during the Battle of the Bulge in Belgium where piles of dead soldiers lay festering by the side of the road on the way to the town of Tillet.

Moses squared his shoulders. They were still fighting men, dammit. "We need medics here, ASAP. Lots of wounded here." He bit his lips as tears sprang once again from his eyes. He gazed up at the blue sky, until his vision cleared. "My Lord... a lot of wounded."

The next seventy-two hours dragged by despite the incredible amount of work that needed to be done. The rest of the 761st went through the same period of horror and revulsion as they entered the camp, but quickly regained their composure and got to work. Makeshift hospitals were set up for the most in need of medical attention. This proved futile when the medical staff came to realize that every prisoner required medical attention and began administering first aid wherever a patient lay, with only the most serious being carried to the hospital. Diphtheria and Typhus went along with the acute malnutrition, open sores, rashes, dehydration and infections all the prisoners suffered from to various degrees and the supply of medicine dwindled far too quickly. The last of the fires were extinguished and the gristly task of filling mass graves was begun at once to prevent the spread of disease.

Prisoners strong enough to be of use did what they could. An international camp committee with sub-committees for the various nationality groups was formed to cooperate with the 761st in running the camp.

Armed patrols went into the woods upon learning that the SS had fled there and might still be hiding. They discovered a farm close by and asked if they could bring food to the camp. When the farmer declared he would rather let his crops rot than give them to sub-humans, one of the soldiers broke the man's teeth in with a rifle butt, then they began loading wagons. The soldiers involved drew some flack for this action, but when the prisoners told them that the ashes from the crematorium had been sold as fertilizer to this farmer for years, the matter was dropped.

There was no end to the relief effort and the work continued into the night before the camp settled into eerie stillness. With no running water or electricity, broken windows from the revolt, doors slamming in the wind and iron sheets from the roofs screeching and clouds of ash, the camp resembled a ghost town. The prisoners had been issued candles from the SS stores and the lights winked like so many stars in the darkness. While the disposal of bodies continued, the camp received word that Canadians had taken Jenseits and the main body of the US 3rd was pressing forward.

Aaron watched and recorded all as conditions slowly improved. He'd observed the arrival of the Americans closely, but they were no threat though his attack sub-routines remained active. The damage to his mainframe logic pathways was extensive and he had trouble speaking and suffered as well from thought-chain progression disruption.

The Americans had marshaled their emotions and set themselves to providing whatever aid the prisoners required. Also, they had marched the surviving townspeople of Jenseits through the camp to bear witness to the horrific crimes their government had committed.

The functional logic centers in Aaron's mind approved of this, confident it would act as a deterrent once the liberators had left. It seemed evident to him that, aside from the few SS hiding out in the forest, evil had been removed from the camp. Many of the guards had been caught and incarcerated, awaiting trial. A camp rumor held that some of the SS, after more than three days with nothing to eat, had come back to the camp, exchanged their uniforms for prison garb in the hope of blending in as prisoners and gaining access to the food and medicine.

For this reason, Aaron restricted his movements, observing the liberation from a distance. He had not been examined by the medics and avoided the Jewish Camp completely since that was where the majority of urgent cases lay. He had no need for rations or drinking water so these places were easily skirted. But the Americans were going over the few surviving camp records, attempting to compile a list of inmates for the Red Cross and he didn't know how much longer he could remain to ensure his work in camp was complete. Especially since he was unable to completely mimic the wasted appearance of his fellow prisoners and might be mistaken for one of the masquerading SS by the Americans.

The morning of the fourth day the Americans advised the prisoner committee that they'd apprehended three SS guards in the process of stripping corpses of their camp uniform and that two others had already infiltrated the prisoner population. Eventually the news trickled down until everyone knew to be on the lookout for the two men. If spotted, the prisoners were to inform the first US soldier they could find to come and take possession of the man. This last part was stressed, re-enforced by promises of trial and punishment if the SS man was convicted.

Aaron found no fault with these measures and kept his eyes open, recording each face he saw and comparing it to his partial records. At the same time, he was aware that it was time for him to leave. He risked detection with every passing hour and his repair/recovery directives had done everything possible to restore him to limited operating efficiency. Also, his presence was no longer required. The Americans had things well in hand. The prisoners were free. The camp had been consumed by fire. The guilty SS were either dead or being rounded up for trial and word had it that the Canadians in Jenseits were doing the same. His mission objectives had been accomplished. The people could live in peace now that the evil had been exorcised.

He set about covertly gathering some meager provisions so he could look authentic if stopped on the road. A bit of food, a canteen and walking stick and a set of green coveralls to replace the camp uniform were all he needed. As was the need for caution. The US had implemented a barrack-to-barrack search for the SS guards. Everyone was wary. Aaron could not slink away without drawing unwanted attention to himself. Better to wait until the hiding men were caught. Still, he wanted to stay out of sight.

The Jewish Camp was the most densely populated right then due to its proximity to the hospital though it was more of a Babel of different nationalities and religions. The SS distinctions between prisoners were used now out of habit rather than ideology. He could lose himself amongst the throng there, then slip away when the crisis was over.

It was his first time back in the Jewish Camp since the incident with the truck. He recognized several faces as he moved through the crowds, but so many of John's followers had been killed during the revolt that a familiar face was a rare occurrence. Those who did recognize him seemed eager to speak to him, perhaps out of genuine surprise that he was still alive. He was careful to elude them before they could catch up. He had no time for explanations. An entire world required liberation and he was set on beginning this new mission.

Aaron saw a group of prisoners making their way towards one of the barracks. They seemed intent, moving with quick short steps through the others. It was a fairly large group and they were doing everything in their power to avoid attention. Aaron saw an opportunity to get away from the men who recognized him. He joined the group, which was so focused on where they were going, they did not notice him.

As things turned out, the group actually entered the barracks with an American detail on their heels. Aaron quickly slipped into the shadows at the far end of the barracks where a large group of men huddled around the tier of bunks there.

"We're looking for those Nazi skunks," a tall sergeant spoke, his wide shoulders filling the doorway. An interpreter stood just inside the door. "Anybody here knows anything, speak up. We'll see the krauts get what they've got coming."

A few of the men near Aaron gave him anxious looks and he thought they might turn him in but his shorn head, just starting to bristle, convinced them that he was one of them. His method of avoiding suspicion if taken into custody was to play Muselmann, avoiding any and all questions until they were satisfied he was not SS and sent him to the hospital. This scenario meant further delay, but there was no other course of action if he were turned over. However the men darting glances his way did not speak up. Even as the Americans quickly searched the barracks, passing within five feet of them, they remained silent.

"All clear here, suh," a corporal called out to the sergeant in a heavy southern drawl. His words were echoed by the rest of the search party.

The sergeant called his men to him and they filed out. The sergeant turned in the doorway. "You see them krauts you sing out, hear?"

When the Americans were gone, all the prisoners began speaking at once. Aaron's translator function could not even begin to isolate the twenty different languages.

The group around him were visibly relieved when the Americans were gone, directing smiles at Aaron for some reason he did not understand. Their relieved looks became instantly savage and sneering as they turned their attention to the bunk they were clustered over.

Aaron had been prepared to begin his Muselmann routine when he realized that the attention of the men was focused solely on the bunk against the wall beside him. The men who had been crouching on the bunk stepped off and joined the group, easing Aaron out of the way and staring down at the bunk.

Aaron craned his neck for a look. It was a man -- bound, bloodied, a wad of filthy shirt wedged in his mouth. A quick scan of the man's overall appearance convinced Aaron that the man was far too healthy to be a prisoner. Here was one of the SS guards the US soldiers had been searching for. Why had the prisoners concealed him from the Americans?

"You didn't think we were going to let them have you," one of the prisoners addressed the bound man. "Scum like you don't deserve a trial." He lashed out with his fist and struck the guard squarely in the face. Blood poured out of the man's nose, soaking the gag.

The guard's wide, frightened eyes darted around at the cluster of men, looking for sympathy and finding none. The group moved en masse and dragged the man to the floor and proceeded to viciously kick and stomp at him. Face, groin, fingers, kneecaps, these they crushed mercilessly while the man writhed like a worm on a hook.

At one point the gag came loose but the man was near death and unable to speak above a whisper. Sobbing past swollen lips and broken teeth he said, "Heimweh." Over and over he repeated that one word until a blow to the temple knocked him unconscious. The prisoners continued to beat his broken body long after he was dead, until what was left no longer looked human.

Aaron watched the scene with a puzzled look on his face, then suddenly pushed through the crowd and headed for the door.

CHAPTER TWENTY-FIVE

O utside Aaron moved haltingly one way then another. His higher logic centers functioned at less than optimum and it was all but impossible to reconcile the conflicting data.

The evil had been expunged, the balance restored. There was no longer a need for violence in camp. And yet the prisoners had reacted with extreme violence. The two facts were irreconcilable. To his limited reasoning capacity, the oppressed could not become the oppressors once the yoke of oppression had been removed. The camp had been liberated. The basic needs of the men were being met. The oppressors had been driven off. Balance. Good over evil. Good must triumph over evil.

Aaron turned all his limited cognitive power to this dilemma. There had to be a logical solution. Good had triumphed over evil, the oppressor had been removed from the equation. The men should be at peace. But the extreme violence was incontrovertible. He had witnessed it, seen it with his own eyes. It was reality and therefore could not be rationalized away. All this left was the validity of his first directive: that the balance be restored so that men could live in peace. This was supposition, the violent attack was fact. Thus the fault must lay in the supposition. It had to be faulty.

Proceeding from this conclusion, a two-pronged conclusion

resulted:

1. Balance had not been restored.

2. Men could not live in peace.

Conclusion One could be verified as the necessary requirements had been met: Freedom from oppression, physical needs satisfied, freedom of body. These constituted balance. His records showed that Conclusion one had to be valid.

This called Conclusion Two into question. If Conclusion One had been verified and error occurred, then Conclusion Two had to be valid. Therefore, if men could not live in peace, then his mission objective was no longer relevant. With TARGET: Solomon Liebman terminated and Conclusion Two/Objective Two unattainable, then his mission in this time was over. Knowing he would require seclusion for what had to be done next, he headed for the clump of trees hiding the Prophet.

The ground was still muddy between the trunks of the saplings since the sun had not penetrated through the fresh canopy of leaves. Aaron kept his footing as he moved deeper into the copse to a clump of rose bushes. When he'd determined he'd gone far enough, he stopped and listened. Birds sang, an insect droned past, the sounds of the camp were distant behind him.

An instant before he gave the command, something seemed to pass over his features as if a new thought was imprinting itself.

"Heimweh," he said aloud and sent the auto-destruct command.

His body imploded with a muffled crump and Aaron fell as if his legs had been cut from under him. For all intents and purposes dead, his limbs continued to twitch as redundant charges made sure his inner mechanisms became a fused mass of useless slag. After several seconds of these contortions, Aaron lay unmoving, one arm bent at the elbow, a twisted claw pointing at the new green leaves.

The wildlife, momentarily startled by the explosions, gradually resumed their noise. But a new sound made them fearfully quiet once more. Staggered footsteps sloughed through the mud, coming closer.

A man appeared leaning heavily on a makeshift crutch made from a broom. This was snug under his left arm which was in a crude cast like the one on his left leg. He could not manipulate the crutch with his left hand and had to use the right to slide the crutch forward before taking a step.

He came and stood over Aaron's body, gazed into the staring, lifeless eyes of his one-time benefactor.

"I thought it was you," Solomon Liebman said. "I couldn't believe my eyes at first."

His good knee wobbled so he lowered himself into a sitting position beside Aaron's body.

"They told me no one else had survived the hill. I was sure they were wrong. They didn't know what I knew." He ran a hand over his shaved scalp just starting to bristle with new growth. "Dear Lord, if a machine cannot survive this place, what hope do any of us have?" He chuckled. "Then again, you destroyed yourself, didn't you? Perhaps that makes you human after all. More human than you could possibly imagine."

He reached out and took Aaron's extended claw in his own hand. Liebman was shocked to discover he had tears in his eyes.

"What was that you said at the end?" he asked, covering Aaron's hand in both of his. "Heimweh."

It was German, loosely translated as 'longing for one's home.'

"Can any of us have a home after this place?" Liebman resumed. "Can we ever get back to it if it does still exist?" He patted Aaron's hand and released it. He staggered to his feet and stood over the body once more. "Well, old friend. You're home. May we all get there someday."

Liebman stared down at Aaron's body, his brow furrowed. "You saved my life. You saved many lives if what I've heard is true. I begged you to rise up but you wouldn't. The timeline, you said. I wonder what changed your mind? As for your precious timeline, I pray to God it has been changed. For the better. By your hand or anyone else's, I pray it has been changed for the better. But, just in case dear benefactor, I shall do something for you. I owe you that much."

Thirty minutes later, he was just patting the last wad of mud in place when he heard the voices coming from the camp.

"I'm telling ya I saw two of them scarecrows go in there and nobody's come out in all this time. Could be the krauts we're looking for."

"All right," a second voice agreed. "But hold up. Let me get a detail together. Be right back."

Liebman got up and shuffled away from the grave. He wanted to put as much distance between it and him before they found him. He managed about ten yards before his knee gave out and he sprawled heavily in the mud. Turning over onto his back, he examined his handiwork. A hollowed-out, rotten log curving out of the thick mud had been the perfect spot and he'd shoved Aaron's body under it. Using the flat end of his crutch, he'd deepened the area beneath the log enough to lay the body out flat. Then he'd covered the body with mud from the furrows piled around the log and scattered dead leaves and twigs over the mound. From where he lay, it was all but impossible to spot the grave unless one knew where to look.

"They went this way." The voices had returned.

"Easy now. They may be armed."

Liebman took one last look at the grave, then threw his head back and shouted, "Over here! Over here!"

The copse went quiet. "You hear that?" one of the soldiers whispered.

Liebman shouted again and heard the sound of men crashing through the trees. They entered the clearing and gathered around Liebman lying helpless at their feet. He looked up at them with expectant eyes. They holstered their weapons and bent to help him up.

"What you doing out here?" a soldier asked, easing Liebman's shoulders out of the mud. "You'll catch your death in this slop."

"Maybe he's cracked," another solider observed, a wide, doughy man swathed in the last of his baby fat combat hadn't burned away.

"We're all nuts in this loony bin," the first soldier said and he helped Liebman to sit up.

The rest of the men were glancing around casually. Liebman didn't want to take any chances. They'd seen two men go in and two had to come out.

"Up ahead," he said, his English impeccable. "The Prophet."

"Who's a prophet?" One of the soldiers turned.

"Up there." Liebman gestured with his good hand. "The Prophet. I wanted to make sure he was all right."

"You are nuts," the man at his elbow said. "Let's get him back to camp."

"Hold up," the doughy one said. "I see something past them trees."

Four of the men raced ahead. There was a moment of crashing noise, then a call came back. "We got another here. Alive to boot!"

"Well, bring him in," the doughy one called. "We'll get this one back."

Liebman hid his relief though a contented smile softened his features. The birds resumed singing and the sun came down through the thin gaps in the canopy, throwing weak shafts of light over the wet mud. "All right, friends," he said. "Take me home."

EPILOGUE

The men buried their noses in the collars of their undershirts and entered the Prophet's hovel.

"Sweet Jesus!" their leader said as they all stared at the sight before them.

The Prophet stank of his own waste and was leaning over so far that, as he continued to sway back and forth, his forehead brushed the mound supporting him.

"What's he saying?" another said, stepping closer. "Maybe he's hurt."

"*...tell me all this if you know, which is the way to the home of the light, and where does darkness dwell...*"

"What lingo is that? Can't understand a word."

"*...evil had come though I expected good, I looked for the light but there came only darkness...*"

"Does it matter? Let's just get him out of here before we pass out from the smell."

"I hear you, brother."

They considered how best to go about removing the Prophet with all the rags and pillows piled around him.

"*...mourn less bitterly for the dead for he is at rest...*"

It was decided they clear away the pillows in front so as not to risk losing their balance when they carted him out. This was done as quickly as possible until finally the way was clear. They pawed at their sweaty black faces and gathered around the Prophet.

"Who wants to do the lifting and toting?"

"Couldn't we fetch a stretcher or something?"

"*...surely you have heard what Kings have done to all countries, exterminating their people, no fire great had force enough to give them light, nor had the flaming stars strength to illuminate that hideous darkness, however there shone on them a blaze of no man's making...*"

"... man's fate is sealed..."

"Look, let's stop dicking around here and get him out. It's hot as hell in here and I'm gonna die if I don't get some fresh air. Come on, now, enough's enough. I want out of this place. I want out of this whole goddamn war for that matter. Let's just get it done."

The men moved forward, two on a side and gently slid their arms under the Prophet's shoulders and behind his knees and raised him up. The sergeant couldn't keep the door open so with a savage twist, he pulled it off its hinges and threw it into the bush.

The fresh air seemed to revive the Prophet and his voice grew in intensity as they carried him through the forest back to camp.

"...for the breath in our nostrils is but a wisp of smoke, our reason is a mere spark kept alive by the beating of our hearts, and when that goes out, our bodies will turn to ashes, our names will be forgotten with the passing of time, and no one will remember anything we did, a passing shadow -- such is our life, and there is no postponement of our end, man's fate is sealed, and none return..."

THE END

Author Bio

Ellis Award nominee **ANDREW SALMON** lives and writes in Vancouver, BC. His work has appeared in numerous magazines including *Storyteller, Parsec, TBT* and *Thirteen Stories.* He also writes reviews for *The Comicshopper* and is creating a superhero serial currently running in *A Thousand Faces.*

He has published two books to date: **The Forty Club** (which Midwest Book Reviews calls *"A good solid little tale you will definitely carry with you for the rest of your life"*) and **The Dark Land** *("a straight out science-fiction detective thriller that fires on all cylinders"* -- Pulp Fiction Reviews). **The Dark Land** is the first of a series.

THE LIGHT OF MEN is his first work for Airship 27/Cornerstone and his work will appear in the upcoming all-new Jim Anthony collection, Volume 1 of the re-issued and re-edited Secret Agent X series and the new Mars McCoy adventures. He is also co-writing the Ghost Squad with Ron Fortier for the line. He is set to release **Wandering Webber**, his first children's book, in the spring. To learn more about his work check out the Airship 27/Cornerstone store and the following links: www.Lulu.com/thousand-faces and www.LuLu.com/AndrewSalmon

ABOUT THE ARTIST

Beginning in 1986 illustrating role-playing game modules and rule books Rob Davis has been a working professional artist/illustrator. Covering a wide range of genre works in comics and illustration Rob has depicted Fantasy and Science Fiction characters from **Merlin** to **Captain Kirk** at a variety of companies from **DC** to **Marvel** and **Malibu Comics**.

The latest projects to come from the drawing board of Rob Davis include a weekly political cartoon that can be found at Philadelphia writer Jack Curtin's website (for which Davis did some logo design work), called **thedubyachronicles.com**.

Several years ago *Dr. Satan*, a 1930's "pulp" fiction online comic strip united Rob with writer Ron Fortier beginning a string of exciting collaborations. Rob and Ron have created the Gothic Romance/Horror graphic novel entitled *The Daughter of Dracula*. Rob has worked with Ron designing and illustrating a number of prose novels and anthologies for Airship 27 and Cornerstone Book Publishers.

Rob, his wife (Theresa) and two young children (Rachel and Ryan) live in Central Missouri near Columbia, home of the University of Missouri just two hours' drive from either Kansas City or St. Louis, Missouri.

Examples of Rob's work may be found at his online art gallery at: http://homepage.mac.com/robmdavis/

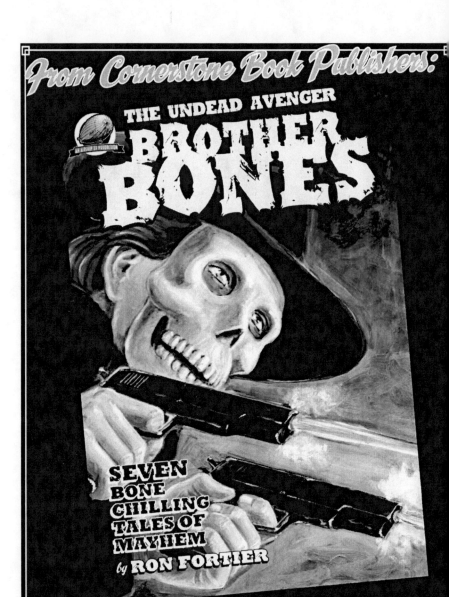

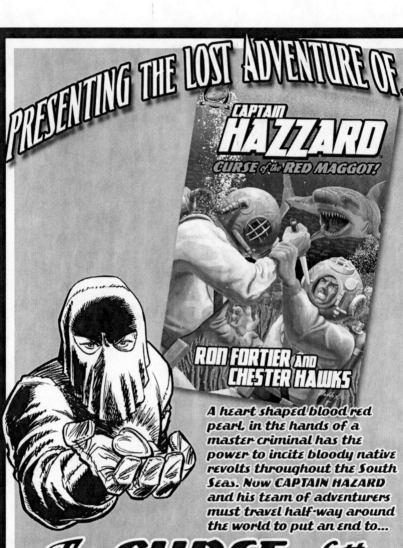

PRESENTING THE LOST ADVENTURE OF...

CAPTAIN HAZZARD
CURSE of the RED MAGGOT!

RON FORTIER AND CHESTER HAWKS

A heart shaped blood red pearl, in the hands of a master criminal has the power to incite bloody native revolts throughout the South Seas. Now CAPTAIN HAZZARD and his team of adventurers must travel half-way around the world to put an end to...

The CURSE of the RED MAGGOT!

Thought to have been lost for all time, this classic CAPTAIN HAZZARD story by writer CHESTER HAWKS has been unearthed and once again been completely rewritten and edited by modern day pulpsmith RON FORTIER. The CAPTAIN HAZZARD exploit 1938 readers never saw is now at long last in print!

COMING SOON IN THE NEXT THRILLING INSTALLMENT OF CAPTAIN HAZZARD...

An evil genius of science has learned how to transform people into throwback savages bent on total destruction and has unleashed them throughout Manhattan.

In the midst of the greatest blizzard ever to hit the gotham. CAPTAIN HAZZARD and his Fighting Five must confront and battle...

The CAVEMEN of NEW YORK!!!

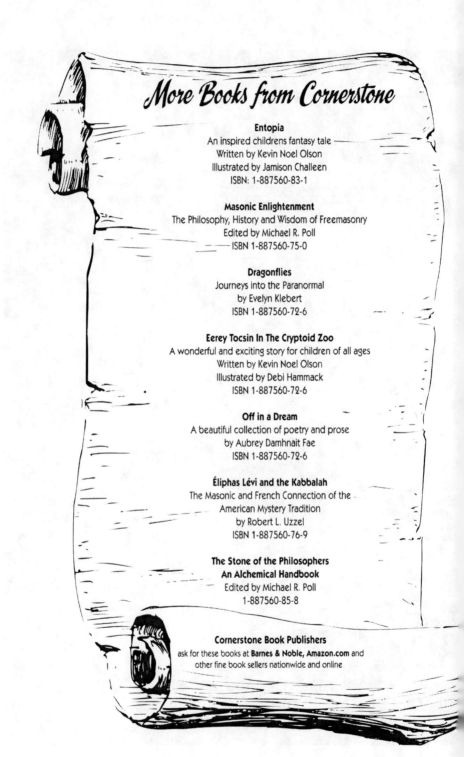

More Books from Cornerstone

Entopia
An inspired childrens fantasy tale
Written by Kevin Noel Olson
Illustrated by Jamison Challeen
ISBN: 1-887560-83-1

Masonic Enlightenment
The Philosophy, History and Wisdom of Freemasonry
Edited by Michael R. Poll
ISBN 1-887560-75-0

Dragonflies
Journeys into the Paranormal
by Evelyn Klebert
ISBN 1-887560-72-6

Eerey Tocsin In The Cryptoid Zoo
A wonderful and exciting story for children of all ages
Written by Kevin Noel Olson
Illustrated by Debi Hammack
ISBN 1-887560-72-6

Off in a Dream
A beautiful collection of poetry and prose
by Aubrey Damhnait Fae
ISBN 1-887560-72-6

Éliphas Lévi and the Kabbalah
The Masonic and French Connection of the
American Mystery Tradition
by Robert L. Uzzel
ISBN 1-887560-76-9

The Stone of the Philosophers
An Alchemical Handbook
Edited by Michael R. Poll
1-887560-85-8

Cornerstone Book Publishers
ask for these books at **Barnes & Noble, Amazon.com** and
other fine book sellers nationwide and online

Printed in the United States
115573LV00005B/213/P